BAND OF BROKEN GODS

RYAN KIRK

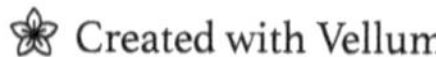 Created with Vellum

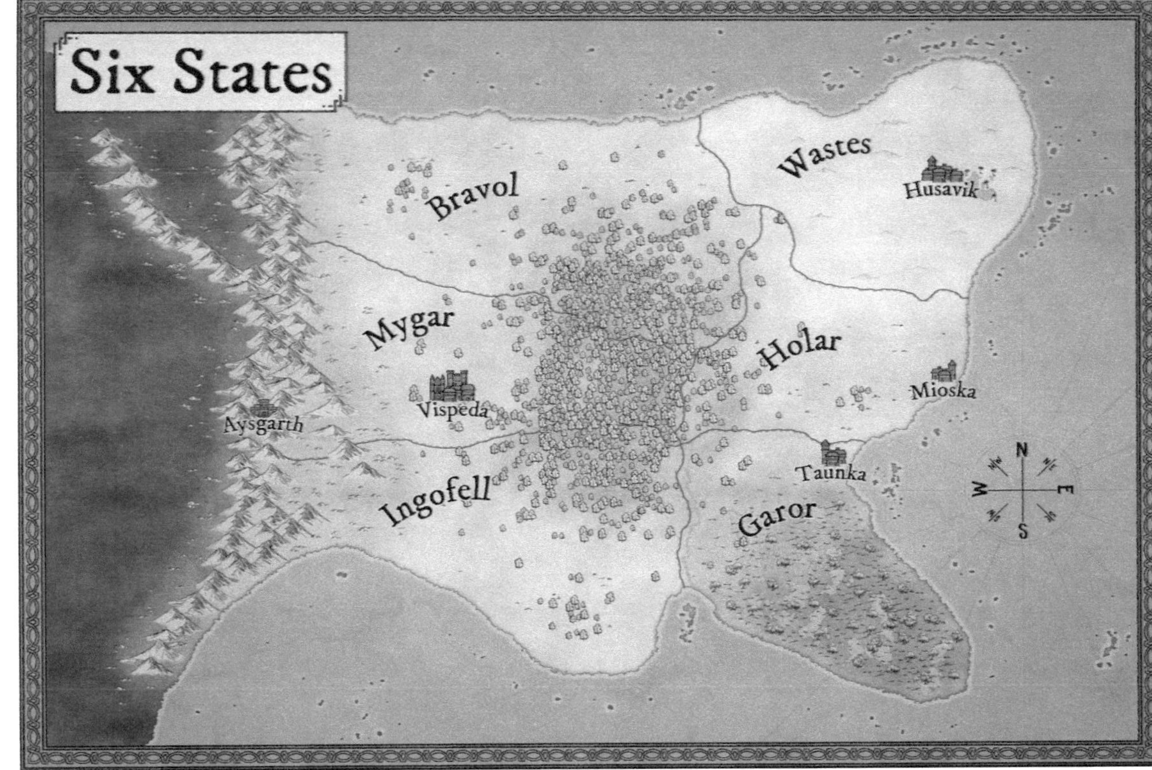

Six States
Bravol
Wastes
Husavik
Mygar
Holar
Vispeda
Mioska
Aysgarth
Taunka
Ingofell
Garor
N
E
S
W

For Juliet

1

———

No one traveled these woods at night. Only a few brave souls risked them under a cloudless, sunny sky.

And for good reason.

This forest did not welcome humans. It hunted them wherever they dared to walk.

Hakon crept through the tightly packed trees like a mouse hiding from a cat, ears alert for the sound of uninvited company. Though birds sang to one another overhead, a heaviness in the air lingered, an unnatural presence the wildlife here either ignored or had grown used to.

His hand reached up to brush against the sword on his back for the tenth time in half as many minutes. An ahula might not notice the presence that permeated these woods, but he was not so easily fooled.

The creatures of the wild were not his only threat this night. Here, humans hunted their own.

His unease grew as the birds above took flight, leaving him with only the pale moonlight for company. He stopped. His eyes roamed slowly over his surroundings. Among the tall pines of this forest, though, he was more likely to hear a threat first than to see one.

As near as he could tell, he was alone.

Hakon took two steps forward and triggered a trap.

Dark bands of teho wrapped around his body, pinning his arms to his sides and his legs together. He lost his balance and fell forward, his restraints preventing him from reaching out with his arms to protect himself. He landed hard.

Hakon sighed.

Once, such a basic ward never would have surprised him. The incident added credence to his unspoken worry that he was too old, too soft now, for this. If any of the band saw him trussed up like a pig ready for the spit, the violence of their laughter would have driven this wood's predators miles away.

In that regard, at least, he was fortunate he traveled alone.

With a deep breath, he shattered the bonds that held him. Then he found a fallen tree to rest on. The one who watched these woods wouldn't let such strength wander uncontested.

His company arrived sooner than expected. A cloud of teho darkened the air before him, then took shape in the form of a surprisingly familiar face. "Good evening to you, Eliav," he said.

The man who now stood before him appeared to be somewhere in his twenties and in the prime of his life. His short black hair contrasted with Hakon's long, unkempt blond mane. But it was Eliav's eyes that belied his youthful look. Dark as his hair, there was a sense of calm behind his piercing gaze.

Eliav was younger than Hakon, but not by much.

"Hakon?" Eliav looked around the forest, suddenly on guard.

"I'm alone," Hakon reassured him.

Eliav's eyes narrowed. "That's hardly comforting." He watched the trees for several long seconds before accepting the truth of Hakon's claim. "Why are you here?"

"A personal matter."

Eliav scoffed. "So important you would risk these woods, and in the middle of the night?"

"I had hoped to avoid drawing attention."

"She would have known no matter what route you attempted."

"I assumed as much, but I still felt this was safer. Figured if it came to a fight, at least no one else would be hurt."

Eliav studied him in silence.

Hakon returned his regard.

For all of Eliav's own experience, he still gave his intent away. His muscles tensed and his breaths came faster as he steeled himself for the fight to come.

He attacked with teho first.

As Hakon expected.

To Eliav's credit, he formed his teho into a beautiful attack. Small darts sped toward Hakon from all directions, seeking his heart.

They bounced off him as he covered the space between them in a heartbeat. Eliav was strong by the standards of this age, but that mattered little.

Eliav danced back as Hakon's sword cut the air where he had once stood. More darts came at Hakon, who swiped them away with the flat of his blade.

Eliav's nimble feet barely kept him out of Hakon's reach. He used a thin, tall pine tree as protection, and Hakon cut it down with one swipe of his sword.

Two dozen darts materialized above Hakon, and he was forced to pause his pursuit for a moment. Eliav put more space between them.

Hakon growled. This became tiring.

He embraced teho and launched himself at Eliav.

The duel ended as suddenly as it started.

The speed of Hakon's pass blew dry brown pine needles away in all directions. Eliav wasn't fast enough to save himself. Hakon held his sword steady, the sharp edge pressed against Eliav's throat, hard enough to draw blood.

Eliav held up his hands in a gesture of surrender. He smiled. "Had to try. She would have been upset, otherwise."

"I might have killed you," Hakon said.

"I hoped you wouldn't," Eliav said. "Rumor has it you're a changed man. Had to see for myself."

Hakon shook his head, but stepped away from Eliav, wiped off his blade, and returned the sword to its sheath. "Still foolish."

He walked back to the tree he'd been sitting on when Eliav arrived.

The other man rubbed at his throat. "You come at a difficult time. She'll want to know why you're here."

Hakon fixed his gaze on Eliav, who had never been a good liar. "She wasn't expecting me?"

"If she was, she's told me nothing of it."

"Would she?"

Eliav thought about the question. "I believe so. She still prefers to keep her own counsel, but I am close to her." The tone of his statement left little doubt in Hakon's mind just how close the two of them were. "I believe she would have told me about anything regarding you."

Hakon's shoulders slumped. If she hadn't been expecting him, she probably knew nothing.

Eliav noticed. "What is it?"

Hakon ignored the question. "Could you take me to her? If you speak true, I doubt I will stay long."

Eliav looked away. "I cannot. If I were to reappear with you by my side, my troubles would never cease. I do not wish to forfeit her trust in me."

Hakon respected Eliav enough not to press the matter. Though Eliav owed him a favor from long ago, completing the journey on foot wouldn't take more than another day. His pace could increase considerably once he was sure she wouldn't send more warriors after him.

It wasn't the forest he feared, but those who used it as a shield.

Eliav gave Hakon a small bow of gratitude for his forbearance and made to leave.

Hakon held him back for a moment. "You say I come at a troublesome time. Why?"

Eliav shook his head. "It is best for me not to say. You may ask her when you see her."

"What is she like, now?"

Eliav glanced away again, but this time, Hakon could see it was because he was imagining her. "She's changed since we saw you last. Much. You'll see. She's done good in this world since the war, but she is afraid, and the threat of death has her clinging more tightly to life than ever."

"Who is powerful enough to threaten her?"

Eliav chuckled grimly. "You truly don't know, do you?"

Hakon shook his head. "I have lived a quiet life."

"You should have continued to do so," Eliav said. "These are particularly tumultuous days."

"How so?"

Elias offered him a sad smile. "The telling would take a

full evening and several pints of ale, and I must return soon with news before she sends others."

"Shall I see you again when I arrive?"

Eliav looked pained. "Is there no way of turning you aside? I fear how she will react to your arrival, though I will try to smooth the way. But she's gathered enough teho to threaten even you."

"I'm afraid not. I mean her no harm, so long as she's done none to me, but I must speak with her."

"Why? What is so important that you would risk so much?"

Hakon looked up to the moon, wondering if somewhere, someone else was also staring at it. He hoped so.

He returned his gaze to Elias. His heart felt heavy as he admitted the truth.

"It's my daughter, Cliona. She's missing."

2

The lone candle in Cliona's room sputtered as it neared the end of its wick. She glanced at it, silently willing the flame to endure a little longer.

Cliona turned her attention back to the ancient book resting on the desk before her. She guessed it had been written over six hundred years ago, based on clues from the text itself. But there was no way to be sure. She pressed the palms of her hands into her eyes.

The list of things she wasn't sure about right now would probably come close to filling this slim book.

She leaned back in her chair and stared at the ceiling. They had been penned up in this decrepit town for almost a month now, and all they had was a series of deep holes in the middle of nowhere to show for it. Agnesse had promised her the home of a god.

Instead, Cliona had discovered that she was a hopeful fool, ready to run off on any harebrained scheme that had the slightest chance of providing her the answers she sought.

Her curiosity had overwhelmed her reason.

The legends of the stamfar were myths. Stories to entertain and instruct, not true reflections of a past long forgotten. They had been as human as her, and no more.

She sighed. Soon it would be over. Agnesse was running out of places to dig, and when she finally admitted defeat, they could begin the long journey back to Vispeda.

Just a bit longer.

Cliona blinked away her tiredness and focused on the text before her, determined to translate at least another half-dozen pages. But soon the flowing script of the long-dead language swam in her exhausted vision. Most of her afternoon and all of her evening had gone into the book, a pile of organized pages of dense handwriting evidence of her consistent effort.

She stumbled her way through two more pages before the candle sputtered again. She tucked a loose strand of long blonde hair back behind her ear. Then she finally sat up straight and stretched her arms overhead.

Though she suspected the expedition would ultimately prove a failure, it wasn't without benefit. Away from the endless demands on her time at the academy, she'd completed more useful work in the past month than she had in the past year. And the expedition was well-funded. They stayed at the nicest inn for many miles, and although Cliona wondered where the money had come from, the long days and nights hadn't been a hardship.

She stood and walked over to the window. The moon was full tonight, its pale light lending the streets of this town a mysterious air. Not that it needed any more mystery.

They were as close to the edge of the six states as she'd ever wandered. Though plenty of unexplored land existed to the west, it was still too wild for humans to live upon.

Though she was in the same state, this unnamed town

couldn't be any more different than Vispeda. Empty streets instead of full. Older, weathered faces instead of young men and women seeking fortunes. And a dedication to the myths of the stamfar that had all but died out in the city. Here they looked to the past for guidance, instead of the future.

A commotion below her feet, from the common room of the inn, snapped her out of her reverie. The voices were familiar, excited, and numerous. Quick, heavy footsteps pounded up the stairs, and a second later a firm hand knocked on her door. "Come in," she said.

As she'd guessed, it was Zachary, perhaps the greatest mystery remaining in this town. His enormous frame filled the door, reminding her of her father. "They say they've found it."

Despite her efforts to resist the reaction, her heart beat faster. "How sure are they?"

Zachary's eyes sparkled. "They're sure." He held out his hand, and she saw he carried something.

She stepped forward to take a closer look. A large flake of stone rested in his hand, the visible side perfectly smooth except for the flowing script etched with care upon its surface. Her eyes went wide as she translated the symbols. "Where did this come from?"

Zachary's grin was almost as wide as his shoulders. "The diggers almost missed it. One of them was widening a hole they were just about to abandon when he chipped this off. As soon as they realized what they were near, they went to work with more care. They uncovered a building, with more of the script etched upon it."

Cliona exhaled slowly. Zachary's explanation had her heart pounding so hard in her chest she worried he would hear it.

It couldn't be real.

But no other explanation came to mind.

And if this was true, it gave credence to Agnesse's other beliefs. Perhaps the stamfar were closer to myth than any serious scholar believed.

"Did you summon Agnesse?" Cliona asked. She tried to imagine how the head of their expedition would react to the news, but failed. Even after a month and more of time spent together, she didn't understand the woman. Her theories at times bordered on madness, and Cliona didn't think she understood a single thing about living humans, but there was no doubting her brilliance.

"Of course. I sent someone looking for her, but she's out wandering again, probably trying to figure out where we went wrong."

Cliona refused to wait for the older woman. "We should probably head over there first and confirm the find."

Zachary stepped to the side and gave an exaggerated bow. "I suspected you might think so."

She smiled. Zachary had made his affections for her well known over the course of their brief acquaintance, but she'd politely rebuffed his advances. Though he was kind, quick to jest, and the center of most conversations, there was something about him that made her wary. It wasn't that she thought him false. But the personality he displayed was only a fraction of who he truly was.

She only caught hints of more. Times when one of his observations startled her with their acuity. Or times when the smile dropped from his face, and he looked east, concerned about something he wouldn't speak of. Until she'd unraveled the mystery he was, she wouldn't let herself fall for his considerable charms.

Cliona gathered any gear she might conceivably need,

stuffed it haphazardly into a pack, and flung the pack over her shoulders. She was ready in less than a minute.

Downstairs, they met with the leader of the digging crew. He was a stout older man, who only came to Cliona's chest when he stood on his toes. But she suspected he weighed twice as much as her, and his arms were as wide as her legs. His name was Vinko, and Cliona believed him to be one of the buried jewels of this expedition.

Vinko flashed her a smile. "We've found it."

There was no doubt in his voice.

And for the first time, Cliona truly allowed herself to believe.

Vinko was no academic. Indeed, he was as far from an academic as one could be. The scholars she knew imagined themselves in lofty towers, looking down over human history with a critical eye, as though their knowledge separated them from the masses of people struggling to make their living every day.

Cliona didn't blame them. She suffered from some of the same and believed it was at least partly due to their training. A genuine scholar distanced themselves from problems, and examined questions without their judgment colored by emotion or empathy.

The skill was a useful one, but she wasn't surprised when those trained in such techniques used them too frequently. When the entire world was nothing but a series of problems and challenges to solve, it made sense that scholars would hold themselves apart, both from their fellow humans and from the world they inhabited.

Vinko did neither.

He loved the earth. He lived for digging holes and exploring underground passages. Dirt permanently stained the tips of his fingers, and the thick calluses on his hands came from years of wielding shovels and pickaxes. He was happiest when surrounded by mud and stone.

When he wasn't digging, he walked among those who were. He knew every detail of every member of his crew. Whenever difficulties arose, he was there, lending a hand or advice.

In her opinion, no one knew more about holes or people.

Vinko led them from the inn.

Though the streets were quiet, they weren't quite empty. They passed an old woman, praying at a shrine to Heiden, stamfar of the hunt. Though the woman's prayer was whispered, Cliona heard her plea for the success of her son's upcoming hunt.

Cliona's gut twisted and she hurried past the woman.

At the outskirts of town they met with the expedition's guards, who escorted them along the path as they always did. The plains that surrounded the town were less dangerous than the woods Cliona had grown up in, but that didn't make them safe. One digger had been wounded by a coyote, and another had been clawed nearly blind by a large bird.

As always, the wild fought back. They'd been fortunate to suffer as little as they had.

Accompanied by the guards, they began their hike.

Dozens of pairs of feet walking every day for over a month had worn a smooth path through the tall grass, making the trail easy to follow. They crested one small rise and dropped into a shallow draw. They stepped over the trickle of water flowing down the heart of the draw, then summited another rise and came upon the excavation.

Holes pockmarked the land, each a dozen feet deep.

Cliona had no problem finding the hole Vinko intended to lead them to.

It was the only one glowing.

When they arrived, Vinko extended his hand and presented the hole as if it was a newborn child.

Cliona took one look and almost leaped for joy. Instead, she settled for wrapping Vinko in a tight embrace. Vinko grunted and patted her on the back.

Several feet below the surface, his team had uncovered a door, partly covered by runes. The symbols seemed to reflect and amplify the light of the moon, glowing with an eerie white light.

Just as the legends said they would.

Cliona shook her head, still not quite able to believe they had done it.

They had found the home of a god.

3

When the sun broke over the horizon, Hakon figured he'd earned a rest. The thick pines held threats all hours of the day, but the ones that hunted during daylight hours were easier to protect against. He found a comfortable position leaning up against one of the ancient trees, a bed of soft pine needles cushion enough to rest on. He twisted the familiar wards around himself and fell into a deep and dreamless sleep.

A deer crashing through the forest woke him several hours later. The animal bounded through trees twenty feet north of him. Something dark and fast pursued it, too fast for Hakon to see.

A shadow wolf, most likely.

The deer had little chance of surviving the encounter, but Hakon was simply grateful the wolf had found the deer before him.

A glance at the sky told him that it was near noon. He'd rested long enough, and the woods were quiet.

She hadn't sent anyone else after him.

Did that bode well for him, or did she just want him closer when she made her move?

He couldn't say, and at the moment, didn't much care.

There were those who thrived in uncertainty, people who found no greater thrill than risking their lives in complex schemes of alliance and betrayal. Once, he had been such a man, and he had schemed with the best of them.

Though the stories of those days were amusing in the retelling, the truth was he didn't miss them.

Worse, he worried that his time away had weakened his skill at the great game, that his talent might no longer suffice for the challenges he faced.

Hakon ran his left hand through his long hair, sighed, and resumed his journey, running through the forest with more grace than the doe that had woken him. He bounded lightly, reveling in the simple pleasure of physical exertion.

The miles disappeared underfoot, and he reached his destination earlier than expected. The sun kissed the tops of the trees when he saw the smoke of cook fires in the distance.

With any hope of surprise a distant memory, he angled south until he found the road. Once upon the hard dirt track, he slowed his pace to a walk that would draw no attention. The traffic this late in the day was light, with most travelers already safely ensconced in whatever shelter they could find. The only remaining adventurers were those who knew they didn't have far left. Come night, no human would travel these roads, and they'd be wise not to.

At night, the wilds drove back the realms of men.

He imagined Dagrun as he had seen her last, and wondered what type of home she had built for herself. He imagined an ornate palace, with highly polished wood in every room, all surrounded by a thick wall four times the height of a man. The fact she had settled in the woods still surprised him. She'd always been one for the solitude of high mountain places.

Dagrun's village revealed itself as he turned a bend in the road.

Hakon stopped, frozen by the sight.

Even if he lived a hundred more lifetimes, he never would have guessed she'd build such a place.

Before him sat a small village, consisting of no more than three dozen small homes, packed together in a cozy arrangement. It reminded Hakon of the village near his home he'd left just a week ago in search of his daughter.

Eliav chose that moment to step out of the shadows of a tall pine, a smile on his face. "I'd hoped to catch you when you saw."

"She built this?"

Eliav nodded and led him forward. "Come, she's expecting you."

They walked, Eliav keeping his pace slow so Hakon could gawk. The village possessed a wall, but not half as thick or tall as Hakon expected. It was designed more for keeping creatures of the forest out than defending against an attack. A man and a woman stood guard at the gate. Both were unarmed.

After they passed, Hakon raised an inquiring eyebrow at Eliav. "Most of the residents are tehoin. Dagrun is believed to be a nelja," Eliav said. "We don't need any special attention from the outside world."

Hakon understood. "This is a refuge."

Eliav nodded.

"From what?"

Eliav glanced at him, as though he didn't understand the

question. "It is not as safe to be tehoin as it once was. Dagrun protects those who seek a quiet life."

Hakon wasn't sure he believed that, but he also didn't think Eliav was lying.

They stopped outside a home that looked like all the others in the village. It was modestly sized, with a small covered porch over the front door. Two chairs sat close together under the awning. The men took off their boots and Eliav led them in.

The scent of roasting meat hit Hakon's nose the moment the door opened. Eliav gestured toward some pegs near the door. Hakon unstrapped his sword and hung it from one. His pack followed the sword onto a neighboring peg moments later.

Then he saw Dagrun.

He tensed, then forced himself to relax. She never would have let him this close if she intended him harm.

Her appearance had only changed a bit since he'd last seen her. She'd grown her dark hair longer, but it was still cut well above her shoulders. Though her appearance had hardly changed, his perception of her did. She was still lean, her bare arms displaying the wiry muscle that developed after too many years on the road. But she now possessed a softness he'd never have predicted.

The years had changed them all.

Eliav began setting the table.

Hakon spoke first. "I come as a guest, Dagrun. Will you welcome me?"

Dagrun gave Hakon a small nod of acknowledgment. She hesitated only briefly before answering, but in that moment he saw a flicker of fear. She was as nervous of him as he was of her.

But he couldn't ever remember seeing her nervous.

His sense was that her concern wasn't really about him. Something else had her worried.

Worried so much she'd let him into her home with hardly a fight.

"Be welcome, Hakon," Dagrun said.

"Thank you." He let himself relax. He didn't know what had shaped Dagrun over the years, but he couldn't imagine her as an oath breaker. Though the world may crumble around her, she would never stoop so low.

Not like he had.

Eliav placed heaping piles of food around the table. Dagrun had prepared a roast, with potatoes, carrots, and bread to serve as sides. Hakon helped himself to hearty portions, enjoying the succulent meat and fresh vegetables. If nothing else, coming here might have been worth it for the food alone.

They spoke only of inconsequential topics over the meal. Dagrun's village supported itself through the bounty of the land. The villagers cleared plots of forest away and converted them into farmland. Some wood went into the construction of the village, but they sent most downstream. Like most of the kolma, Dagrun possessed a deep reverence for this world. Her village cut what they needed and no more.

She'd found a balance here.

Hakon had little to share. Any story of his life would lead to his purpose for being here, and etiquette demanded that story wait a while longer yet.

Later, while Eliav cleared away the food, Dagrun's gaze settled on Hakon. She'd always been beautiful, and the years had done nothing to change that. But it was her sharp mind that had always been her most attractive and dangerous quality. When she leaned back in her chair,

Hakon couldn't help but think of a predator at rest. "Eliav tells me your daughter is missing," she said.

Hakon nodded, the very thought of it constricting his throat. "He speaks true. Do you know anything of it?"

"No. Until last night, I was not even aware you had a daughter. I never figured you for the type."

"That makes two of us."

"How long has she been missing?"

"I'm not sure."

Dagrun raised a disbelieving eyebrow. Hakon shrugged. "She's grown and no longer lives with me. All I know is that she disappeared about two months ago. Not even her closest friends know her whereabouts."

"Why did you think I might know anything about her?"

"She's a scholar, a master of the first language of the stamfar."

Dagrun almost choked on her wine. Eliav looked over from his cleaning, concerned. "*Your* daughter became a scholar?" she asked.

Hakon shot her a pointed glare and ignored her outburst. "Someone told me she'd been approached by a small team seeking the grave of a stamfar in these woods."

Dagrun nodded. "Ah. I remember those two. Old men, but clever. They came close to finding Heiden's grave." She paused. "Unfortunately, they met an untimely demise."

"I had worried as much, and so I came here first."

"They were alone."

Hakon bowed his head toward her. "Thank you for letting me know."

"I'm sorry that I couldn't be more help."

"Perhaps you still might be. I know you protect Heiden's grave, but what about the other known stamfar? Has there been any news about scholars searching for them?"

Both Eliav and Dagrun tensed at the question. Hakon caught the look that passed between them. "What?"

"Do you believe your daughter might be involved in such a search?"

"It's the only reason I can think of for her disappearance," Hakon admitted. "If something had happened to her on my account, I would expect my antagonist to inform me of her predicament. But there has been only silence. She is known for her skill at translating the works of the stamfar. No other reason comes to mind."

"Perhaps she just ran off with a lover? It does happen."

"Not my daughter," Hakon growled.

Dagrun held up her hands in mock surrender, but he saw she enjoyed needling him.

"So what is it?" Hakon demanded. "What's happening that I don't know about?"

Dagrun turned to Eliav. "Get us another bottle of wine, would you?"

Eliav nodded and rushed to obey. There was no humor in Dagrun's expression any longer. She placed a cup in front of him. "Drink up. You'll want it."

He took a sip, the wine rich on his tongue.

Dagrun looked down at her own cup, spinning it slowly in her fingers. "First, I must tell you why I'm here, and then I must tell you about the war that is coming for us all."

4

———

Cliona descended the rough wooden ladder down into the hole that Vinko and his team had dug, becoming the first scholar to examine the discovery closely. Under Vinko's careful supervision, his diggers had widened the hole and cleaned off the strange markings as well as they were able.

It was the markings on the door which first drew her attention. The door itself was little more than a thin, perfectly straight line in the stone. At least, Cliona assumed it was a door. It was just slightly greater in size that the height and width of a human. If she could figure out how to unlock it, who knew what discoveries might lie on the other side?

Recording the information came first, though. Zachary joined her at the bottom of the hole, carrying two lanterns, and together they began the painstaking process of sketching out the runes. A small chip in the lettering marred the script, but Zachary held the missing fragment in his hand. The pale light emanating from each symbol made translating the runes a simple matter, even in the dark of night.

She finished her translation and whispered it softly to herself.

Zachary looked up from his work. "What does it say?"

Cliona read the words louder.

"Here lies the home of Marjaana,

Sealed upon the conclusion of the second and final war.

Let no usurper pass."

Zachary looked up at the door. "Think it's cursed?"

Cliona scoffed. "No. But I think it's worth examining with care. Assuming the legends are true, Marjaana buried her home herself. It stands to reason she would have put other measures in place to protect her property."

Zachary grinned. "I guess that's why you brought me, then, huh?"

"It wasn't for your ability to copy runes," Cliona said, pointing at an obvious mistake he'd made.

Zachary was one of a very few vilda, the weakest class of tehoin, in the academy, but the strongest by far. Though Agnesse had never said so out loud, it was most likely the reason he'd been selected for the secretive expedition. He was a middling scholar at best, sent to the nearest academy to prevent some political crisis in his hometown. His father was a magistrate, and Zachary was tight-lipped about the details. Still, he bore his exile with a smile.

She turned her attention from Zachary to the wall with the door. Marjaana was the stamfar of knowledge, and a shrine to her sat in Cliona's academy. It was the legends of Marjaana, in part, that had inspired Cliona to pursue a scholarly life. She didn't believe the legends, but she respected the truths they hid.

She believed someone named Marjaana had existed,

someone who had been a scholar, or whatever equivalent the stamfar had.

And now she sat outside her home.

It didn't seem real.

Zachary finished his corrections and put the papers away. "Should we try to open it?"

"Agnesse would flay us alive."

"I know you're just as curious as I am to know what's in there."

"Flay. Us. Alive."

Zachary sighed and sat down next to her. After a moment, his impatience got the better of him. "Do you think our friends back at the academy miss us?" he asked.

"Me, probably. I can't imagine anyone missing you."

Zachary stabbed an imaginary knife into his chest and twisted it. "You wound me."

His antics, as always, brought a smile to her face. Even if his jovial nature masked something deeper, he rarely failed to entertain. She hadn't known him well at the academy. They hadn't had much reason to interact beyond exchanging greetings at the dull gatherings some of the senior scholars invited them to.

Her respect for him had grown this past month. His self-depreciating humor and loudly proclaimed laziness masked a sharp mind and observant nature. When he focused his attention on her, it felt as though she was the only person that mattered in the whole world.

Once he recovered from his imaginary knife wound, Zachary continued. "You should know there are several beautiful scholars awaiting my return. Agnesse couldn't believe I had so many letters to leave behind." He laughed. "I imagine even she blushed when she read some of what I'd written."

The thought of Agnesse blushing made Cliona laugh out loud, the sound echoing hollowly in the hole. "How many letters did you leave?" she asked.

"Nearly a dozen. Forgot my father, though. But I suspect he won't even notice that I went missing for several months."

"They were *all* letters of affection?"

"Every single one."

"You best be careful when we return. You may have a dozen women vying for your attention."

"Such a fate would be a dream made reality." He fixed her with his attention, and the hole seemed to shrink around them. "How many letters did you write?"

"Not nearly so many. I struggled to find a half dozen handsome men within the academy to write to."

He laughed, but his attention didn't waver.

"Just two," she confessed. "One to my father and one to a friend. I'm afraid neither would have made Agnesse blush."

Secrecy had been a part of this expedition from the first moment Agnesse had approached Cliona. Now that Cliona knew the aim of the expedition, the secrecy made sense. The home of Marjaana had the potential to be the greatest find of their generation, and perhaps of all time. It promised answers to mysteries that had plagued humanity since the stamfar had hidden so many secrets.

Cliona, like Zachary, had been allowed to write letters to those she left behind. She couldn't reveal anything about the expedition, but she was allowed to reassure her loved ones that she was safe and healthy and would return in several months' time. She'd delivered her letters to Agnesse to examine and then send off a day before their departure.

Before they could continue their discussion, they heard sounds of people stirring to action above. Soon after,

Agnesse's stern face peered over the edge of the hole. "You two haven't attempted to enter, have you?"

"We've been waiting for you," Zachary reassured her.

"Good." Her face disappeared and Cliona heard her giving sharp orders to the diggers. She wanted defensive earthworks surrounding the hole by daybreak, as though she was worried they would have to fight off an invading army come the rising of the sun.

The creatures of the wild were a more reasonable concern, but the contingent of guards hadn't had any problems fighting them off yet.

If Vinko had any questions for Agnesse, he didn't ask them. When the dig had started he had tried making suggestions, but after a few arguments that shook the inn, he'd stopped questioning Agnesse and settled for blind obedience.

Cliona let her hand brush against the door. She could feel the mechanism within, an empty reservoir waiting to be filled with teho. She frowned. The door would require considerable effort to open, and despite Zachary's strength, she wondered if he would even be able to open it.

Agnesse's boots appeared and stepped firmly on the wooden ladder. Caked dirt and mud from the bottom of them shook loose from the impact and rained down on Zachary and Cliona. Their leader joined them in the bottom of the hole, and now it felt cramped.

Agnesse was a short and thin woman, her gray hair tied back in a tight bun. She gestured to Zachary. "Well, I'm here now, so open it."

Zachary gave Cliona a quick look, one that literally passed over Agnesse's head. But he turned and examined the door, looking for a latch or a handle. Then he felt what

Cliona had, and placed his palm against the door. Cliona took a step back to watch.

Zachary closed his eyes. Cliona sensed teho gathering and filling the locking mechanism. To an ahula, it would seem as though nothing happened. The gathering of power was invisible to the eye, the only sign of effort the small beads of sweat gathering on Zachary's forehead.

"Well," Agnesse demanded, "what's taking so long?"

Zachary, lost in the demands of his task, didn't respond. Agnesse stomped her feet, and the frown that permanently decorated her face deepened further.

Cliona bit her lip to stop herself from expressing her frustration. She'd met other scholars like Agnesse over the years, but Agnesse was the worst of them. Agnesse lived in a world where only ideas were pure and worth understanding. People were nothing but an unnecessary distraction.

But it was Agnesse's research, fueled by Cliona's translations, that had led them here.

She might be a terrible person, but her results were beyond question.

The door opened, sliding back and to the side through a mechanism Cliona didn't understand. Zachary, deprived of his support, collapsed. Cliona knelt beside him and helped hold him up.

"I'll be fine," he said, his voice weak. "Took a lot out of me."

Agnesse stepped around Zachary without so much as a word.

"Please be careful," Cliona said. "The writing on the door warned against entering."

"This is no time for curses," Agnesse replied. "This is a time for answers!" She picked up a lantern from the ground and stepped inside the home. "You two remain here."

She disappeared into the dark, and Cliona tended to Zachary. He hadn't been injured by his efforts, but appeared exhausted.

She kept glancing toward the door, but there was no sign of Agnesse. Her light had completely faded from view. "Do you think we should follow her?" Zachary asked.

Cliona shook her head. "Not without her permission."

Her determination to follow orders lasted until they heard Agnesse's scream echo down the halls of the ancient home.

5

———

Hakon followed Dagrun into the cool night air. Eliav had retired for the evening, resigned to spending most of this night alone. The younger man showed no bitterness, though, accepting Dagrun's absence as a matter of course. Following Dagrun's example, Hakon carried no weapon as they left the comfort of her home.

His host led him through town, their steps soft and slow.

"If you had told me, years ago, that all of this," Hakon gestured to the homes, "was because you'd fallen in love, I would have laughed you out of town."

Dagrun's answering smile was brief. The tale of her journey to this place wasn't a happy one, and the tragedies she'd related weighed heavy on his heart. "But you understand, don't you?" she asked.

Hakon thought of Sera and the smile he missed so much. "All too well, I'm afraid."

"Eliav struggles with it, occasionally," Dagrun said. "Though he will never say so, I know he sometimes feels like I only accepted his companionship because I needed someone to fill the boots of a ghost."

"He seems devoted."

"He is." She paused. "I don't feel like I deserve the kindness he has shown me. But I've at least learned to stop questioning the desires of the heart."

They walked for a minute in silence. Hakon's history with Dagrun held far more battles than parleys. This new familiarity seemed unreal. It wasn't friendship—such relationships were exceedingly rare between their kind, and only more so as time passed. But they shared an understanding no ahula could comprehend. He smiled at the thought.

Dagrun caught the expression. "What?"

"We're getting old."

"We *are* old."

Hakon chuckled. "Had this meeting happened a hundred and fifty years ago, we would have come to blows before even greeting one another."

Dagrun nodded her agreement. "You've changed, too. The fire that once drove you still burns, but is no longer out of control."

Hakon shrugged. "Love. The world's most painful blessing."

"I'd like to hear your story, if you're willing."

"There's not much for the telling. The imprisonment broke my mind. After I was awakened, I wandered for years, contemplating ending my own life. I was a shell of the man I'd once been. But I eventually met a woman who gave me something to live for. We fell in love and started a family." His voice trailed off as memories attacked his composure.

Dagrun walked beside him, waiting for him to finish.

"She died several years ago."

"I'm sorry. Illness?"

"The wilds."

"What was her name?"

"Sera."

"Did she know who you were?"

Hakon nodded. "We had no secrets between us."

"And your girl?"

He shook his head. "She believes I'm nelja, as is she."

"Why have you not told her?"

"Sera and I discussed it at length. We decided that we wanted her to live a life as free from my past as possible."

"Noble, but our pasts have a tendency to haunt us, even as we run from them."

They reached the wall of town and walked beside it. The gates were locked and guarded, and a raised platform stood nearby. Dagrun led them toward it.

"You speak of a war?" Hakon asked, eager to change the subject.

"I do." She reached the ladder of the platform and climbed it with an easy grace. Hakon followed. Once they reached the top they could see into the forest. Hakon's sharp eyes saw several shadows moving between the trees.

"Have you truly managed to put the great game behind you?" she asked.

"I have. Few things interest me less, now."

She sighed. "What I'm about to tell you might drag you back in, and I fear you've become too soft for what is coming."

"My choices are my own, Dagrun. You believe my daughter's disappearance might have something to do with this war you fear?"

Her face twitched, a flicker of emotion quickly

suppressed. "I cannot say for certain, but if your daughter is a scholar of the stamfar, it stands to reason."

"Tell me."

One of the dark shapes emerged from the forest, eyes glowing in the dark. A shadow wolf. Darker than spilled ink, its eyes watched them for a long time, intelligent and fierce.

Eventually, it retreated to the woods and Dagrun spoke. "It's Damion."

Hakon swore softly.

"He's become obsessed with the stamfar. If the rumors are true, he believes that their power can be his. He's building a movement, larger than anything we've seen since the rebellion. I'm not sure whether to call it a cult or a state. And he's become frightfully strong."

"Why do you believe it will come to war?"

"His ambition is boundless, and he continues Torsten's work. When the dust settled after the rebellion, he rebuilt Aysgarth, where he now reigns unchallenged. I don't believe he will stop until the empire is reborn and he has enough power to challenge Isira."

"She hasn't stopped him?"

Dagrun shook her head. "She hasn't. I don't know if it's because she has a soft spot for the boy, or if she's that committed to her oath of not interfering with the affairs of the world. As far as I've heard, you're the last person who's seen her."

The revelation made him take a step back. That had been over forty years ago.

Surprising as the fact was, though, it was only a distraction from what Hakon really cared about. "You believe my daughter got caught up in this?"

"I hear rumors of digs and expeditions, attempts to pull the past from the grave the stamfar buried it in. Say what you will about Damion's ambitions, but he has become a great patron of the scholars, even if few of them know it. Much of our new knowledge is due to his influence. Who knows, he might even be the one who saves humanity."

"You don't really believe that."

"I don't. But I'm old enough to know that I don't know anything. It's not my battle anymore."

He wondered at that. "If he's continuing Torsten's work —" He left the rest unspoken.

She gestured back at the village. "He's approached me several times."

He noticed the sudden tension in her voice. Between the story of her past and what he knew of the events of the day, he realized the source of her fear. "You stand against him by creating this refuge."

She nodded.

Dagrun's change beggared belief. When they'd last met, she had been one of Torsten's staunchest allies. "Why?"

"Freedom." She looked over her village, the pride obvious on her face. "Damion promises us the world, but the price is endless obedience, enforced at all costs." She shivered. "He's sent me parts of friends, of kolma who fought him. Every year, there are fewer of us to stand against him. And as his strength grows, fewer yet who have any chance against him."

Dagrun wasn't one to exaggerate her claims. If she was that worried about Damion, the fear was reasonable. And Cliona might be involved.

"Do you have any idea where my daughter might be?"

"West. Most likely near one of the buried stamfar artifacts."

"Do you know their locations?"

"No, but Solveig might, and she's not far."

Hakon swore.

"She was one of your band." Dagrun's remark was half a statement and half a question.

"None of them have reached out to me since I was woken, and I never tried to contact them."

"The band is no more?"

Hakon grunted, realizing the weakness he'd inadvertently revealed. But he had a guest's protection, and he believed they were no longer enemies. He found Dagrun's company pleasant, his first interaction devoid of pretenses since Sera had died. It reminded him of all that he missed. "They never forgave me," he admitted.

"I'm sorry," Dagrun said. "Will you go to Solveig?"

"I suppose I have little choice," Hakon said. "Where is she?"

"She's one of the head scholars at Vispeda."

Hakon's eyes narrowed. "She is?"

"For many years now."

"Vispeda is the academy that supported my daughter."

"A coincidence?"

Hakon shrugged. "I doubt it."

After a few seconds, Dagrun reached out and grabbed his arm, surprising him. "Would you consider returning here, once you've found your girl?"

Hakon frowned. "I hadn't planned to."

"Would you consider it? With your strength, we might stand together against Damion."

A knot formed in Hakon's stomach. "If what you say is true, my strength may no longer be sufficient."

She looked puzzled at that. Her eyes went to the hand on his arm. "Don't you feel it?"

"What?"

"That you've grown so much stronger over the years."

Hakon shook his head. "I've barely used teho in decades."

She let go of his arm. "If you continue down this path, you will, and I think it will surprise you. We're all much stronger. But Damion has improved even more than the rest of us."

Hakon took a deep breath and looked around the forest and at the life Dagrun had created for herself. It was rare for the space between them not to be filled with bared steel.

He liked the change.

Which made his choice even more painful. "I'm sorry, Dagrun. All I want is my daughter safe. My wars are all in the past."

His words struck her like punches. Her shoulders dropped and her eyes fell to her feet.

Part of Hakon grieved for his old enemy. He would help if he could, but Cliona was all that mattered. He'd made an oath over her crib to keep her safe, and that was one he never planned on breaking.

Dagrun gestured toward the ladder. "I am sorry, too, Hakon. I understand your desire, but it's naive. You hope for peace, but war is gathering at your doorstep, and there is no hiding from it. As Damion grows more powerful, he will come for you, and your pacifism won't protect you from his bloody sword."

6

Cliona stepped through the door before she realized what a poor idea that was. Zachary cursed as he rushed to his feet and stumbled after her. He, at least, had the presence of mind to grab the second lantern on his way in. Its yellow light illuminated part of the long hallway.

She reached out her arm to block Zachary's advance. "You shouldn't come. You're exhausted."

He pushed her arm down. "I'm tired, but I can still use teho." Somehow, he found the strength to smile. "And anyway, if something happened to you," he paused, letting the suspense build for a second, "I'd get terribly bored out here."

She rolled her eyes, but understood Zachary intended to join her no matter her objections. And they didn't have time to argue. "Fine, just stay behi—"

Her suggestion died on her lips as Zachary stepped ahead of her, willfully oblivious to her wishes.

Cliona growled, but Zachary seemed struck by a temporary deafness. He proceeded farther into Marjaana's home, lantern held up high before him.

She huffed, but followed the fool. If nothing else, she supposed, his enormous frame would shield her. Though she'd never forgive herself if he was seriously injured. She settled for cautioning him. "Slow down," she whispered. "Who knows what surprises Marjaana left for us?"

"Sounds like Agnesse found one," he replied.

Glib response aside, he heeded her warning. His every step was deliberate, and Cliona was pleased to see the earlier evidence of his exhaustion fade. He stood straighter and his breaths came easier. Opening the door had tired him, but not broken him.

Her attention turned to the hall they were in. Works of art hung on the wall, protected by an invisible layer of teho. She brushed her hand against one of the barriers, eyes widening when she sensed the strength of the working. Who would harness such powers merely to protect a painting?

Cliona knew the answer, of course. They stood in her home.

Marjaana. One of the stamfar.

A woman who had more legends attributed to her than a single human could possibly create in a lifetime. One of the greatest scholars and explorers the world had ever known. The woman who had a shrine in every academy in the six states.

And they were in her home.

Cliona blinked and focused. There would be time to explore later.

Zachary came to an open doorway. He stepped to the side so Cliona could join him and thrust the lantern inside. The room appeared to be a study, with a massive desk near the back of the room. More art hung on the walls, and two chairs were angled toward one another in a corner, but the room was otherwise empty.

They ventured deeper in.

Another open doorway revealed a bedroom, designed with many of the same principles as the study. One bed, one chair, and three pieces of art on the wall.

Cliona heard short, quick gasps from someone nearby. The light from Zachary's lantern couldn't penetrate the gloom ahead.

Agnesse might have been alive, but she wasn't alone. Something skittered across the floor, concealed by the unnatural shadows.

The sound of Agnesse's distress wore down the last of Zachary's patience, and he hurried toward the darkness. Cliona's eyes narrowed. Though Zachary, and thus the lantern, approached the gloom, the shadows didn't retreat from the light. Either Zachary hadn't noticed, or the sounds of Agnesse's labored breathing alarmed him enough to ignore the danger.

She dashed forward and reached out to stop him before he entered the darkness.

She arrived too late. He took another step and the shadows reached out and obscured him from view.

Cliona drew back, afraid of the dark's embrace.

She heard the skittering sound once again, almost close enough to touch but impossible to see. Without the lantern, all Cliona had to see by was the pale moonlight coming in through the door far behind her.

Zachary yelled and she felt him lash out with a blade of teho.

She hadn't realized he possessed the skill.

There was a dull sound she didn't recognize, followed by

a grunt. Then, "Cliona, run." The words sounded heavy, as though their utterance had taken all his remaining strength. A body thumped against the hard floor of the home.

Cliona ran.

She hated herself, but what choice did she have? She didn't have the first clue what foe or trap waited within the shadows. The ways of the stamfar, for all her study, were still fundamentally a mystery. To think she stood a chance against whatever Marjaana had left to guard her home was the height of hubris.

Cliona looked over her shoulder to ensure she wasn't being pursued.

She was.

At first, it appeared as though the darkness was expanding to fill the entire house. But when she heard the skittering sound again, her perspective shifted. The shadows weren't expanding, but they were moving, a living creature that quickly overcame her. A chill ran over her skin as the shadows enveloped her.

The moonlit door faded from view, and Cliona slid to a stop.

She faced her opponent.

She summoned teho, strengthening her body the way her father had drilled into her every day when she was young. Something sharp took shape from the shadows, thrust square at her chest.

It was too fast to dodge.

It hit between her breasts, not far from her heart.

She stumbled back from the force of the blow, and as she did, her opponent came close enough to see. It resembled a spider, except with six limbs instead of eight, and stood as tall as her. Its limbs were thicker than a spider's, though, and ended in sharp points. One of which had just tried to kill her.

A teho demon.

The name came to her even as her rational mind rejected it as impossible. Such creatures were legends, nothing but myths told around campfires when one had finished a few too many drinks.

Another limb came for her, and she caught it with her left hand. The demon made no sound, not even when Cliona used her right hand to chop through the creature's limb. Teho drained from the amputated leg, and the creature took a step back, rearing onto its two back limbs. It stabbed out with the remaining three legs as Cliona approached.

She let them hit her, then drove her fist into its center, feeling the flow of teho around her hand. She pulled, ripping a face-sized chunk of the creature's carapace away.

The creature collapsed, its limbs flailing wildly.

Cliona stepped back and watched it die.

As soon as its body went still, it began to dissolve, flecks of teho floating into the air and out the door. The living shadows faded and Cliona found herself alone in the hallway. She rushed back down it, hopeful she wasn't too late to save Zachary and Agnesse.

The lantern lay on its side in a large, circular room. Zachary was on the floor, blood pooling near his stomach. His chest still rose and fell, and Cliona breathed a sigh of relief. She kneeled next to him and saw that he'd been struck through the side by the demon's limbs. The wound didn't look fatal. It didn't even look like it should have knocked him over. The cut was deep, but hadn't sliced through anything but skin and muscle.

"Don't worry. I'm fine," came a bitter voice from another part of the room.

Cliona jumped. She'd forgotten about Agnesse.

"It's just a broken leg," Agnesse continued. "One that I'm worried might have cut an artery. So if you're all done looking over your young lover there, how about you make yourself useful and go get some help!" By the time Agnesse finished, her voice had risen nearly to a yell.

Cliona stood, checking once more to ensure Zachary was fine. For the briefest of moments, she considered telling Agnesse to go find her own help. She bit down on the words, though. It would do no good.

"Yes, ma'am," she said.

Once again she ran to the entrance, but this time, nothing followed.

7

Dagrun offered Hakon a place in a small trading caravan traveling to Vispeda.

The offer reminded him of the Dagrun of the past, always turning events to her gain. He admitted the idea was a win for them both. He earned the first real opportunity for rest since he'd left his home. In return, the caravan would enjoy Hakon's protection through the wilds.

Before he left, she pulled him aside once more. "If you find your daughter, return here. Together, perhaps we can stand a chance against Damion's advance."

"I'll make no promises," he replied. "But I will consider it."

Dagrun wasn't pleased by his lack of commitment, but she settled, knowing she wouldn't get more.

Then they left, the refuge disappearing behind them as the dense forest swallowed it up.

Fortunately, the caravan required little of him. His presence allowed them to bypass the series of inns that preyed on travelers' purses while protecting their lives.

Each night he placed some of his strongest wards, sufficient to deter any creatures in this area that wandered close looking for human flesh. During the day he rested and spoke with some of the others. They knew little about the events of the larger world, but Hakon learned plenty more about Dagrun.

Those who lived within her refuge loved her, according her a status somewhere between a hero and a legend.

It made him glad he'd visited.

She was proof they could change. They could become more than the stories now told about them.

The caravan reached Vispeda after five days of hard travel. Hakon thanked his companions and parted from them at the edge of town. They rumbled off, leaving Hakon to marvel at the changes in the world since he'd last been a part of it.

Vispeda was the largest city in the state, but Hakon had heard it paled in comparison to the grand cities of the east.

Which meant those cities must be marvels beyond comprehension. Vispeda stretched out as far as his eye could see, its streets filled with people. The noise and the smell, even at a distance, was almost too much to endure.

Cliona had written of the place, of course, but her descriptions didn't do justice to the actual experience of the city. She had written of the energy of Vispeda, the shared excitement of a people forging a new path forward. Here she'd met people from all over the land.

She loved living here. He could tell as much in every stroke of her neat handwriting.

If not for her, though, he would have turned around and walked away. This place was not for him.

For several long minutes he stood on the outskirts, gathering his courage.

This was what he had fought for. The least he could do

was experience it for himself, to see and listen to the fruits of the sacrifices he and his friends had made.

He gritted his teeth and walked into the chaos.

The people he met were kind enough, nodding to him as he passed and wishing him a good day, but many eyed him warily. Most gave him plenty of space, moving to the other side of the road as he approached. He saw few swords in the city, and no one carried a blade as massive as his.

He didn't mind. The space almost allowed him to believe the streets weren't as crowded as they were. Shopkeepers shouted from open doors and groups of people spoke amicably wherever he looked. In his entire life, he'd never felt so small. Not even in the midst of the clash of armies.

He had to ask for directions to the academy three times. The countless intersections and tall buildings confused his sense of direction, and if not for the sun in the sky serving as a guide, he was certain he would have become completely lost. How people found their way when everything looked the same was beyond him.

Eventually, though, he came upon a cluster of buildings surrounded by a short wall. It wasn't a defensive fortification so much as a divider. But once he stepped inside he felt like he could breathe again. The noise of the city faded to a din. A garden, small but well maintained, welcomed him and almost allowed him to believe he wasn't surrounded by the chaos of so many lives in one place.

He took a few minutes to gather his wits.

People were infinitely adaptable. No doubt, those who lived here were used to the sights, smells, and sounds of the city. But he'd spent the last forty years of his life in places where three families together was considered a crowd. And buildings squatted close to the ground, like they were supposed to, not reaching up to touch the sky.

As he recovered, he examined the academy where his daughter had come to live and work. It consisted of three taller buildings and one that appeared to be a dormitory. Here and there, men and women in their scholars' robes walked from building to building. Everyone was so lost in thought or debate they didn't even notice him.

He smiled. No wonder his daughter felt so at home in this place.

How many times had he called to her, perhaps for a meal or for a chore, only to be answered by silence? And then he would search for her and find her, curled up in one of her favorite nooks, bathed in sunlight, reading whatever stories she could get her hands on.

Cliona was, in many ways, the perfect balance between him and Sera. He was a man of the earth, happiest with tools in his hands and a task ahead of him. Sera had been a dreamer, obsessed with the legends of days long past and the futures that might one day be possible. Cliona somehow found a way to keep a foot in both worlds.

He set his shoulders and approached the largest of the buildings. A man wearing the robes of an apprentice scholar greeted him as he entered. He stared at Hakon as though he was seeing an illusion, then remembered his manners. "Is there something I can do for you?"

"I'm here to see Solveig," he answered.

The boy's eyes had landed on the enormous sword strapped to Hakon's back. He couldn't seem to tear them away. Hakon waited, and in the prolonged silence, the boy remembered his duties again. He shook his head. "I'm sorry. Who did you say you were here for?"

"I'm here to see Solveig," Hakon repeated.

The boy glanced again at Hakon's sword. Soon, Hakon was worried he'd have to pull it out and show its edge to the young scholar. But the boy cleared his head faster this time. "Do you have a scheduled meeting?"

"No, but I'm an old friend."

The scholar frowned. "Solveig is very busy. People don't just come and see her."

Hakon was thinking about picking the young scholar up and throwing him out the door when a voice from his past echoed down the hallway. "It's fine, Petyr," Solveig called. "Send him back."

Hakon didn't wait for the boy. He strode past Petyr. After passing a few open doors he came to the room the voice had come from.

He stopped before the threshold. His hands were sweating. He shook them out, then entered.

A hundred and fifty years was a long time to go without seeing a friend.

"Hakon," she said, her voice cool. "It's been a while."

The tone of her voice made him think she would have been happy not to see him for another century and more.

She was a smaller woman, but she held herself in such a way as to make most men cower before her. Her blue eyes were equally adept at melting hearts and freezing them solid, often within moments of one another.

There was no warmth in her gaze today.

Hakon swallowed the lump in his throat. Just looking at her opened up wounds he'd thought had scarred over decades ago.

He'd missed them all so much.

"Solveig," he said, "it's good to see you."

She gestured for him to take a seat, and he noted his sentiment hadn't been returned.

"You're here because of Cliona, I assume?" she asked.

He nodded. "How did you kn—?"

His voice trailed off. He was a fool for not having realized it the moment Dagrun told him Solveig was here in Vispeda. "You wrote to me."

A storm of emotions crossed over her face, quickly suppressed. "I did." She leaned back in her chair. "I take it Dagrun knew nothing?"

"The scholars mentioned in the note had visited, but Cliona wasn't with them."

Somehow, Solveig's eyes turned even colder. "I suppose that means she killed the scholars, then?"

Hakon nodded. Solveig cursed and stood up from her desk. At his surprised glance, she said, "They were good men. With good ideas."

"You sent them after Heiden's grave?"

"No, I tried to dissuade them, but I lack the authority to stop them."

"You do?"

"Being a senior scholar comes with responsibilities, but not many privileges. The comings and goings of most scholars are beyond my control."

"Who leads the academy?"

She smiled as if he were a child who had just asked a foolish question. "No one."

"Then how does anything get done?"

She arched an eyebrow. "You sound like an imperialist."

Hakon knew it for a jest, but it stabbed all the same.

She answered his question. "We have councils that gather. Most decisions require a majority, but some require unanimous consent. It's messy and slow, but voices are heard."

The weight of her cold gaze finally snapped something inside him, a tension that had wrapped around his spine from the minute he'd read that Cliona had gone missing.

He couldn't fight, not against Solveig. He slumped into his chair and looked at his feet. He gestured, meaning to encompass all of Vispeda and what it represented. "None of this is for me," he admitted.

Solveig returned to her chair and waited for him to say more.

"We built this world, and it left us behind," he said. "I don't want any more part in it. I just want to know my daughter is safe."

The weakness in his voice pained him, but there was no shame. Not with Solveig, who knew him inside and out.

"It left you behind," she said. "Not us."

"What?"

"We were released much earlier than you. And all of us have rejoined the world, finding our roles within it. Only you ran and hid."

The words were bitter, but true. Regrets pulled at him, and he longed to ask the questions that had troubled him for decades.

He reminded himself of his purpose. Nothing else mattered. Cliona needed him. He sat up a bit straighter. "How long did you know Cliona was my daughter?"

"Not long after I met her. She takes after you, you know. After befriending her, I eventually figured out who she was. You never told her who you were."

Hakon shook his head, but kept his focus on the problem at hand. "What can you tell me about her disappearance?"

"Not much more than was in the letter. It wasn't until a few weeks ago I even realized anything was wrong. Scholars come and go all the time, and Cliona was no different. It was only when I was speaking with one of her friends I began to worry. No one knew where she had gone, which is very unusual. We may not exercise much control here, but we are well informed. Scholars don't just leave without letting someone know."

"Have you looked for her?"

Solveig shook her head. "I'm not even sure she's in trouble. It could just be an oversight and she reappears here next week, confused about the fuss. But I was worried enough to send you a message."

"You haven't looked for my daughter at all?" Hakon clenched his fist again and leaned forward.

Solveig wasn't impressed by his display.

"She's not even my most pressing problem today, Hakon. The world nears the brink of war again, and I am doing all I can to prevent it."

With an effort, Hakon mastered himself. He forced himself to lean back in his chair. "When I spoke with Dagrun, she was also concerned."

"And she should be. She told you about Damion?"

Hakon nodded.

"Are you thinking of getting involved?"

"I only want my daughter. But Dagrun said she might be a part of whatever Damion is planning."

Solveig grimaced. "It's one possibility among many. I'd rather not speculate without further information." She reached into a door and pulled out a key. "This will get you into her room. Have Petyr take you there. See if you can find anything worthwhile, and we'll speak tonight over supper."

Hakon recognized a dismissal when he heard one. He stood up. "Thank you for letting me know, Solveig."

She was already turning to her next task, though, his presence already a part of her past.

8

———

Every time Cliona passed through the door of Marjaana's home, a brief but uncontrollable shudder ran down her spine. She understood she had little to fear. The house had been mostly explored. Only one trap remained, and she had no plans to set it off.

Still, as she stood in the hallway, she couldn't help but think of the shadows coming for her, opening up their cold embrace.

Vinko entered behind her, holding several lanterns aloft and banishing the darkness.

Every other digger, understandably, had refused to enter the home. Which left the task of exploring the buried building to Vinko and Cliona.

In truth, Cliona couldn't imagine a more pleasant companion to delve into the mysteries of the past with.

Vinko might not be a scholar, but his curiosity was boundless. His interest wasn't just in dirt and stone, but in everything buried within. Over the past few days they had spent countless hours in Marjaana's home, and as Cliona documented every item within, he told her stories of some of his own discoveries.

"Spend enough time with your hands in the dirt," Vinko said once, "and you'll find everything you were looking for and more." He'd unearthed lost jewels, old weapons engraved with unknown languages, and strange materials that were not natural, yet flummoxed everyone he had shown them to. And corpses, of course. Everywhere he went, he claimed, he found corpses in the most surprising places.

"Everybody believes they can bury the past," he once told her, "but the past refuses to stay buried." He'd gestured around Marjaana's home as further evidence of his theory.

She enjoyed his stories. His years of experience held a wisdom any scholar would be hard-pressed to find in the pages of a book.

In exchange, she taught him what she knew of the stamfar and their world.

Today they walked straight through the round room where Cliona had first encountered the demon and into the master bedroom, larger than any of the others within. It, more than any other place they'd explored, had been a trove of information.

The art on the walls depicted natural scenes in the same style as every other room. But here Cliona had found a small writing desk with a bound book. Though most of its pages were blank, tiny, neat handwriting filled the first thirty or so pages.

It was a journal.

One of Marjaana's.

Though she couldn't say how, the leather cover and the pages within bore none of the familiar signs of aging. From the way it appeared, Marjaana could have been writing in it just a few days ago.

She ran her hands over the cover. Marjaana was real. Though she'd spent the last few days translating the journal, it still seemed like a dream. Thanks to the magic of the written word, when Cliona translated the elegant stamfar script into imperial, she felt as though she was having a conversation with a myth made reality.

The wonder of it all made Agnesse's restrictions bearable.

The expedition leader had given strict orders not to remove anything from the site. When Cliona pressed for an explanation, Agnesse had ordered her out of the room. Now, Agnesse had guards search them every day when they emerged from the home. More were stationed constantly around the site, deterring anyone who came near.

Cliona could almost understand some of Agnesse's decisions. If they discovered some secret about the stamfar here, there was no telling how the information might be used. Knowledge was a powerful tool, but like all tools, it could either help or harm. If even half of the legends of the stamfar were true, the knowledge locked within this house could change the course of the world.

But they were in the middle of nowhere. Certainly it would be easier to take the journal back to the inn and work on it there.

But Agnesse didn't bend. Everything stayed within the home. And then she added even more restrictions to Cliona's work.

Every morning, the guards gave her a certain amount of materials to work with when she went into the home, then expected every material returned upon her exit. Even a missing scrap of paper was enough to cause a commotion, as Cliona had discovered on the first day of translating the journal.

Thankfully, Vinko's presence made the entire ordeal less bothersome.

Like her, he was naturally deliberate in his work, and could mimic writing the symbols of the stamfar well enough. They would sit side by side, and he would copy the marks of the stamfar, his hand slow and deliberate. As he did, Cliona would work on a direct translation on another paper.

The work was slow. Marjaana's vocabulary was wider than any stamfar text Cliona had encountered before, and many words in her translation were guesses.

But page by page, the journal revealed a world that long ago had passed into history.

Though most entries seemed mundane upon first glance, Cliona knew the scholars back home would salivate over every word.

She did.

She opened the journal to where she had ended the day before. Then she placed it carefully on the writing desk. Vinko watched. "Do you mind if I ask you something?" he asked.

"Anything." She was almost hurt he felt he needed to ask.

"The way you treat that journal, it's clear you think the stamfar were special. But I've never seen you pray at their shrines."

"They weren't gods," Cliona asserted. "Not even when they were alive. They had more teho, but not so much they could defeat death. They were people, just like us." She glanced down at the journal. "It's not who they were I'm fascinated by. It's what they knew."

Her eyes narrowed. "I've never seen you at the shrines, either."

Vinko chuckled. "Oh, I pray often enough. When a mine's about to collapse, or when a tunnel is filling with water. Just can't seem to remember whenever I'm near a shrine." He looked down at his hands. "I like the stories. But if I can't feel something in my hand or see it with my eye, I don't worry too much about it."

"We should all be so wise."

She swore he blushed. "Nonsense. I'm just an old man who talks to much. Come, let's get to work."

So they did, falling into their familiar roles.

Vinko finished copying his page and waited patiently for her to finish the translation. She saw he had something on his mind, but the translation consumed most of her attention. When she completed it, she leaned back and carefully turned the page over. The book was in unbelievable condition, but she would have treated a newborn infant with less care. Then she turned to Vinko. "What's wrong?"

He looked around, as though making sure they couldn't be overheard. He studied her for a moment, then spoke in a low voice that barely reached her ear. "Do you ever have doubts about our work?"

"What do you mean?"

He gestured around the room. "This is Marjaana's home. Buried by her own hand to prevent discovery. It is an incredible find, but there is power here. What will be done with it?"

"It will be used by the scholars to improve our world," she reassured him. "We'll make new tools to fight against the wild, and we'll make lives better for thousands."

His look was unreadable. "Do you truly believe that?"

"I do. It's the work I've dedicated my life to. I want to better understand the past so I can build a better future."

Vinko stared down at his feet, and Cliona saw his right heel bouncing rapidly up and down. After almost a full minute of silence, he looked back at her. "You don't know, do you?"

She frowned. "Know what?"

He looked around again, then whispered so she had to lean even closer to hear him. "This is no academic dig."

She laughed. "What are you talking about? Of course it is."

He shook his head. "I'm sorry. I thought you knew, or had guessed."

She couldn't decide if Vinko was joking or not. But his claim was ridiculous. "Why would this not be an academic dig?"

"Because I've been on academic digs. Far more than you. And every one has been a disorganized mess. Few scholars even remember to hire guards, and those that do usually hire locals just as likely to steal from them as protect them from the wild. Scholars never pay on time and will argue over every copper you spend. Does that sound like this dig to you?"

Cliona shook her head. Though she personally detested Agnesse, there was no doubt this expedition had been run well. She knew the guards who protected them were skilled. Her father had given her enough martial training she could recognize the skills in others. The diggers griped about the work, but never about the pay.

"I assumed all this was normal," she said. "If that's your only concern, perhaps you've just been on the wrong digs."

Even as she said it, though, she doubted. Her own life in the academy was never as efficient as this expedition. It had all the hallmarks Vinko had just mentioned. She tried again. "Perhaps this dig is just an exception."

"Not with the kind of money that's gone into this," Vinko said. "I'm being paid enough to take the rest of the year off, if I wish. And maybe the next. We all are. Even the guards."

There was no piece of evidence more convincing. The academy was always desperately searching for funds. Their advances might change the course of humanity, but they had to beg and borrow to fund those discoveries. Cliona leaned back in her chair. Agnesse had sometimes confided to them, in oblique ways, that their dig had a secret bene-factor, a patron who wished to remain anonymous. But Cliona had always assumed a gift had been given to the academy.

She felt as though a veil had been ripped from her eyes. Everything they'd done over the past two months took on a new shape.

She looked down at the journal. They were in the home of a stamfar, and she was suddenly uncertain of what that meant for the future.

She pushed her chair away from the writing table and stood up.

Vinko watched her. "I take it, then, you share my concerns."

Cliona wasn't sure how she felt about the revelation. But she didn't like the secrecy. Where it had once seemed a wise precaution, it now had a more sinister feel to it. "I feel like a fool."

"Don't. This is your first expedition, so you had nothing to compare it to. And it's easy to let our assumptions spin stories that aren't true. If I had a silver for each time someone had taken advantage of me over the years, I wouldn't be digging holes out here."

Vinko's reassurances did little to settle Cliona's unease, though.

She looked at the journal, but she'd get no other work done today. "I need to speak with Zachary," she decided.

Vinko helped her pack up everything they'd brought inside. They left the bedroom, but Cliona stopped before she reached the main room in the center of the house. A single door, larger than any other in the home, stood before her.

It alone remained locked.

When she examined the door, she felt the same type of locking mechanism that had been on the front door. It required teho to open.

A lot of teho.

More than she could manipulate by far. It required a kolma, at least, if not a stamfar. And neither existed anymore.

Given what had waited behind the first door that required teho, it was probably safe to assume even more dangerous surprises waited behind this one.

But what else was hidden behind the door? That was the question that had been keeping her up at night, her imagination running rampant with possibilities. Maybe it held one of the machines of the stamfar. Or weapons that put edged steel to shame. There were legends of gasses, invisible to the eye, that killed any who breathed them.

Vinko had offered to work on the door, but she had refused. She didn't think the constructions of the stamfar would fall to even Vinko's sharpest axe. And she didn't want to face the consequences if it did.

Her stomach clenched a little tighter as she abandoned her examination of the door. That was a mystery she would need to solve another day. But it loomed ominous in her thoughts. If they weren't here for the academy, whose hands would such secrets eventually end up in?

After enduring the usual inspection from the guards after leaving the home, she began her return journey to the inn, escorted by a pair of guards. Vinko remained behind, claiming he needed to supervise his diggers as they continued to excavate around the home.

Zachary greeted her warmly when she knocked on his door. A very competent physician had stitched up his wound. After another day or two of rest, he would be strong enough to join her on the dig. If it had been up to him, he'd already be helping.

"My hero," she said, enjoying the way he blushed at the compliment.

Zachary shook his head and looked down at his hands. Some part of him, she guessed, didn't believe the story she'd told him after their confrontation with the demon. But he'd stopped arguing, at least. There was no evidence to contradict her tale. He'd been unconscious from the overuse of his teho, and Agnesse had been around the corner and out of sight. And so, despite his reservations, he was the hero of the hour, the man who slew a teho demon.

"What brings you here so early?" he asked. "I figured you'd be in there another few hours at least."

"A question," she said. "Do you know who we're working for?"

He frowned. "The academy. Why?"

She shook her head, the lie coming easy to her. "Vinko told me some of the diggers were having trouble getting paid. Wanted to know who to write a letter of complaint to about Agnesse."

Zachary laughed at that. "When he writes the letter, let him know I've got about a dozen complaints to add." His expression changed. "Speaking of Agnesse, she wanted to see you."

"Well, I better not leave her waiting, then," Cliona said. She bid him well, then left the room and went to Agnesse's. She decided not to reveal her concerns to the woman, not yet. Let Agnesse think her more ignorant than she was.

She knocked on the door to Agnesse's room and entered when invited. She almost stopped in her tracks when she did.

Agnesse was smiling.

She was confined to her bed, but that didn't seem to matter in the least.

Cliona quickly recovered. "Zachary said you wanted to see me?"

Agnesse nodded. "We finally got some good news. I've just received a letter from our benefactor. He is most pleased with our progress, and distraught over the injuries we sustained."

"Our...benefactor?"

Agnesse looked again at the letter and then back up at Cliona. "Yes. You haven't met him yet, but he's been absolutely vital in convincing the academy to send us out here. His name is Damion, and he'll be visiting within the week."

9

———

Petyr led Hakon to Cliona's room, which Hakon unlocked with the key Solveig had given him. He pushed open the door, then looked over at Petyr. "You can go now," he said.

Petyr opened his mouth to protest, then saw Hakon's sword, like a demon on his back. The words died on the young man's lips. He nodded, then retreated down the dormitory hallway as though he had someplace very important to be.

Hakon watched him leave, then took a long, slow breath and stepped into his daughter's room. He closed the door behind him.

Cliona had never described her room in her letters, and it was easy enough to see why. It was a small space. A neatly made bed was pushed into one corner. A small writing desk sat underneath the window, where it could catch the light for as long as possible. One whole wall was consumed by a bookshelf that stretched from floor to ceiling.

The sight brought a smile to his face. She had always been one for stories, and her passion for collecting books hadn't abated since he'd seen her last. When he'd hired the cart to take her to Vispeda, he remembered packing more books upon it than clothes. Her collection, it appeared, had grown since then.

The only remaining piece of furniture was a small dresser, which also made him smile. It reflected Cliona's preferences for simple clothing, a taste she'd inherited from Sera. Two necklaces rested on top of the dresser, both pieces familiar.

He swallowed the small lump in his throat. Both necklaces had been Sera's, and Hakon had given them to Cliona when she'd moved to the academy. Over the years, his grief for his wife had faded, but it never left. Once it had threatened to tear him apart, but Cliona had held him together. Now Hakon welcomed the sorrow like an old friend, because it reminded him of what had been best in his life.

Hakon turned from the sight, unwilling to touch the necklaces.

He swore he felt Cliona's presence in the small space. He easily imagined her at her desk, her face furrowed in concentration as she translated a text older than he was. The thought of it brought him joy and pride.

She loved it here. She'd stated as much in her letters, but even if she hadn't, he would have guessed from the energy that radiated from her descriptions of a scholar's life. Hakon had always encouraged her passion, and had delighted in her sharing of it, but it had never been his. Here, though, she'd found others who shared her intersts and pushed her to new heights of inquiry.

He started his search at her writing desk, but a quick examination proved fruitless. It held stacks of paper and writing supplies, but little of interest. There were a few drafts of papers she'd started, mostly dealing with the translation of old stamfar texts. He read through them quickly, but saw nothing that gave him any hint of where she might have gone.

Next he turned his attention to the bookshelf. It was the only other place in the room he might find clues. He ran his fingers across the top shelf of books, smiling as some of the books brought memories bubbling to the surface of his thoughts.

One book on Heiden made him laugh out loud. He had purchased the book for her eleventh birthday, and she had spent the next three weeks explaining to him how it was full of inaccuracies. Even then, she'd had a confidence in herself that Hakon admired.

His fingers stopped on another book, the spine well worn. It was an illustrated book of stamfar legends, one meant for younger readers. He pulled the book out and flipped through the pages, a smile growing on his face. Even after years separated from this book, he remembered the illustrations and the specific phrases the authors had used to tell the myths every child on the planet knew. How many times had Cliona demanded he read her these stories? And when he got tired of reading, she'd demand Sera pick up and continue from where he left off.

He put the book back, right where he'd found it. Cliona had organized her books by subject, and he could imagine her anger if she found a book where it didn't belong.

Hakon's eyes stopped their search near the bottom of the bookshelf. There was a gap in the books.

There was a knock on the door, and it opened a moment later. Solveig looked in. "Would you care for some supper?" she asked.

At the mention of food, Hakon's stomach rumbled. He

looked out the window and noticed for the first time the fading light. "I would."

The corner of Solveig's mouth turned up in a smile, reminding him of the woman he'd once known. She was warmer to him now, which encouraged him. "Come on, then. I know a place I think you'll like."

As SOON AS they stepped outside the academy walls, Hakon felt like a stranger in a new land. The sun was setting, but the pace of life within Vispeda didn't seem to slow down at all. Couples walked arm in arm down the street, and merchants shouted from almost every shop.

Solveig noticed his discomfort. "Not much for cities?"

Hakon shook his head. "I've avoided them. At home, we'd all be locking our doors for the evening."

"The wilds rarely threaten Vispeda. Most creatures avoid the city at all costs."

"Perhaps they are the ones possessing true wisdom."

Solveig smiled and gestured for him to turn down a small side street. They passed one store and stopped before a nondescript building. Solveig led him in.

The smells that permeated the air within almost brought him to his knees. It was a small place, with only a few tables, but they found one in a corner that afforded them a degree of privacy. Before long, Hakon had before him an enormous mug of ale and enough food to feed a small state. He filled his plate and began the work of clearing the table of anything edible.

In between bites, he asked Solveig, "Do you truly like it here?"

"I do, although I'm not here as much as I used to be. My responsibilities send me throughout the lands."

He shook his head. "It's too chaotic."

"You're sounding like an imperialist again." She took a gulp of her own ale, then held up a hand to stop him and continued before his anger could build. "I understand what you mean, though. Vispeda is unlike anything we knew back then, and we never could have predicted it would arise as a result of our actions. But *this is* what we fought for. It's what our friends died for. It feels chaotic because it is. And that chaos has produced some of the greatest technology and art we've ever seen."

"You sound like Cliona in her letters. She said she felt energized just walking the streets."

"For good reason," Solveig said. "There are people from every state here. There're more cultures and ideas in one square mile of Vispeda than even existed when we fought. Don't you feel it, even a little?"

Hakon grimaced. "I don't." He paused, looking at his cup. Once, he'd shared nearly everything of his life with this woman. Maybe it was time to do so again. "Sometimes, I don't think I'm supposed to live in this world we built. I think that perhaps my time has ended and I should be content to exist only in legends."

His confession elicited a sympathetic smile. Of all the band, he was grateful to meet with Solveig first. She'd always been the gentlest of them.

Though, compared to the others, that wasn't saying much. She danced with a sword better than almost anyone.

Still, she was the one least likely to kill him. She turned the conversation back to the reason he'd left home in the first place. "Did your search reveal anything?"

"She's looking for Marjaana."

"How did you figure that out?"

"All her books on Marjaana are gone."

Solveig sighed and leaned back. She gave him a look he couldn't decipher.

"What?" he asked.

"I wish it was easier to hate you," Solveig said, "but you're still the same, even after all these years."

Hakon wasn't certain what she meant.

"Do you have any idea how many scholars I've trained over the years?" Solveig explained. "I could have sent almost any one of them into that room and they wouldn't have come out any wiser. They only look for what they can see. No one else instinctively looks for what's missing. Only you. It's one of the reasons why we accomplished everything we did."

"But without you putting the pieces together, my observations wouldn't have amounted to much," Hakon said. "The same is true today. I know Cliona is searching for Marjaana, but that means little to me. It doesn't help me find her."

"She's probably to the west," Solveig answered. "We have a scholar here who is probably closer to locating Marjaana's home than..." Her voice trailed off.

Solveig cursed. "She's gone, too," she said, more to herself than anyone else. When she saw Hakon's look, she explained. "Agnesse, one of our senior scholars. Like Cliona, she specializes in the stamfar, and probably knows more about Marjaana specifically than anyone else alive. When I learned that no one knew where Cliona had gone, I had Petyr make a list of everyone absent from the grounds. Agnesse was on it."

"It's safe to assume they're together?"

Solveig hesitated for a moment. "Probably. I'll dig further into Agnesse's absence when we return. If no one knows where she went, I'd stake anything she's with your daughter."

Hakon finished up his meal. He couldn't remember the last time he'd felt so full. One question still worried at him. "What is Damion up to?"

"He wants to rebuild the empire and become emperor, as he believes he was destined to."

She made the claim so nonchalantly Hakon was taken aback. "Is that all?" he asked, sarcasm dripping from the question.

Solveig grinned. "He doesn't say so publicly, of course. According to the official record, he's a duly elected official, the leader of one of the fastest growing and most secretive areas on the continent. Rumors are that he'll soon apply for statehood, becoming our seventh governor."

"And that doesn't concern anyone?"

"It concerns plenty of people, including the other governors. But not as much as feeding their citizens or protecting them from the ever-increasing threats of the wild. Despite what places like Vispeda might lead you to believe, we're not winning the war against this planet. Damion promises peace and safety, and that's more than most governors are willing to commit to. Tehoin, in particular, have found his promises appealing."

Hakon turned the news over in his head. It wasn't surprising. Damion had always been a staunch imperialist, and they'd been on opposing sides of the rebellion.

"How might Cliona be helping him?"

"He's grown quite obsessed with the stamfar. His own strength surpasses that of most kolmas, if what I hear is true. I don't know exactly how her research will aid him, but I'd rather it not." Solveig looked at him, clearly holding something back.

"What?" he asked.

"Damion has made no secret of the fact that if he finds you, he will kill you in a heartbeat. If he finds out Cliona is your daughter..." She left the rest unspoken.

"Then I need to hurry. Can you help me?"

Solveig nodded. "I have notes from some presentations Agnesse gave a few years ago. I recall her mentioning potential locations of Marjaana's home. It'll give you something to pursue, at least."

"Thank you," Hakon said. "Both for this, and for letting me know about Cliona. I'm grateful you've kept an eye on her."

Solveig accepted the thanks, but he felt as though she was still keeping him at arm's length. She might not be trying to kill him, but she wasn't forgiving him, either. They paid an exorbitant amount of money for their meal, then stepped into the streets. Though it was dark, many were still out.

They walked slowly, Solveig allowing Hakon to take the city in and ask whatever intrigued him. He pointed to a shrine. "Those don't seem too popular."

"They aren't. It's an age of progress, and few here pray to the stamfar anymore. The tehoin fade, and the legends start to sound an awful lot like lies."

"The tehoin continue to disappear?"

"If anything, faster than ever before. Even vildas are uncommon among the students at the academy now. Soon we'll all start to sound a lot like myths."

"Have you found a reason?"

Solveig looked up at the stars. "I've imagined dozens of reasons, but not one I believe. Those of us who continue to live grow stronger by the year, but a child born today has perhaps one chance in a hundred of being able to manipulate teho. And if they can, they are increasingly considered outcasts among the youth."

He shook his head, then answered her inquiring look. "I just had the terrifying thought that I'm starting to understand Isira better."

"She is frustrating, but I can understand her philosophy."

He felt a flash of teho from above. He tensed and looked up, preparing to defend himself.

Solveig laughed. "One of Damion's spies, I believe. He keeps a close eye on me, and now he'll know I have company. Fortunately, you've been gone for so long I don't think anyone will recognize you."

"He's spying on you? And you let him?"

There was a twinkle in her eye. "Don't worry, I return the favor. But I'm sure Dagrun told you. There's a war coming, and in this war, even the scholars will matter."

10

After Agnesse's announcement about their benefactor's arrival, Cliona slowed her efforts to translate the journal. She couldn't stop work completely, but with no one except her and Vinko in the home, it was easy enough to generate excuses for slow progress. Agnesse didn't even notice. She spent her time at the inn, supported by two guards, preparing the place for a feast.

Even if Agnesse had been staring over her shoulder, there was little the woman could do to help.

Agnesse's primary skill, as far as Cliona could tell, was an ability to gather information from disparate sources and form it into a cohesive story. Give her five different legends and she would extract the single thread of truth from within.

But Agnesse relied on the work of others to do her own. She couldn't translate the language of the stamfar. So yes, thanks to Agnesse, they'd found Marjaana's home. But once found, she became little more than a glorified administrator.

Zachary eventually joined her and Vinko, but wasn't much more helpful. Cliona couldn't begin to guess what scholarly skills he possessed, but even after he was healed there was little for him to do but wander through rooms that were already explored. She and Vinko had their system, but Zachary insisted on accompanying them anyway.

Cliona suspected the silence of Marjaana's home was far superior to the chaos of the inn. Any distance from Agnesse was a welcome relief.

Three days after Agnesse's declaration their benefactor would soon arrive, Cliona felt an incredible release of teho. It was late afternoon, and she and Zachary were dragging their feet on the way back to the inn. Despite the power of the release, she kept her face expressionless.

Beside her, Zachary started, the event kicking him out of his reverie. "Did you feel that?"

Almost as soon as the question was past his lips, he apologized. "Sorry. Of course you can't. Someone just used a lot of teho." He gulped. "Too much." He kept staring in the direction the burst had come from. "I think that was a kolma."

Cliona laughed at the thought. Kolmas were dead, the legends of an age long past. She had felt the power, too. But it had to be a very strong nelja. It was the only logical explanation. He glared at her. "I know what I felt."

"The last kolma died a few years after the end of the rebellion."

Zachary didn't respond. But he kept looking in that direction, his expression worried.

When they reached the inn, there were several new horses in the stables. They were fine beasts, taller than Cliona and built of muscle. The warhorses seemed out of place in the small stables, and Cliona had no desire to be on the opposing side of such creatures.

No doubt, this was Damion. He'd transported himself, a horse, and apparently two others, also mounted. She faltered for a moment at the thought. No wonder they'd felt so much teho. Zachary stared at the horses with wide eyes, and she wondered if he was thinking along the same lines.

They entered the inn, where all appeared normal, at least by the standards of the past few days. They went to their rooms, and Cliona found a note on the floor of hers, hastily pushed under the door, telling her to appear for supper that evening.

As if she had planned on skipping the meal.

She bathed and relaxed, trying not to think of their mysterious patron and failing completely.

When she went down for supper, the common room was more crowded than she'd ever seen it. The scene looked more like a formal presentation to a governor than a meal. Vinko and most of his senior diggers were present, as well as the captain of the guard and his officers. Agnesse presided over everyone like the queen of the world's smallest court.

She saw Zachary and their gazes met. He rolled his eyes and she smiled.

If there was one thing she hadn't missed about being at the academy, it was the endless formal dinners and ceremonies. The scholars in her corner of the world had become masters of fanfare.

Her eyes traveled over the rest of the crowd. She had no trouble finding Damion.

He wasn't a large man, but he commanded the room in a way Agnesse could only dream of. His dark hair was cut short, and from her position on the stairs, Cliona saw how others shrank under his attention. He seemed to intimidate as a matter of course. Not by shouting or belligerence, but by the strength of his presence.

The effect was heightened by the two warriors who trailed him like shadows. A man and a woman, dressed completely in black.

Cliona paused at the sight of them. When they moved, it was like watching water pour from a pitcher. Then they would stop behind Damion as he endured yet another introduction, and they would become perfectly still. Not only that, something about them seemed to pull her eye away from them, as though they didn't want to be seen even though they stood in the middle of a crowded room.

The captain of the guard and his soldiers were well trained. But they were nowhere near as dangerous as this pair.

By the time Cliona made it to the bottom of the stairs, the introductions were over. Agnesse had seen her come down, but made no effort to bring Damion to her. Instead, the leader of their expedition called for everyone to sit. Cliona looked down at the long tables and saw that place cards had been set, indicating people's assigned seats.

Agnesse might have been restricted to the inn due to her injury, but she'd been busy. The calligraphy on the place cards was exquisite.

Cliona found herself across from Zachary at the far end of one of the tables, about as far from Agnesse and Damion as it was possible to be and still remain in the same room.

She was frustrated and relieved in equal measure. At least back here, she didn't have to pretend to be respectful toward Agnesse. But at the same time, it was her work that had started to crack the mysteries of Marjaana's home.

"Feel like we're being disrespected?" Zachary asked with a smile.

"Starting to get that impression," she said.

Despite their location near the back of the room, or perhaps because of it, they enjoyed their meal. Agnesse had clearly spoken with the innkeeper, as the food was the best they'd eaten since their arrival, and it had been good to start. If Cliona had a few extra cups of wine, it only made the food taste that much better.

As the meal drew to a close, Damion stood to address the assembly. The room went silent without him having to say a single word. When he spoke, he wasn't loud, but his deep voice carried easily through the room.

"I'm honored to be among you today. Through your efforts, you have uncovered a secret long buried, a discovery that will change the lives of everyone struggling to make a living on this planet. The work has been hard, but I do not think it an empty boast to say that one day, your descendants will look back on this work and say, 'This is when the world changed. This is when humans started to win.'"

He raised his cup, and everyone in the room mirrored the gesture.

From another, Cliona might have laughed at the absurd claim. But there was something about Damion that made her think he might actually have the right of it. And at that thought, she was proud of her contribution to the work. When she held up her cup, she had the sudden certainty that she was part of something important.

"Thanks to Agnesse's translations," Damion continued, gesturing to the expedition leader, "and the tireless support of everyone in this room, we will build a world safe for our children to live in."

Cliona squeezed her cup until her knuckles turned white. Zachary was grimacing. Of course Agnesse would claim Cliona's work as her own. Cliona swore that the next time she was alone in a room with the older woman, she would give Agnesse a piece of her mind and more.

But Damion currently consumed too much of her attention. He raised his cup even higher. "For a better future," he toasted.

"For a better future!"

The rational half of Cliona's mind was surprised by the enthusiasm the diggers and soldiers took up the toast with. But she had shouted just as loud, her anger at Agnesse's betrayal temporarily forgotten.

The rest of the meal passed quickly, and Zachary and Cliona had to support one another to make it up the stairs. She liked the feeling of his sturdiness next to her, and she was just drunk enough to consider inviting him into her room.

She didn't, though she couldn't say why. Zachary made sure she made it to her room, then went to his own.

Cliona flopped into the chair beside her writing desk, watching the moon in the sky. Despite her inebriation, she had little desire to rest. There was something about Damion that captured her attention and prevented her mind from wandering aimlessly. No matter which path of thought she took, it always led back to him.

She didn't know how long she sat and stared at the moon, but she nearly jumped out of her skin when someone knocked firmly on her door. She opened it and found herself face to face with the very man she'd just spent too long thinking about.

"I saw the light under your door, and I wondered if I might speak privately with you."

His two shadows stood behind him, their backs to the door, watching the hallway.

Cliona had trouble finding words. Close to him, it was as

if there was suddenly no air to breathe. She nodded and stepped aside, gesturing him in. He shut the door behind him, leaving his shadows outside.

"I'm afraid we haven't been properly introduced. Damion," he said.

"Cliona."

His eyes narrowed as he looked at her. "There's something familiar about you. Have our paths crossed before?"

She shook her head, finally remembering how to string a sentence together. "I only just learned about you a few days ago," she said.

His regard didn't waver. He looked at her for nearly a full minute, then blinked rapidly and looked away. "I've listened to many people tonight, and they all speak highly of you. They say you know a good deal of the stamfar."

"I've been interested in them since I was a small child."

"Why?"

His gaze returned to her, and she almost wished he would look away. Then she found her spine. Her father had raised her to fear no one. She stood up straighter and met his gaze. "My father was a gifted storyteller. I'm sure he told the same stories as any other parent, but when he told them, I felt as if I was in a different time and place. A time when teho allowed us to beat back the wild." She paused. "Unlike other children, though, the stories weren't enough for me. I wanted to understand the stamfar and their power. Not just as a story, but in truth."

"Why?" Damion asked again.

"Because they had the strength to change the world. Maybe, with their knowledge, we can do the same."

Damion nodded, then paced the room slowly. "If you had the knowledge of the stamfar, what would you do? You say you want to change the world, but how?"

"I want humans to defeat the wilds," Cliona said.

She regretted the claim the moment it left her lips. It was true, but it was the dream of a child, one who hadn't grown enough to realize the impossibility of it. Not something to admit to the patron of their expedition. She might as well have claimed she wanted to fly among the stars or defeat the gate of death itself. All were equally foolish. She blamed the drink.

Damion didn't dismiss her dream as she would have expected. Instead, he smiled. "An audacious dream, and one I happen to share."

Cliona stepped back. "You...do?"

Damion nodded. "You lost someone to the wild, didn't you?"

Cliona swallowed. "My mother. When I was twelve."

"I'm sorry," Damion said. "But with your help, I believe we can turn our dream into a reality. We can prevent what happened to your mother from happening to anyone else. The stamfar are the key to unlocking the mysteries of this planet." He pulled a slip of paper from his pocket. "And speaking of help, this was why I actually knocked on your door tonight. One of my scholars found a fragment of stamfar text, and I was hoping you might translate it for me. I'd ask Agnesse, but I'm afraid she's asleep after tonight's festivities."

Cliona bit back her retort. She couldn't guess how Damion felt about Agnesse, but now she had an opportunity to show their patron her skills directly. She nodded and he handed the paper over to her.

She took it to her desk. Most of it was easily translated, but one word in particular caught her eye.

She glanced back at Damion, who watched her with an expressionless face.

"You're testing me."

He smiled, though he showed no regret for being caught in the act. "I am. But please, write your translation down."

An odd request, but she supposed wealthy patrons were entitled to them. She turned back to her desk and wrote the translated phrase, hesitating only a moment at the questionable word. Then she handed it to him. "It's an epitaph."

Damion read her translation out loud. "Here lie the remains of our father, who has flown among the stars." He smiled. "Most would translate it 'who dreams of the stars.'"

She knew the word had been the test. "I don't think so. We see the same root of the verb in other words, and we are certain those words all have to do with movement."

"And most scholars argue it means to dream, or to move the mind."

Cliona hadn't expected Damion to be so well versed in current academic debates. "It's possible, but in all the other uses of the root, the motion is physical. I believe the same is true here. They are speaking of physically flying through the stars."

Only then did she realize what she was saying. "Wait. Where did you find this? I've heard legends of stamfar who could use teho to fly, but never so high as to be among the stars. Is it a metaphor? Is there more text?"

Damion smiled again, and she knew he had answers to at least some of her questions. But he wasn't offering them up. "It was a test, and in more ways than one," he said. He held up her translation. "You have small and neat handwriting, whereas Agnesse's is large and difficult to read. It's your translations of Marjaana's journal I've been reading. Not hers."

Cliona nodded.

His grin grew even wider. "So, do you want to unlock the

final mysteries of Marjaana's home? You're clearly the one I should be asking."

"Now?"

"Did you have other plans for tonight?"

"No, but—"

"Then let's go. I'm guessing you want to know what's behind that final door just as much as I do."

"But it's sure to be a trap."

"Of course. So are you coming?"

His confidence astounded her. And she couldn't say how, but she was certain that his confidence was deserved. If she went with him, she would finally have answers. And she felt safe in his presence.

"I wouldn't miss it for the world," she said.

11

———

Solveig came to Hakon's room around mid-morning the following day. She looked like she hadn't slept at all since they'd parted ways the night before.

She handed him a folded piece of paper.

"What's this?" he asked.

"The best map we were able to make," Solveig said. "It's based off our most recent surveys and all the notes any of us have on Agnesse's work. There are three areas where it's plausible Marjaana's home was buried. They're large areas, but you don't need to find the house, just the scholars."

He unfolded the map and studied it. It was a good map, but she was right. The spaces in question were large. Dozens of miles wide and long. But if he got close, he could find the dig without much difficulty. "Thank you, again."

"Someday, after their anger has cooled, you should thank the scholars here. Almost a dozen of us stayed up through the night to make this."

He nodded. Given their history, he couldn't think of any words sufficient to express his gratitude. Fortunately, also due to their history, he didn't have to.

Solveig knew.

"If there's ever anything I can do in return," he said, "please ask."

She offered him a thin smile. "I will." She looked around the room, taking in his preparations to leave. Then she reached into a pocket and pulled out a small stone. When she held it out to him, he felt the complex weave of teho around it.

"What is it?"

"In case of crisis," she said.

He reached out tentatively and took it, half surprised it didn't explode in his hands. It had been decades since he'd encountered a weave of such complexity. "What does it do?"

"When you unravel the weave, help will come. It can only be used once, though, so it's best to use it only if you really need it."

He looked up from his examination. "You think I might need this?"

"I hope not. But the wilds are fighting back, and you'll be close to land Damion controls. If he knows you're near, he'll go to any lengths to flay you alive. Let's just say that of the two of us, I think you have a greater chance of needing it in the near future."

"Reassuring."

Solveig reached out and grabbed his arm. "Hakon, be careful. I suspect Damion is far stronger than you now, and the world has changed since you left it. I don't want to stop you from finding your daughter, but I fear what this pursuit will cost you."

"Whatever the cost, she's worth it," Hakon said. "And thank you. I will be careful."

They said their farewells then, and Hakon could tell Solveig feared this parting would be their last.

He couldn't help but wonder. Was her confidence in his skill that shaken? Or was this search that dangerous?

He left the academy and put Vispeda behind him. Though the danger was greater out in the wilds, his shoulders relaxed a little more with every mile he put between him and the city. The wilds, at least, he understood.

He opted to spend his first night by the side of the road with a caravan that offered him shelter. The caravan had hired a nelja, and she cast a powerful net of wards around the wagons. A few creatures explored the defenses that night, but none were much danger against the wards.

He was on the road before the sun rose, ignoring the worried glances from the caravan owner. Dusk and dawn were widely considered some of the most dangerous times in the wild. But thoughts of Cliona pushed him forward.

Hakon didn't allow himself to imagine the worst possibilities of what might have happened to her. He tried to convince himself she was fine. Even if she had found herself in a dangerous situation, she was more than capable of looking after herself. He'd raised her to be strong, both mentally and physically.

His attempts at reassuring himself did little to ease his fears. If anything, he walked faster.

The day seemed a busy one. Vispeda's size and thriving market attracted hopefuls from all corners of the known world, and though he was more than a day out of the city, the road was far from empty. Farmers on carts lumbered past, trailed by caravans ranging in size from three wagons to nearly a dozen.

Hakon walked on the side of the road, studying his fellow travelers from under the brim of a wide hat. He was one of the few who walked the road without wares. From the well-worn ruts in the road, he suspected thousands of carts and wagons had made the journey to and from the city.

When he'd been a boy, there had been no such trade.

Of course, there'd been no cities the size of Vispeda either. The emperor had detested such concentrations of humanity.

In the empire, goods had moved because the emperor, or one of his designated vassals, determined that the goods needed to move.

Now gold pushed the states forward.

Hakon wasn't sure how he felt about the change. It was less orderly, which clashed with the world he remembered best. But as Solveig said, out of that chaos progress emerged. Give people the freedom to do what they want, and inevitably, some will push society forward.

The meal Solveig had shared with him two nights past was a perfect example. Though expensive today, such a meal would have been impossible for all but a few under the empire's rule. Progress inched forward. And yet, he felt that something had been lost, too. He didn't doubt the power of gold, but he quietly longed for the days when people worked for something more important than coin.

He shook his head.

Perhaps he *had* lived too long.

A familiar face on the road caught his attention that afternoon. He'd seen her yesterday, a short blonde woman with sharp eyes. She remained well behind him, but like him, she carried nothing to sell or trade. It was that detail that had brought her to his notice the day before.

Of course, he wasn't the only one traveling this direction, and there was no law stating that the road was only to be used by merchants.

He gave no indication that he'd spotted the woman.

One advantage to being a large man was that many people tended to underestimate his intelligence. They saw his size and his enormous sword, and thought him good for only cracking skulls or chopping wood. He did little to convince people otherwise. Better to be considered a fool and alive than be known as cunning and treated as such.

That night he stopped at an inn, but she did not enter.

As night fell, he sat near the corner of the common room, listening to the tales of the wild. If anything, it seemed that Solveig hadn't warned him strongly enough about the dangers. Creatures no one could identify seemed a common occurrence. Everyone had a story of family and friends lost to the never-ending battle against the planet.

And yet they traveled, risking it all for greater fortunes.

In time, the conversation turned to the rebellion, and the deeds of the band. Tonight, they spoke of the battle outside Hognastir, a town that no longer existed. The band's names had been lost to history, no doubt influenced by Isira. The deeds grew with time and retellings, but the seed of truth was still enough to raise unpleasant memories. Hakon finished his drink and left before the story ended.

He knew well enough how the stamfar had come to be worshipped. That the deeds of the band were on the same journey bothered him.

He welcomed his dreamless sleep that night.

The next day he didn't see the woman, and he relaxed a bit.

By the day after that, the number of people on the road had diminished considerably. Several roads had branched off the one Hakon followed, and it seemed most saw more traffic than the one that headed west.

The road diminished into a rutted track that only saw occasional use. More than one traveler he passed going the other way cautioned him about dangers ahead, but so far, Hakon had come across nothing that worried him.

He spotted the same woman again late that evening. She made no particular effort to hide, but with nothing but rolling grasslands for miles, there was little point in trying.

He felt fortunate to find an inn that night. Given the hazards of traveling the wild, innkeeping was a particularly lucrative business, but risky. The best inns had nelja standing guard day and night, and the poorest relied on small armies of ahula. Either way, they were expensive to run and expensive to stay at, and usually only found on main roads.

This inn was a squat building, guarded by two vilda, if the strength of their wards was any indication. The innkeeper confirmed it was the last protection for a long ways.

So it wasn't much of a surprise to see the woman enter not long after him.

She paid him no particular attention, though. There were a handful of travelers that night, but unlike the inns closer to Vispeda, no one seemed much in the mood to talk. That night he dozed lightly while sitting against a wall, sword propped up in front of him in case he was attacked.

He could have warded the room, but he didn't want his pursuers to know he was tehoin.

When he sensed someone transport themselves twice that night, he was grateful for his caution. It was probably the woman. With any luck, she didn't know who he was. But she was reporting to someone else.

Most likely Damion.

The next morning he resumed his journey. The woman didn't follow him. He hadn't seen much in the way of wildlife, nor did he feel particularly tired. So he walked into the night. With any luck, he would either draw out his pursuit or leave it behind.

Sometime near the middle of the night, he saw three figures, all wearing dark clothes, standing in the road. He hadn't seen another soul for miles, and of course, no one traveled at night.

It was a perfect place and time for an ambush, if one was interested in such activities.

Hakon paused for a moment, then shrugged to himself and continued on.

They met before long. Hakon stopped, a dumb smile on his face. He didn't recognize any of the three.

"Greetings!" he said.

For a long moment, no one responded.

Then the man in the middle spoke. "Who are you?"

"I'm Petyr," Hakon said, the smile growing wider on his face. "It's a pleasure to meet you."

The woman on Hakon's right began to gather teho. Not much. No more than a vilda. He gave no sign he'd noticed.

"What business did you have with Solveig in Vispeda?"

Hakon pulled the folded map from his pocket, leaving it folded. "She asked me to deliver this message to a friend."

The man held out his hand. "We'll be taking that, now."

Hakon shook his head. "I promised her I'd deliver it."

The man laughed. "You're outnumbered, and all of us are tehoin. Even if you can use that oversized monstrosity on your back, you have no chance."

They had no intention of letting him live. But they were overconfident, and too close. Hakon dropped the map and closed the last few paces between them in a heartbeat. He drove his elbow into the face of the speaker just as he formed a teho blade. The man's nose crunched under Hakon's elbow as his eyes rolled up in his head.

As the leader fell, Hakon shifted toward the woman who had been quietly gathering teho. She stepped back, a thin knife of teho in each hand.

She hadn't been prepared, though, and hadn't adapted to his speed.

No one expected big men to move fast.

He wrapped one of his hands around her wrist and drove the hand toward her head.

Too late, she realized his intent. But his strength was far greater than hers, and he didn't give her time to respond.

She killed herself with her own teho blade.

As Hakon spun to fight the third warrior, he drew his sword from his back.

The final warrior was a tall man with long arms. Like his partners, he'd formed a teho blade, except one that was longer and narrower than any sword of steel.

Hakon paused. If he drew upon teho, the fight would be easy enough. These three, as near as he could tell, possessed no special skill. But if he didn't, he wasn't sure how he would get inside the warrior's long reach. The teho blade would carve him into pieces.

Hakon stepped forward, encasing his sword in a thin layer of teho. He barely drew upon what he was capable of, but it would protect his weapon.

When their swords met, Hakon reveled in the man's look of surprise. He'd expected his teho blade to slice through Hakon's sword. He probably hadn't even felt Hakon's weak technique.

The third man died with that look frozen permanently on his face.

Hakon let the blood drip from his sword as he picked up the map and returned it to its pocket.

A quick swipe of teho cleaned the blade and he returned it to his back.

Then, off in the distance, he felt someone transport. He looked, but saw nothing.

Hakon swore.

Someone had seen him.

12

———

Cliona left the inn with Damion and the two warriors who shadowed him. They caught the guards at the edge of town by surprise. Work had effectively stopped for the night so people could attend the feast. Before the guards could hurry to rouse an escort, Damion waved them to ease. "We'll be fine. Rest tonight, as there is much work still to be done."

The head guard looked uncertain, but Damion held the purse strings, and there was no contradicting his wish. The guard made just enough fuss to absolve himself of responsibility, then let them pass unaccompanied.

Damion and Cliona walked side by side, the moonlight providing more than enough illumination to see the path. Off in the distance, she thought she saw shadows stalk among the tall grasses of the plains, but none neared the small group.

The sight reminded her of his bold claim. Damion seemed content to walk in silence, but she needed answers. "Do you really believe it's possible?"

"To defeat the wild?"

She nodded.

"I do." A simple statement of fact.

"How?"

"Through the lost knowledge of the stamfar, in part. Through our own will, ingenuity, and determination for the rest."

"That's vague."

He smiled, but didn't elaborate. Instead, he questioned her. "You say you've spent your life studying the stamfar. Tell me, what did a typical day look like for the average stamfar?"

She frowned. It was a simple enough question, but one she had never spent much time considering. The legends told of great feats, of people with the power of gods who walked the planet and carved out the first places for humans to live in peace.

She knew of no tales of the stamfar washing their laundry. The only stamfar hunts she could recall involved great beasts, not the more common hunts that brought back food for the family. "I have no idea," she confessed.

Damion grinned. "A scholar willing to admit when they don't know something?" He turned to the two warriors following them. "Now I do believe in miracles!"

To her surprise, the warriors chuckled. She glanced back and saw they were relaxed. After their posture and demeanor at Agnesse's feast, they seemed like completely different people.

Their laughter put her at ease, even if it was at the expense of her profession.

Damion hadn't finished his questions. "Who or what came before the stamfar?"

"Most scholars believe that humans lived in small tribes, roaming the land for food, fighting off the wilds."

"Were those who came before the stamfar tehoin?"

Cliona faltered.

"Because if they were," Damion continued, "why do we not tell stories about their deeds? And if they weren't, how did they survive the wilds, and how did the stamfar develop their abilities?"

Cliona's head spun. The questions weren't new. Scholars had been asking them for a generation, at least. But all attempts at answering those questions fell woefully short of being believable. "I don't know," she said.

For all they had learned, they had barely begun to scratch the surface of the past.

"Neither do I," Damion said, "but the answers to these questions are vital. Learning the answers isn't just a matter of increasing our knowledge of the past. We need those answers to survive into the future. The stamfar changed this world. If we could understand them, we could too."

Damion looked at her, but she did not let the intensity of his look intimidate her. "You criticize me, rightly, for vague statements, but they are all I can make. I won't know how to change the world until you tell me how the stamfar did it first."

"Me?"

He nodded. "Agnesse is a useful administrator, and she will be rewarded as such. But it's a translator I need, a translator who will unlock the secrets of the past. Will you?"

He didn't ask it as a simple question, but as a promise.

She didn't hesitate. "I will."

"Good."

They had covered a little more than half the distance to the excavation when Cliona sensed teho behind her. She turned a second after the others, surprised to see someone else now with them. The visitor was a shorter woman with light hair.

The others relaxed when they recognized her, so Cliona did the same.

"Sir," she said. "They questioned the man traveling west, as you requested. He killed them."

Damion raised an eyebrow. "He's tehoin?"

"Vilda, at least. He didn't use much, but he was a skilled warrior."

Damion sighed, but didn't seem too distraught over the loss of his warriors. "She wouldn't send someone without talent this way." He looked out into the distance, but his decision came quickly. He looked to his two shadows. "Go with her. Find out what you can, then return when you are able."

The woman who'd just arrived protested. "Sir, both of them?"

"I don't want to take chances."

"I won't be able to transport them out for at least a few hours."

"That's fine."

Cliona watched the exchange with interest. At Damion's order, the two warriors became the people she recognized from the feast. In a moment, they'd taken up the mantle of killers. They stepped away from Damion and held hands with the woman. Then they were gone in another burst of teho.

The woman had to have been nelja. No vilda was so strong to transport three people. "Do we need to return?" she asked.

Damion shook his head. "Those two are more than strong enough to handle almost any warrior on this planet," he said. "Besides, this is more important to me."

He risked the wilds at night alone without a second thought. Had he been almost anyone else, she would have called him mad, or a fool. But he was clearly neither.

Though it was impossible, she wondered if Zachary was right about Damion's strength. Perhaps the kolma hadn't disappeared the way everyone believed.

They made their way to the excavation without incident. The guards at the site recognized Damion and allowed him past the checkpoints without so much as a question. Cliona had never received such an open welcome, even though she came through every day.

Someday, she wanted to be the funder of an expedition, instead of working for one.

They descended the ladder to the entrance. Cliona prepared to light one of the lanterns they left at the bottom of the hole, but Damion shook his head. "I don't think we'll need that."

She put the lantern down. Damion's confidence infected her, but a part of her wanted him to be wrong about something, just to see if he had any humility at all. He stepped into the house and she followed. He reached out his hand toward the wall and smiled.

She felt him manipulate teho, and suddenly there was light everywhere. It wasn't the soft yellow light of the lanterns, but brighter and whiter, emanating from previously invisible strips on the ceiling.

The whole house began to hum with power, a soft background noise unlike anything Cliona had heard before. She took a step back.

"There's nothing to fear," Damion said. "This is just a small part of the ability of the stamfar."

"How did you know such a thing?" She had studied

every inch of the house she could, and she hadn't even felt whatever Damion had interacted with.

He spun in a slow circle, looking around. "I've been studying the stamfar for a very long time."

"If saving humanity doesn't work out for you, there's always a place at the academy," Cliona replied.

"Not for me, I'm afraid, but I appreciate the offer. Now, come, let's see what's behind that last door."

She pointed the way and he led, though he didn't seem to be in any particular rush. He poked his head into every room to examine the decorations. They passed the locked door so that he could briefly check the master bedroom. He flipped through the journal casually and tossed it back on the desk.

To see him treat it so dismissively after all the work she'd put into translating it pained her.

He caught her expression and laughed. "You're looking for flakes of gold when there's an enormous vein just a few feet away," he said.

"You know what's behind that door, don't you?"

He gave her that smile that was so quickly becoming familiar. The smile that reminded her he knew exactly what was happening and that he enjoyed watching her figure it out. "A pretty good idea, yes."

"And?"

The grin widened. "Telling you would spoil the surprise. And this way, you'll never know if I was wrong."

She grumbled under her breath, but she couldn't be upset with him. She had the feeling that by his side, she would learn more about the past in days than she would in years on her own.

They went to the door and he placed his hand upon it.

He whistled softly. "No wonder your vilda couldn't open this."

He stood there for a while. Cliona studied the door again, her imagination painting vivid scenes of what lay beyond. She realized she was tapping her foot and stopped. Then she looked at him, saw the smile on his face, and swore at him. "Just open it already!"

Damion grinned. "Your wish is my command."

An enormous amount of teho flowed into the door. Cliona angled herself so that he couldn't see her face, couldn't catch her reaction to his strength.

She'd never felt such power. Not even close.

Zachary could have worked on the door for years and not made progress.

Damion opened it in a heartbeat.

The massive door slid to the side, just the way the door to the house had. Cliona took a step back, remembering the demon that had greeted them then.

But curiosity soon overwhelmed fear. Damion was here, and he would protect her from whatever was within. She stepped forward and saw the greatest treasure she could have imagined.

It was a large room, half again as large as the master bedroom.

Shelves lined every wall, and upon every shelf, more books than she believed a single room could hold.

Damion turned to her, and she realized her mouth was hanging open. "I feel the same," he said.

He took another step in, and the light in the room faded. Not because the strips had stopped glowing, but because a new shadow took shape within the library. The darkness was alive and familiar, and Cliona had no problem distinguishing its shape. It was the same form as the teho demon that had attacked them earlier, just twice as large.

Cliona's limbs froze. She wanted to run, but her legs refused.

The enormous demon rose on its hind legs, then stabbed out at Damion with its sharp limbs, almost too fast for Cliona to see.

13

Hakon wanted to kick himself.

Of course someone had been watching. Damion was no fool, and those who served him wouldn't be either. He'd caught them by surprise once, but not again.

When Hakon had been younger and playing the great game with every breath, he wouldn't have made such a simple error.

There was nothing to be done for it, though. The mistake had been made.

He continued west, hoping the consequences weren't too much to bear. He rubbed his thumb along the stone Solveig had given him. It resisted all his attempts to examine it, the weave far beyond his skill. Such manipulation of teho had never been his strength.

Hakon expected retaliation.

He didn't think it would come so soon.

Not more than a few minutes after his first fight had ended, he felt the use of teho behind him. He turned to see the familiar woman, now accompanied by two new arrivals. The blonde woman collapsed, no doubt exhausted from the effort of transporting so many people so quickly.

He sighed and drew his sword.

The two newcomers, dressed in black, ran at him.

Hakon reinforced his sword with teho. In response, both of the warriors formed teho blades.

They were strong, too. The power in their blades would have awed a vilda.

And he hadn't had a real fight in decades.

His lack of practice showed in the first exchange.

His sword clashed against the teho blade of a dark-haired man, the muted *thunk* sounding almost like wooden practice swords. The instant Hakon's sword was stopped, the woman took position in front of him, dark knives in hand. She sought vital organs with quick stabs, and he had no choice but to surrender ground.

They didn't pursue.

The initial exchange had given the two strangers a sense of confidence. Hakon saw it in their relaxed stances. He was a dead man, at least in their eyes.

As he was, they were right. Unless he unveiled his true power, he had no chance against them. He had hoped to travel in secrecy for a bit longer.

"Who are you?" the woman asked, twirling her knives as though bored.

"Told the first group that asked me. Name's Petyr."

"And what business did you have with Solveig?"

"Just delivering a message."

The man replied. "I don't believe you."

Hakon shrugged.

The man watched him for a few moments, then sighed. "So be it."

Hakon didn't have many cards left to play. If he didn't use his full strength, he wouldn't see the sunrise. And it was possible the blonde woman was too tired to transport back to Damion. There was a chance he could maintain his secret.

But he had to kill these two first.

He waited until his assailants attacked, then filled his body with teho.

The world slowed as his perception quickened.

He attacked with his sword, handling the giant weapon as if it were as light as a knife. It met the man's attack and sent him stumbling backward. Hakon advanced. His sword carved the air between them, and the man barely kept his feet.

The woman attacked from the side, and Hakon smoothly shifted his stance to meet her. Her short knives were fast, but not fast enough to break through his guard. His sword was too long.

She kept her partner alive, though. The dark-haired man regained his balance and joined the fight.

Swords and knives met and broke apart, the dark blades barely visible in the light of the moon. Hakon's sense of where the teho weapons were kept him alive.

They broke apart.

The man's eyes narrowed. "Who are you?" he asked again.

"It's Hakon," the woman said. "No one else uses teho like that."

The man took a step back at the mention of his name. "I thought he was dead."

The woman dropped into a crouch. Her teho knives grew longer, becoming a pair of short swords. "He will be, soon."

The man took courage from his partner. He let his teho blade dissolve, then bounced from one foot to the other. He shook out his arms and legs, then assumed a fighting stance. The teho blade reappeared, as did several teho needles, suspended a few feet above his head.

Hakon took his favorite stance, ignoring the fear twisting his stomach.

Guessing his identity was problem enough. It didn't change what he needed to do. What worried him was that they knew who he was and didn't retreat.

In his experience, almost everyone retreated when they knew who he was.

"My name is Gunvald," the man said.

"Valdis," said the woman.

Hakon gestured respectfully to them with his sword. Damion had taught them manners, at least. He could show the same respect, especially given that he had nothing to hide anymore. "Hakon."

They took their positions.

Gunvald led with the needles.

Hakon swiped them away with the flat of his blade.

The moment he moved, Valdis responded, sprinting forward. She slashed at him, and he parried her strikes.

As soon as he was distracted, Gunvald formed and threw several more needles.

Hakon couldn't protect himself from every threat, but he didn't have to. He ignored the needles and focused on the greater threat—Valdis and her blades.

She was a clever fighter, always fending his sword off with one weapon while striking with the other.

But Hakon was stronger and faster, thanks to the teho running through his body. He didn't let her close enough to strike.

The needles annoyed him, though.

Gunvald threw them hard, and his points were sharp. The teho running through Hakon's body prevented the needles from shooting through him, but they still penetrated a bit and drew blood. Nothing even close to fatal, but it was as if he was forced to fight while being stung repeatedly by angry bees.

Those needles made it too easy to make a mistake.

For several moments he held them off successfully. He even brought the fight closer to Gunvald, so that he might attack the man if Valdis ever gave him a moment of freedom.

Unfortunately, she didn't seem so inclined.

Gunvald changed tactics. Most of his needles had been aimed at Hakon's torso, a sensible target on most people. It contained plenty of vital organs to pierce, and was easy to hit, particularly on Hakon. He had a lot of torso to aim for.

When they didn't kill his enemy, Gunvald aimed at Hakon's face.

Hakon sensed the change just in time. He ducked as the needles came for his eyes.

Valdis took advantage of the distraction, her weapons slicing through Hakon's clothing even as he backed away.

The battle was, in many ways, like an enormous stone balanced on the edge of a sharp ridge, precariously shifting between one of two descents. So long as it was balanced, victory was possible for either side. But once it tilted in one direction, it quickly gained a momentum that made it nearly impossible to stop.

The stone began to fall on top of Hakon. If he gave Valdis the attention she required, Gunvald attempted to blind him by poking needles of teho through his skull. If he protected his face, Valdis cut at him with reckless abandon. With every step he took in retreat, the stone tipped further.

The battle was lost before he realized it.

Valdis deflected his sword with her own and broke through his guard completely. He filled himself with as much teho as he could, but it didn't feel like it once had. Teho responded to the will and focus of its user, and he lacked both. She swung hard, her sword cutting into his skin.

Teho met teho and the assault transformed more into a blow than a cut.

Hakon felt his ribs crack under the assault. He gasped as the breath was violently pushed out of his lungs.

Then the needles finally found his face. Half a dozen sharp points lodged in his forehead, cheeks, and nose. One found his right eye. A blinding flash of pain exploded in his skull, and for a moment, he could make no sense of the world.

Valdis hit him again, just above where she'd struck him last time.

The blow knocked him to the ground.

Belatedly, he realized his sword wasn't even in his hand anymore.

He focused as much teho as he could into his body, but it felt like he was filling a bucket riddled with holes. As fast as he brought teho in, it drained even faster.

Valdis cut at him again, her black blade digging even deeper, slicing through at least one rib before being stopped by Hakon's teho.

He coughed up blood. Out of his good eye, he could see two pairs of feet approach. One of the smaller feet prodded him in the chest. "This was who he was so worried about?" Valdis asked.

"He's out of practice. You could sense his strength as well as I. Just couldn't use it."

Valdis grunted. "Should we kill him?"

"Damion won't like it."

"We're going to have to wait to get back, and I don't really want to guard him. No telling what tricks he might still have."

"Fine." Gunvald squatted down next to Hakon. A long needle of teho appeared in his hand. "I don't suppose you're going to tell us why you're actually wandering this close to Damion's lands, or what you spoke with Solveig about?"

Hakon glared at him with his one good eye.

Gunvald shrugged, then stabbed the teho needle into it.

Hakon roared in pain. His world flashed, hot and white, then black and cold.

And then it was just black.

He writhed on the ground.

When he could think again, he reached into his pocket and unraveled the teho around the stone Solveig had given him.

Nothing happened.

A blow, which felt like it came from Valdis' short sword, curled him into the fetal position. "What was that?" she demanded.

Hakon heard a shuffling of feet in front of him, then, "It's a stone," Gunvald said.

"He did something complex."

Hakon couldn't see, but he could still sense teho. He felt Valdis raise her sword, ready to cut at him until he finally died.

There wasn't even time for regret.

A burst of teho, stronger than any Hakon had felt today, erupted behind him. Valdis and Gunvald reacted immediately, skipping backward and away from the new arrival.

The stranger swore. Both the voice and the rich combination of vulgar language were familiar. "Hakon?" The voice swore again. "Should just leave you here to die."

Hakon grunted.

The new arrival might have, too, except that Valdis and Gunvald attacked him first.

They attempted the same approach they'd used against Hakon.

Except Ari, the one who had appeared at the summons of the stone, wasn't Hakon. Teho bloomed around him, a defensive shield easily repelling both warriors. Nothing the pair attacked with came close to him.

Ari's response to their assault was a withering storm of teho that sent both warriors scrambling backward. Hakon heard a grunt, and he wondered if one of Ari's attacks had broken through.

The two attacked again, with similar results. Ari drove them back with ease, and this time, he didn't relent until they'd given up hundreds of feet of ground.

Feet shifted near Hakon's head. When Ari spoke again, his voice was closer. Hakon imagined the thief had squatted down beside him. "You look pathetic," Ari said. There was no sympathy to be found in his cold words.

Hakon grunted. "I've had better days."

Ari didn't laugh.

Hakon imagined the thoughts going through the other man's mind right now. He could guess them well enough, and decided not to say much. If he said the wrong thing, he believed Ari would leave him here to die.

Ari exhaled sharply and swore. "You never change, do you? A hundred and fifty years, and you still ruin my day."

Before Hakon could reply, a cold but firm hand gripped his wrist, and Hakon felt himself transported.

A moment later he felt stone underneath him.

He couldn't see where he was.

But he believed he was safe for now.

He gave up fighting and let a deeper darkness swallow him whole.

14

The limb of the enormous demon stopped less than a foot away from Damion.

Another limb stabbed out, but was also stopped by Damion's teho shield.

The demon didn't seem as impressed by Damion's strength as Cliona. It stepped forward, striking with even more power. Damion tilted his head to the side, as though the encounter was little more than an opportunity to study one of the legendary abilities of the stamfar.

The demon struck with four limbs at once.

Damion didn't even flinch.

His expression changed from interest to resignation. Then, with the flick of his hand, a long teho blade, at least twice as long as Cliona was tall, appeared in his hand. He snapped it forward, slicing the demon in half with a single cut.

The battle was over before Cliona had time to be properly terrified.

Damion's only reaction was to watch the demon fade from reality. Flecks of teho drifted into the air like ash from a fire, returning to its mysterious source. Without even turning to check on her, he stepped over to the nearest bookshelf and began perusing the titles.

When her body and her brain finally worked in tandem again, all she could do was stare at him. "Who are you?"

He glanced back, as though surprised she also wasn't buried in the books. "Surely you've guessed by now."

"You're kolma." The words didn't sound like they could be true, even though she was the one who had said them.

He nodded.

"But they're all dead."

Damion made a show of examining himself. "I beg to differ. There aren't many of us left, and most tend to keep to themselves, but I am far from alone. You know one."

"I do?"

"Solveig," Damion said. "She is, in fact, one of the band that overthrew the empire."

Cliona laughed. Damion might be one of the most powerful people she'd ever met, but somewhere along the line, his beliefs had become unhinged. "Solveig wasn't one of the band. I don't even think she's tehoin."

Damion shrugged, then turned his attention back to the books. It was that casual dismissal that made her doubt her own beliefs. He didn't care what she believed, and he knew far more than he was telling her.

How much of what she believed was wrong?

"You're looking for something specific," she guessed. "What?"

The corner of his mouth turned up in a smile. "A rumor," he admitted, "but one I believe."

She waited for him to explain further.

"There are stories of one artifact, in particular, that interest me. One with a power even the stamfar feared.

Few stamfar were ever made aware of its location." He nodded at the books in the library. "I hope to find answers in here."

Cliona frowned. "You went to all this trouble and expense, only to find a clue to something else?"

"Why wouldn't I?" He turned so that his full attention was on her. Though there was nothing hostile in his look, she still felt as though she would wilt under his gaze.

Her heart raced as he looked at her.

"You're no fool," he continued. "So you know how powerful the stamfar were. You stand here, amazed at what I can do, but before them, I am nothing. If an artifact exists that gives one power even a stamfar would fear, it would be worth all the gold in the world, don't you think?"

"There are many who claim their goals are worth more than gold, but most rarely part with any."

He stepped toward her and held her eyes with his own. "You speak true, but know this. I am not like others. I would give not just my gold, but my life, to right the wrongs of the past. Helping humanity thrive on this planet is all that I care about. It is a dream of my former master that I pursue with every waking moment."

Standing in his presence, she felt small. Not just because of his incredible use of teho, though that was part of it.

It was the scope of his ambition. Perhaps their dreams were the same, but in her scholarly pursuits, she had only hoped to chip off some small shard of that dream. Before today, that had always been enough. Her own efforts suddenly felt meaningless.

Damion dared mighty feats.

And as she stood here next to him, she thought he might just succeed. "What comes next?" she asked.

"The work," he said. "Finding Marjaana's home was the

easy part. Now we need to learn her secrets. I'm going to be transporting these texts further west."

"West?" She didn't understand. There was little except the wild further west. "Wouldn't they be safer back at the academy?"

He shook his head. "With so many potential dangers in these books, they must be translated in private, first."

She frowned at that. "The knowledge within this room needs to be shared."

"And it will, but in an orderly fashion. The stamfar weren't just the most powerful tehoin to ever live. They had sciences we can't begin to comprehend." Damion gestured at the strange lights above them as an example. "It's not the secrets about teho I worry most about. It's the stories of powerful weapons that might be made again by anyone with the proper knowledge. Those weapons may serve us, but only if we are wise about how we share what we learn."

The flaw in his logic wasn't hard to find. And she wasn't so intimidated by him she wouldn't challenge him. "You overlook the fact that with all the books in your possession, you become the most powerful person in the world."

He smiled at that. "I already am. The books make no difference."

She hated how he made ridiculous statements sound perfectly plausible. But again, she believed him.

He shifted, just slightly, and Cliona realized just how close they were to one another.

"You're right, though. Let's put aside the fact that I bought and paid for this dig, and that I own this land. Though all that is true, and it makes these books mine, none of it addresses your concern. And I want to address it, because I need you."

Her cheeks flushed and the room suddenly felt warm.

"You fear an abuse of power, and rightly so. But I assure you, there is no kolma in the world stronger than me. There hasn't been for a very long time. And yet, you didn't even know who I was. Would that be true if I were the type of man to abuse my power?"

He didn't give her time to answer. "I'll tell you no lies. To save humanity from the wilds, I believe we need to bring the empire back. And I intend to lead it. Not for wealth or power. I possess plenty of both already. But because I believe I am best suited to lead us into a new age."

Cliona swallowed the lump in her throat. She'd grown up in a household where the rebellion, when it was spoken of, was the greatest event in the history of humanity. Personally, she'd never wasted much thought on it, but Damion stood directly against the beliefs she'd been given growing up.

Damion continued. "I intend to take these books back with me. I have other translators, but none whose work I trust as much as your own. It would please me greatly if you would join me. Your skill would be invaluable, and you have my word that I would value your counsel in all things, even if we disagree."

"You want me to come with you west?"

He nodded. "For as long as you please. I have several tehoin capable of transport, and I'll never ask anyone to stay against their will. You can leave whenever you wish. And," he said, his smile returning to his face, "you'd have constant access to everything here."

She knew her answer already. "That's a shameful bribe."

He chuckled. "But an effective one."

It was.

15

———

Hakon woke to silence and pain.

He didn't move. Previous experiences had taught him that to do so would only bring more agony. His curiosity would be sated soon enough. He took a deep breath and worked his awareness up his body.

Someone had healed him. At least as much as it was possible to heal a body so wounded.

Only one person was that capable, so he knew where he was.

Despite the healing, several injuries lingered. His ribs were still knitting back together, and his face burned as teho hastened his recuperation. He fought the urge to scratch at his face.

His eyes still hadn't healed, and so his blindness remained.

Though it was about the last course of action he desired, Hakon rested. The fastest way to Cliona was to do nothing.

In his enforced darkness, memories ran endlessly.

He'd been a fool out there, and outclassed to an embarrassing degree. His cheeks burned even hotter when he thought of the ways he'd been beaten.

He had no one to blame but himself. Those two shouldn't have even been able to scratch him.

Eventually the door to his room opened. Her soft steps gave her away. "Solveig," he croaked. "Thank you."

She closed the door. He heard something being dipped into water, and then a funnel was at his lips. "Drink," she said.

He did, the water cooling his throat. She gave him more, doling it out a little at a time.

He couldn't remember a libation ever tasting better.

She sighed. "I should be the one apologizing. I feared something like this might come to pass, but I didn't feel like I could stop you. Still, I should have done more."

"You saved my life with that stone."

"That remains to be seen," she said. He heard the smile in her words. "Ari's been pacing the grounds since you both arrived."

"He saved me," Hakon said. "He didn't have to."

Solveig's laughter was soft. "That's been driving him to madness, too. He knew the stone was mine, so he's been upset with me. He thought I was in danger."

"How long was I out?"

"Just a day. I healed the worst of your injuries, but didn't dare attempt anything with your face. Better to let your own body handle that."

He smiled, and it was worth the flash of pain. "Didn't want to ruin my good looks?"

"Can't ruin what wasn't there to start." She dipped something else in the water. Then she placed a cool cloth over his forehead and eyes. The relief was immediate.

"How long will it take?" he asked.

"From what I've seen? Maybe another day before you're able to see and move without too much pain. Two and you should be back to your typical strength."

"Thank you, again."

Solveig's footsteps retreated. "You should talk with Ari. That will decide a lot of what comes next."

Hakon's stomach clenched. "That bad?"

"We're on thin ice. The rest of us have stayed in touch, but you're still an open wound. Your reappearance in the world—"

"That's never what I wanted."

"I know. It's the only reason we're speaking. But you need to talk to Ari."

"Will you let him know I'm ready? Maybe in an hour or so?"

"I will."

She stepped out, leaving Hakon to his thoughts.

He clenched and unclenched his fists. More than forty years, and he'd largely managed to keep thoughts of the band at bay. He'd started a new life and put the past behind him. It wasn't redemption, but most days, he could look in a mirror and claim he was at peace.

A lie, perhaps, but a comforting one.

Even after forty years, he wasn't ready for this. Deep down, he wasn't sure he ever would be.

He swallowed his fear.

One way or the other, it was time.

He tested dozens of different explanations, each true, but none of them complete. He had failed them. Were their positions reversed, he wasn't sure he'd even show the forbearance they'd offered him.

All his explanations vanished the moment someone

knocked on his door. It didn't feel like it had been an hour at all.

"Come in," he said.

The door opened and closed. Hakon didn't hear Ari come in, but he wouldn't. The man was quiet enough to make a single mouse sound like a roaring dragon.

Hakon knew he should say something, but no words suitably expressed the feelings squeezing his heart dry.

Ari broke the silence. "I've seen week-old corpses that look better than you."

Hakon laughed, then groaned as his face reminded him it was still healing. "It's good to see you."

Ari grunted. "You can't see a thing."

"Best you've ever looked." Strangely, Hakon wished he had his sword in hand. Not because he intended to fight, but because he often took strength from it. "Thank you. I didn't deserve your help."

"You didn't," Ari agreed. "And I'm furious Solveig gave you that stone. She gets herself into enough trouble, and now I'll have to make another one for her."

Hakon was grateful Ari still planned on aiding Solveig. He took a deep breath. "I'm sorry."

There was the scrape of a chair against the stone, followed by a soft creak as Ari sat down. "So, we're doing this?"

"It's past time." Hakon clenched his hand, imagining the familiar contours of his sword in his palm. "I'm sorry. I wish there was something more I could say, but nothing comes closer."

Ari didn't respond for almost a minute. "Would you do it again?"

The truth might get him killed, but Ari deserved it. "I would."

The chair creaked again, and Hakon imagined Ari had stiffened.

"But I would have told you," he added. "I don't regret the murder. Just—us."

"Why did you do it?"

Hakon grimaced. "You know why."

"I want to hear you say it."

"I believed it had to be done. I still do. We never would have had a lasting peace with him still alive."

"That's not what I asked."

Hakon knew. But the truth was a pain far worse than his healing eyes. "I told myself it was because I wanted the responsibility and consequences on my shoulders alone." He held up a hand, silencing Ari's retort. "But the truth was that I was a coward. I knew the rest of you disagreed." He swallowed the lump in his throat. "I didn't trust you enough."

He let the last line hang in the air. There was so much more he wanted to say, but with Ari, it was best not to speak much. The man wasn't much for talking in the first place.

One last claim had to be made, though. "I know it doesn't matter now, but I truly didn't believe you would be punished with me."

He sealed his lips shut after that.

The rest was in Ari's hands.

Hakon waited.

Ari swore.

"Do you have any idea how many times I've thought about just killing you myself? Maybe every week since my release, the thought bubbles up at least once. And yet, when given the opportunity, I rescue you instead."

Hakon let his friend vent.

Ari sighed. "You did lay waste to his entire castle, though. I wish I could have seen the look on his face."

"It was satisfying," Hakon said. "But not worth the price I paid to see it."

"Why didn't you reach out to us when you were released?"

"I didn't think you wanted to see me, in part. But mostly, I was too scared to face any of you."

The chair scraped against the floor again. "Sometimes," Ari admitted, "I wish it was easier to hate you."

Hakon nodded.

When Ari spoke again, he was closer. Hakon hadn't heard him move at all. "I didn't agree with your decision back then. With the benefit of hindsight now, you might have been right. There's no telling. But I don't care about the murder. I care that you broke the oath we took. I thought we meant more to you than that."

He spoke softly, but even a dull, rusted dagger would have cut less painfully.

The next thing Hakon heard was the door open. Ari spoke again. "I can't forgive you, yet, but I won't kill you, either." He paused. "But if you do anything like that again, I will not withhold my blades."

16

———

The next morning, Agnesse had half a dozen orders for Cliona, all courtesy of Damion. The woman listed them with a sneer. Watching Agnesse quietly seething made Cliona appreciate Damion all the more.

Zachary joined Cliona as she left the inn. The whole place buzzed with a new energy, and Cliona was no different. She'd only slept a handful of hours, but felt ready to tackle any problem the day could throw at her.

Cliona slowed her pace for Zachary's injury, but even the delay didn't dampen her mood. For so long she had begged and bled for every scrap of knowledge of the stamfar. But no more. Now she would have access to a feast for as long as she wished it.

Zachary, unfortunately, didn't share her excitement. For a change of pace, she was the one who did most of the speaking, while he listened and smiled amicably. Something bothered him, but she assumed it was the nagging pain of his injuries. He should be resting, but he claimed he didn't want to miss the sight of the library.

She didn't believe that for a moment. Zachary was a lover of many things, but books was not one of them.

They found Damion and Vinko near Marjaana's house, huddled over a set of maps, discussing how the diggers could be best put to use. Cliona and Zachary waited patiently while the two of them finished. It didn't take long. Damion clapped Vinko on the shoulder, a blow powerful enough to throw the sturdy foreman off balance. Then he turned to the pair of scholars and smiled. Cliona handled introductions.

Zachary gestured to the work of Vinko's crew. "Are they filling the holes back in?"

Damion nodded. "Whenever possible, I try to minimize the damage my projects leave behind. Vinko and his capable workers will do most of the work, and a few of my soldiers will come in after we're done and use teho to move the rest. Within a few days, this land will look almost as it did before we arrived."

Cliona noticed Zachary frown, but she appreciated Damion's sentiment. It sounded like something her father would say.

Damion wasn't certain about allowing Zachary into the library, but when Cliona told him Zachary had been instrumental in helping her translate the books, he relented.

Their instructions were simple enough. Cliona was to organize the books into crates however she saw fit. Once the containers were full, tehoin stationed nearby would transport the crates to Aysgarth, Damion's fortress to the west. Though Damion didn't say so explicitly, it sounded to Cliona as though she was being placed in charge of the whole translation of the library.

Damion left them to it.

Given Zachary's tenuous grasp on the language, it took

Cliona a few minutes to figure out how best to use him. But once she did, their work proceeded smoothly. She translated the covers by sight. Zachary wrote the translation, then copied the stamfar symbols when Cliona handed the book to him. Then he noted what crate it had gone in.

Zachary's lists grew quickly. But even so, there were an enormous number of books to catalog. Cliona settled for good translations instead of perfect. She reminded herself that this was simply the first step in what might well be the work of her life.

During one break, Zachary interrupted her thoughts. "Are you sure about all this?" he asked.

"What do you mean?"

He gestured around the room. "You're always talking about the power of the stamfar, of the abilities their knowledge might unlock. Now Damion controls it all. Doesn't that make you nervous?"

"A bit," she admitted. "But I think I trust him."

Zachary bit his lip and looked around the room, as though there might be someone listening. "I've heard of Damion before. In my father's court. I'm not sure you should trust him."

Cliona often forgot Zachary came from a magistrate's household. She knew the vague outline of his past, but he didn't speak often of his days prior to the academy. And he didn't act like most administrators she'd met. "What was said?"

Zachary hesitated. "That he's clever and ruthless. My father thinks he is building a new state out west, carving out spaces for humans to live that were once only the domain of the wild."

"If anything, that last part only makes me like him more."

Zachary pressed his palms to his forehead and closed his eyes. "I think there's a good chance that Damion is up to more than he says."

Cliona remembered her conversation with Damion and his plan to start a new empire. She hadn't had time to decide how she felt about such a goal, but she could guess how Zachary would feel. He was, even in his exile, the son of a magistrate, one of the most powerful people in the six states. She decided it was best not to speak of Damion's plans. Soon the two of them would part ways, and she hoped to do so on good terms.

They finished just before the sun fell. Damion's tehoin took the last of the books, and Cliona and Zachary stared at the walls of empty shelves.

"You're going with him, aren't you?" Zachary asked.

She nodded. Given how quickly Damion acted, she judged it likely she wouldn't even spend the night in the inn. Once her own belongings were packed, Damion would have her transported back to his fortress. After the months of time together, her parting with Zachary seemed far too abrupt.

"Would you reconsider?" Zachary asked. "We could go back to the academy together and let people know what we found. I'm sure if you agreed to secrecy, you could even bring some of the books with you. You wouldn't have to risk going to Aysgarth."

"No," she said. "I've already told him I would go. And the library will be there. It's where the answers I seek are."

"You really will do anything for knowledge, won't you?"

"Maybe not anything, but a lot."

"Why?"

It wasn't a story she told often, but Zachary had earned that, if nothing else. "My mother," Cliona answered. "She was an herbalist, and a great one. She knew the wilds well, but one day, she and my father went out and she never came back. They'd separated for a while, and a shadow wolf caught her by surprise."

"I'm sorry," Zachary said.

She shook her head sharply. "It was a long time ago. But it's past time we learn how to really fight back against the wild. The stamfar knew, and so must we."

Zachary considered her story for a few moments, then said, "Well, if I can't convince you not to go, I would like to come with you."

She started. "Really?"

"You need someone to protect you."

She glared and prepared a pointed retort, but he held up his hands. "Not like that." He looked at his hands for a moment. "Cliona, I know you're tehoin. I know you saved me and Agnesse."

"That's foo—"

He cut her off. "Don't lie to me, please. It doesn't suit you."

Cliona stopped. She'd always suspected there was more to Zachary than he let on, but this was the first time she'd seen it surface. She liked it.

"I just figured it out today. You react to teho, even if it's just a quick glance behind you when one of Damion's soldiers transports away." He met her gaze. "I don't know why you chose to hide your ability, and I don't care. I know you can fight your own battles." He took a deep breath. "But you don't have to fight them alone. Damion is about as persuasive a person as I've ever met, and I grew up around people who lived or died based on their ability to lie. It's worth having another person around you can trust and talk to."

Her momentary anger faded. And the idea of having Zachary join her wasn't without its appeal.

"Anyway," Zachary continued. "I'm not ready for us to part ways yet."

She smiled as a warmth spread through her. "You make a compelling argument."

They were interrupted as Damion came through the door. "Good work, both of you." He focused on Cliona. "We leave tonight. Is that a problem?"

She shook her head. "I would like Zachary to come with us. He continues to be helpful, and he's someone that I trust with the work."

Damion studied Zachary. "Do you want to come?"

Cliona swore something unspoken passed between the two men then. She almost rolled her eyes at them trying to impress the other with the hardness of their stares. Then the moment passed.

"I do," Zachary said.

Damion thought for a moment, then nodded. "Be ready to leave shortly after supper tonight."

With that, he turned and left them.

They made one last sweep of Marjaana's house, but they didn't find anything more. The house had been picked clean. Damion's people had even taken the paintings from the walls.

Packing didn't take long, and Cliona sent her belongings with a tehoin who came to transport them.

At supper, Cliona said farewell to Vinko. She would miss him more than anyone on the excavation, and she swore she saw a tear in his eye when he bid her well. "You be careful, now," he said.

She assured him she would, and they made plans to meet when he passed through Vispeda next.

Her goodbye with Agnesse was curt. It was almost as if the older woman had completely forgotten Cliona existed already.

They met with Damion after. He held out his hand, and Cliona took it. Then, with her other, she reached for Zachary. Her friend took her outstretched hand and gave it a squeeze.

"Ready?" Damion asked.

Cliona nodded, and their world vanished as Damion transported them across the continent.

17

———

By the time Hakon woke the next morning, his vision had returned. He greedily drank in the sights of his small room, certain he'd never been so relieved to see bare walls and worn stone floors. He'd never been blinded before, and he had no desire to endure it again.

Solveig checked in on him twice, but her appearances were brief. Once she was assured of his recovery, she ordered him to stay put until she could visit him that evening.

The restriction chafed, but he obeyed.

His confidence healed far slower than his body.

He was no longer a master of the great game. If he wanted to see Cliona alive again, he needed to learn what he'd allowed himself to forget.

He threw himself into long-neglected physical training. The past forty years of his life hadn't been sheltered, but he'd become complacent in his superiority. He'd let the weapon that was his body rust.

Though the cell he occupied was barely large enough to

swing his sword, Hakon did anyway. Over and over, his repetitions climbing from the hundreds to the thousands. Not once did he call upon teho. His arms, shoulders, and back burned. Sweat puddled in the cracks in the stone beneath his feet. When his cuts failed to meet his standards, he stopped and sat cross-legged on the floor, eyes closed.

The sunlight crawled across the floor of his room.

Once his breath evened out, he stood and began again.

That night, when Solveig arrived, she brought with her food, drink, and Ari.

In so many ways, Solveig and Ari were as different as two people could be. Solveig was short and fierce. Ari was tall and withdrawn, and looked like he might just fold in on himself at any moment. She preferred light-colored clothing, while Hakon had never seen Ari dressed in anything but black.

The differences went far deeper than superficial appearances. In her heart, Solveig was a healer. Ari was a killer. He was the most successful assassin Hakon had ever known.

And yet, there was something about the way they entered that caught Hakon's attention. He looked at them again, and was sure. "Are you two—?"

Solveig smiled, and that was confirmation enough.

With no good place to eat the food Solveig had brought, they opted to sit on the floor, spreading the food out on a few plates in front of them.

Ari sniffed the air. "You smell."

Hakon grunted. "Training."

As had always been their way, they dug into the meal first. Few words were exchanged as every scrap of food vanished into their waiting stomachs.

For Hakon, who'd barely eaten all day, the simple meal tasted like a sumptuous feast.

Before long, the food was gone and Solveig passed around the ale. They offered up the bottles in a silent toast, then drank deep.

Hakon interrupted Solveig before she could start. "You two?"

Solveig smiled again. "We found each other a few years after Ari was released. The years were difficult, but we chose to confront them together. Then one day, we realized we were content, and that something more had developed between us."

"Are you married?"

Solveig shook her head. "There is no need. We're together. Someday we might not be. You know how it is."

Hakon nodded. Years meant less to them as to ahula, and if there was one constant, it was change. "Congratulations."

Ari had no patience for the diversion. "Can we begin?"

Hakon gestured for them to continue, a smile on his face.

Solveig spoke for the two of them. "When you first arrived, I had hoped Cliona's absence was a misunderstanding. But it's becoming increasingly apparent that she's involved in something more ominous, and it most likely involves Damion. Which means you're going to get pulled into this incarnation of the great game."

Hakon shook his head. "I'm only here for Cliona. Besides, I can't play the game like I once did."

Ari scoffed. "That we can agree on."

Solveig gave him a stern look, then turned to Hakon. "You know what this means. If you return home now, we can keep your whereabouts secret. We'll do our best to find Cliona, but she's one problem among many. Or you continue, and you rejoin the game, with all the risk that entails."

Hakon stood up and paced the small cell. He sought a third way but found none.

"Fine," he finally said. He returned to the floor and took a long swig of his ale.

Solveig nodded. "Then you need to know the board." She looked over at Ari, who barely shook his head. She sighed, then spoke. "We might as well begin with our story." She took another drink. "The imprisonment caused each of us incredible suffering, and it took time to heal. Once we did, though, we found ourselves in a world we no longer understood. We broke the empire, but we had no real part in anything that came after. We were imprisoned before the peace came into effect."

Resentment lurked in Solveig's voice. Their suffering was his fault. She didn't say so, but there was no need.

She made no accusation, but every word cut.

"Ari and I decided that we wanted to help guide the development of this new world. Not just as warriors, but as something more. I became part of the burgeoning development of scholarship. Ari, as you know, prefers to work from the shadows. We fight, when the need arises, but we've grown to prefer subtler methods."

"The others?" Hakon asked.

"Weren't particularly interested. They aid us from time to time, if they're needed. But like you, they wanted to cut their ties with the past. They've decided to shape the world in their own way."

"What's your aim?"

"Spreading humanity successfully across this planet," Solveig said. "Through my connection with the scholars, I try to advance what knowledge we have. Ari runs a network of informants throughout the six states. We do our best to maintain something resembling a balance in this new world."

Hakon nodded along. "Very well. But what does any of that have to do with Cliona?"

"Nothing," Solveig answered. "Until her path crossed with Damion's."

"And what about him? I've never seen Dagrun scared in her life, but she was of him."

"She's right to be concerned," Solveig said. "There are only a few dozen kolmas left, and he is intent on either recruiting or killing the remainder. Not only does he continue to get stronger than I can explain, but he is eliminating his competition."

Hakon glanced between them. "If he's such a problem, why haven't you two just killed him?"

Solveig grimaced, but Ari answered. "He's stronger than any of us individually, and knows we fear Isira's reaction. It didn't hurt that he had a few decades of a head start."

Hakon grew tired of being reminded of the consequences of his decision. "Why haven't *you* just killed him?" he asked Ari.

Ari growled softly. "I've tried."

Hakon blinked. In all his memory, Ari had never failed to kill a target. Even if Damion was as powerful as his friends claimed, strength hardly mattered when the blade was hidden until the last possible moment. But Ari sat here, staring holes into the floor.

That shook Hakon more than anything he'd encountered yet.

What had Damion become, to render such a man useless?

And his daughter had fallen into the monster's path.

That thought, once it occurred, consumed him. "How do we find Cliona?"

"The same as before," Solveig answered, "but now together. I must remain, as my prolonged absence would be noted by Damion's spies. Besides, this is not the only problem in the six states. You and Ari will investigate the same areas you intended to before. When we learn more, we can decide next steps."

Solveig spoke again before he could ask his next question. "Hakon, you should know this decision wasn't easy for us. We regret that your daughter has gotten swept up in the game, but we almost decided not to aid you. This is a second chance, but one very easy to lose. None of us will risk Isira's wrath for you again. Do you understand?"

Hakon swallowed hard and nodded.

"Good," Ari said. "We leave at first light."

Hakon almost insisted they leave earlier, but the timing made sense. He needed another night of rest and healing, and with Ari by his side, they would travel much faster.

He just hoped Cliona would stay safe until he found her.

18

Transporting from one place to another was less disorienting than Cliona expected. One moment she was standing outside the inn, the next she was someplace else. There was no sense of movement.

She found herself in a large room lit by lanterns. The walls, ceiling, and floor were all made of stone, but beyond that detail and the size of the room, there was little to notice. Damion let go of her hand and stepped forward. "Follow me," he said. "We'll go up and then I'll have someone show you to your rooms."

Damion opened a thick door and greeted two guards posted on the other side. Cliona followed, with Zachary only a few steps behind her.

They climbed a wide stone staircase, and Cliona had the sense that they were underground. The air was damp and all the rooms were windowless. They reached another door, this one even thicker than the one below. Here there were guards stationed on both sides. They stepped through and into a long hallway.

Damion turned right, nodding to the guards as he

passed. Like everyone in Damion's service, they were dressed in dark clothing. Cliona glanced back at them. The guards were relaxed but wary, and few carried any visible weapons.

Tehoin.

They guarded a door within what was apparently a large fortress, a door very few people were likely to use. If he could spare tehoin for a task like this, how many were in his service?

She got a better idea soon enough. They passed another door, this one without guards, and stepped onto a balcony.

Vertigo hit Cliona like a fist to the stomach.

She wasn't scared of heights.

As a young girl, climbing trees had been one of her favorite pastimes, much to her mother's chagrin. She understood that heights worried others, but she felt nothing except a thrill when looking over some steep drop.

No, she felt sick because somewhere, deep in her body, she still assumed she was on the plains where Marjaana's home was buried. One moment in the open proved her body wrong.

The balcony overlooked a valley. By the light of the moon, Cliona guessed the valley was about two miles wide. She closed her eyes. The vertigo quickly passed, and she took in her surroundings with a more careful eye.

Lights flickered in the valley below, and as her eyes adjusted to the dim light, she could make out the shape of fields and homes.

She frowned and pointed down to the valley. "Why aren't the homes together?"

"There's no need," Damion said.

Cliona didn't understand. Nothing stopped anyone from living by themselves wherever they chose, but that was a lifestyle few would choose. Even in the forests where she had grown up, families always built houses near one another. Doing so kept the wild at bay and allowed families to come to the aid of others quickly.

When one built alone, one faced the wilds alone.

"The wilds don't strike us here," Damion explained.

Behind them, Zachary laughed, then tried to disguise it as a cough.

Damion didn't take offense. "It's hard for most to believe at first. But those who live below live without fear. They have their own space, and need never worry about the wilds attacking."

"How?" Cliona asked.

"Through the organized efforts of a great many people," Damion responded. "But that is a story for another day. Come." He gestured, and Cliona saw that the balcony was actually a lower landing for a steep and narrow flight of stairs.

At the top of the stairs, she saw Aysgarth for the first time. Damion's fortress was the most impressive structure she had ever seen. Built into the side of a mountain, it made every palace and guard tower she'd ever encountered pale in comparison.

The stairs led to a small door, which opened up into another narrow hallway. There were more people here, but the sense Cliona got was of order and discipline. Several servants were waiting for Damion, and he quickly assigned them a variety of tasks.

Damion then turned to his guests. "You'll now be shown to your rooms," he announced. "Tomorrow morning breakfast will be brought to you. You are welcome to wander the fortress as you wish, but until the guards know you by sight, it's likely your movements will be restricted. I'll summon you tomorrow for a more complete tour."

Before either Cliona or Zachary could respond, Damion was off.

Cliona watched him go. The kolma didn't seem tired in the least, but all the same he was in a hurry to get someplace.

Zachary was right. There was definitely more to him than he let on.

But there was nothing that she enjoyed more than solving a good mystery.

She woke up feeling well rested the next morning. When someone knocked on the door, she assumed it was her host.

Instead, Zachary stood there. "Mind if I come in? I don't feel like waiting alone."

She let him in and he took a chair. "So, what do you think?" he asked.

"Not much, yet."

"Do you think he's telling the truth about the wilds?"

"If so, it could change the way we live."

Zachary nodded, then stood up again, his rest short-lived. "You feel it, too, though, don't you? That there's more here than he's telling us."

She agreed. "I don't assume it's malicious, though. Not until I learn more."

Zachary gestured to her room. "Do you think he built this?"

"No."

"Me neither. I'm not sure anyone now could."

"Stamfar?"

"Probably."

Damion arrived before long. The pair followed him through the palace and out to another overlook.

In the light of day, the valley below was stunning. Cliona saw a small river ran down the center of the valley. The fields below looked healthy. Cows and sheep chewed contentedly. From their vantage point, the scene was nearly idyllic.

In contrast to the valley, the fortress was busy. Men and women walked with determined strides. No one wandered or idled. Passersby greeted Damion with respect, but didn't defer to him in any particular way. In some ways it reminded Cliona of the academy at Vispeda. It felt of shared purpose.

Cliona also noticed there were no shrines. Though they lived in a place built by stamfar hands, the citizens here didn't worship the stamfar the way so much of the six states did. She wasn't sure what that meant, but she found the fact curious.

Again, there were few guards with weapons in sight. Zachary, apparently, noticed the same. "Just how many tehoin are here?"

"Hundreds."

The casual answer stopped both Cliona and Zachary in their tracks.

Damion stopped, turned, and smiled at them. "There's a reason I told you the wilds don't threaten us here. We have enough strength to turn it back." He stretched out his arm, encompassing all the valley. "We have the advantage of the land, too. But it's not enough. The tehoin fade, with fewer vilda born every year. If we are to win against the wilds, it needs to be soon. Which is why I need your help."

Cliona frowned at that. "Why go to all the trouble? You said you had scholars here."

"I do, but they have no imagination."

"What?" Zachary spoke for both of them.

Damion focused on Cliona. She felt the same instinct to hide she had when they first met. "Why did you translate the epitaph as 'fly' instead of 'dream'?"

"Because it's the most reasonable explanation of the text."

His gaze didn't waver. "Do you believe that what the text said was literally true?"

Cliona shrugged. "That's not for me to decide. I only know the word is more likely to mean fly than dream."

Damion broke off his gaze and smiled again. "And that is what separates you from the scholars I have here. They fit their translations to their current reality, instead of allowing their reality to be shaped by the translations. They tell me it must be dream instead of fly, because no one, not even the stamfar, could fly among the stars. How can one accurately translate the stamfar if one is trapped in the mindset of an ahula? What is possible is not bounded by our knowledge, but by our imaginations."

Cliona felt her heart skip under his look. He was a man of conviction. Not blind belief, but well-reasoned rationality and breathtaking courage.

She understood why so many had come to the mountains with him.

He continued, leading them to another vantage point. He directed their attention to the mouth of the valley, perhaps another mile distant. A wall stood there, easily fifty feet tall.

Another reason why they didn't fear the wild here.

"I'm going to transport us there," Damion said. He held out his hand. Cliona took it quickly, then offered her free hand to Zachary. She closed her eyes, and when she opened them, she was on the wall, looking out to the wilds.

The sound of masons working reached her ears. She looked over the edge of the wall and saw repairs being made.

"The wilds still attack at night," Damion said. "But they haven't broken through in years."

Cliona's eyes wandered across the wall. From the looks of the exterior face, it wasn't for a lack of trying. She leaned back from the edge and took in the top of the wall. Tehoin guards walked everywhere, more here than anywhere they'd been yet.

She didn't doubt he had hundreds total. Even a thousand wouldn't surprise her.

If he attacked, she didn't think any of the states would stand a chance.

Damion's surprises weren't over yet, though. After they'd walked for a while, he stopped, his focus elsewhere. After a few moments he turned to them, a delighted gleam in his eye.

"Cliona, you share my dream of a wild subdued. I'm grateful you chose to come out here, and I'd like to express my appreciation. Would you care to see the shape of the future?"

His grin grew wider at her puzzled look. "Someday, the wilds will obey us. They will fear us, as we do them now."

Zachary scoffed, but Damion just held out his hand. "Let me prove it to you. Let me introduce you to my dragon."

19

Traveling with Ari made Hakon's previous journey seem downright foolish. They traveled more distance in one transport than Hakon had walked in his first failed attempt.

Hakon blinked and found himself in an expansive prairie. Nothing but rolling hills and wild grass met his gaze. "You couldn't have gotten us any closer?"

The assassin's reply was flat. "If there are tehoin in the town, I didn't want to warn them of our presence."

Hakon clenched his fists tightly and breathed out through his nose. He knew the reason just as well as Ari, but let it go. Ari set off in the direction of the nearest town, forcing Hakon to hurry to keep up.

In spite of the circumstances, it felt good to be wandering the wild again. He had loved his life in the woods with Sera and Cliona, but there had been many days when that world felt small. Out here, *he* felt small, exploring a vast world they were just beginning to understand.

He much preferred feeling like this.

With Ari at his side, he could almost convince himself this was like the days of old.

Almost.

Once, Hakon would have trusted Ari to walk through flames to save him. Now he wasn't sure the assassin would endure a stiff breeze on his behalf.

Ari wasn't the most pleasant of traveling companions. Even when they'd been close, he'd tended towards silence, and the years had done little to change that. Though there was much Hakon wanted to talk about, he guessed it would only irritate Ari. So he kept his peace, content to have an old friend at his side once again.

The trip to the village didn't take more than an hour. The small collection of homes sat near the eastern edge of the first area Solveig and her scholars had defined.

Hakon asked around about the expedition.

The old man he spoke with remembered a large caravan coming through about two months past. Said they had passed through without much fuss, heading west. He didn't remember any specifics, but it was the first and only large group that had traveled out this way in years.

Hakon also learned that the road west was busier now than it had ever been. The village had always been quiet, but in recent years more people had started passing through. Never a large group, but a steady trickle. A family here, a young couple there. Almost always escorted by a warrior with dark clothing.

Ari found that tidbit more interesting than Hakon. The two wished the old man well and left the village.

"Do you think they might have stopped somewhere nearby?" Ari asked.

Hakon thought for a moment. "No. They must have planned to be out for a few months, at least. I doubt they brought enough food to last that long. I think they ended up near a town or village. And it wasn't this one."

Ari nodded. "I can take us close to the next village, then."

They transported again and repeated the process. This village was a bit larger, and Hakon spoke to a few people. They, too, remembered the caravan. One woman remembered the head of the expedition, and none too fondly either. Apparently there had been some disagreement over the price of some food the expedition purchased.

As they left the village, Ari said, "The woman's description matches Agnesse's."

It was a start, at least. No one remembered seeing Cliona, but Hakon didn't think she would have stood out. Soon, he'd see his daughter again.

First, though, they had a choice to make. Solveig's map indicated that the first search area included a large expanse of empty land to the north of their current location. No doubt, there were villages scattered about, but Ari had never visited the area, so he couldn't transport them there.

It was certainly possible the caravan had passed through this village and then turned north. But to find out would take time.

Or they could transport another fifty miles west, to where a second search area began.

Hakon voted for west. Ari wanted to investigate the first area more completely. He hated the idea of a place half-explored. They stared at one another. "We can always come back," Hakon said.

"I don't want to be transporting you back and forth forever," Ari retorted.

Hakon's desire to hurry overpowered Ari's desire to be thorough. With a sigh, Ari transported them further west.

They had luck at the first village they stopped at. The caravan had also passed through here, and the young farmer they spoke with believed it had stopped at a nearby town. The innkeeper in town had been purchasing food faster than he ever had before.

They were getting close.

Not having been any further in this area, Ari's ability to transport was of little use. But the sun was only just past its midpoint. The two men received directions and continued on.

About an hour into the walk, Ari turned to Hakon. "Why start a family?"

Hakon glanced over at his friend and smiled. It was the first meaningful question he'd asked since their surprising reunion. The very fact that Ari asked meant it had been bothering him for some time.

"I never planned to," Hakon admitted. "After my release I wandered for a long time. I was angry. I didn't trust myself to be around others much. Then I met Sera."

"How?"

"She was an herbalist, out gathering plants, but not paying as close attention to the wilds as she should have. I came across her high in a tree, hoping a pack of wild dogs would eventually get bored and leave her alone."

Ari chuckled at the thought. Few creatures in the wild willingly abandoned prey.

"After I drove them off, I escorted her home. She wasn't quite of age yet, but even at that first meeting, I sensed something different about her."

Ari looked skeptical, and Hakon didn't blame him. When one lived long enough, one came across all sorts of people. Truly unique people were few and far between.

He tried to explain. "This land makes most people hard. That's no secret. But she wasn't. She was still gentle."

Hakon caught Ari's look of disdain.

"Not weak," he added. "Anything but. She wouldn't hurt an insect. But she was a healer of uncommon skill. And she would fight any illness or injury with every bit of energy she possessed. She won most of her battles, but her losses didn't deter her."

They walked in silence for a bit. "Sera had a strength I didn't understand. She opened herself up to suffering, and it didn't break her. If anything, it made her more compassionate." He smiled at the memories. "She made me want to be better. I left her that first day, but I asked permission to write her, which was granted. I earned a small fortune and our relationship deepened. After she came of age, I told her who I was and asked for her hand. She said yes."

Hakon pulled a canteen out and took a sip. "We waited for a while, but eventually decided to have a child."

"Why?"

"If I'm honest, it was mostly because she wanted one so badly."

"Is it worth it? Knowing that she'll likely die before you?"

Hakon had thought long and hard on this in the past, and his choice remained the same. "It is."

Ari considered the assertion for a time, then shook his head. "I'm not sure I could do it."

"Have you and Solveig discussed it?"

"Once, long ago. Neither of us wanted to welcome that suffering into our lives."

They continued on, much the same as they had all day. But the space between them felt different. Less cold.

Just as the sun touched the horizon, they came upon a small group of travelers heading the opposite direction.

They had a handful of horses, a cart, and a wagon. Ari paused as they neared one another. "They're carrying an awful lot of weapons," he remarked.

The assassin wasn't wrong. One didn't go into the wilds unarmed, but this particular group of men had taken caution perhaps too far. "Maybe they need so many to feel safe out here. We are a ways from a truly secure town."

Ari glanced at Hakon, trying to decide if he was serious.

Hakon shrugged. "It's possible."

"They're going to attack us. There's at least a dozen of them. And that monster on your back is probably worth as much as everything they've got in that wagon."

"You could just transport us well behind them. Once they realize we're tehoin, they'll leave us alone."

Ari shook his head. "I want to know where they found so much loot. There aren't many places that could have come from out here."

Hakon sighed. "Will you at least ask nicely first?"

Ari chuckled. "Sure."

They didn't get the chance. Ari's prediction turned out to be accurate. As soon as they were in bow range, arrows arced into the air. At the same time, the riders kicked their horses into a gallop.

Ari and Hakon charged toward the riders, and the arrows fell behind them. Hakon strengthened his limbs and sword with teho.

If the riders were surprised by the charge, they didn't turn away. Hakon leaped when he was still twenty feet from the nearest rider. He swung his massive weapon as though it were no more heavy than a dagger, cutting clean through the lead rider.

Two other riders fell as Ari joined Hakon.

The remainder of the bandits realized they'd picked a more difficult fight than they thought.

It was too late for them, though. Hakon and Ari carved their way through the group. Hakon's sword, edged with teho, cut through any blade that tried to stop it. Beside him, Ari felled any opponent with quick, efficient cuts.

Ari beat Hakon to the last bandit, a young man who hadn't shaved in far too long. Ari knocked the bandit's blade aside with ease. "Where did you get all this?" he asked.

The bandit pointed west, to where Ari and Hakon were heading. "The town!"

Hakon's stomach sank. What had happened to the town where his daughter had been?

20

———

Damion barely gave her or Zachary time to prepare. Poor Zachary hadn't even had time to tell her it was a terrible idea. He'd reached out for her hand just in time.

Cliona suspected that if Zachary had been a few seconds slower, Damion would have left without him.

It was like blinking, although she was sure she hadn't.

They were a long, long ways from the wall.

Damion had transported them to what could best be called a slight widening of a mountain trail, no more than nine or ten feet across. A flat slab of dull gray granite rose to her left, and to her right, emptiness. The drop pulled her eyes toward it, and she guessed any fall from the trail would result in several hundred feet of descent followed by a sudden and final stop.

Damion's hand tightened on hers as another wave of vertigo slammed into her. For a moment, her knees threatened to buckle. She fought to remain upright. The only thought in her mind was how embarrassed she would be to collapse in front of Damion.

On her other side, Zachary didn't fare so well. He had appeared closest to the edge of the trail, and he sank to hands and knees, dry heaving.

She could do nothing for him until she helped herself, though. She fixed her gaze on the solid wall of rock to her left and took several deep breaths. The vertigo passed in short order.

Damion watched Zachary, still on hands and knees, crawling closer to the slab on their left. Cliona thought she saw a hint of a smile pulling at the corner of his lips. Then he turned his focus to her. "Sorry to bring us to such an inhospitable place, but the dragon has a complex relationship with teho. I fear to transport too close to it. From here, though, it is less than a mile to a place where we might meet it."

In front of them, Zachary placed his hands on the wall of the slab and used it to push himself to his feet. His face was pale, but he seemed otherwise fine. Cliona had a sudden urge to reach out and take his hand, but she feared the gesture would not be welcome. Not under Damion's gaze.

Cliona wrapped her arms around her body as the wind stabbed like daggers into her skin, ignoring what clothing she wore. Though it was still late summer, there was little warmth in the air here.

She didn't know where they were, but they were high. Her lungs had complained within the walls of Damion's fortress. Here, they couldn't even summon the energy to do that much. With every breath she felt as though she lost more air than she gained.

Damion led them farther up the mountain, and it didn't take long for Cliona to realize Damion's choice of location had actually been a generous one. The path they walked was rarely much wider than Zachary's broad shoulders. It hugged the face of a mountain like a lover afraid to let go.

Their elevation did provide spectacular views, though. From this path, even the other peaks seemed short in comparison. For as far as her eye could carry, and up here it could carry for some ways, there was no place higher.

Her breath never came easy, but the exertion of the climb at least warmed her body to the point where she didn't fear freezing.

The distance felt farther than Damion had reported, but Cliona suspected that was due more to the extreme circumstances of the hike than to any objective measure of distance. Eventually, though, they came to a crack in the granite, twice as tall as a person and not quite wide enough for Zachary to walk straight through. Damion led them in.

As soon as they were out of the constant wind, warmth returned to Cliona's limbs. Up ahead, she could see a light and knew that this tunnel probably didn't travel more than a few hundred feet. She guessed it led to the other side of the mountain.

Damion stopped somewhere near the middle of the tunnel and turned to them, little more than a silhouette against the daylight. "It is very likely that when we emerge on the other side, the dragon will be close. It is drawn to tehoin, and so will seek me. It and I have... an agreement of sorts... and you should be safe. But all the same," he cautioned, "it would be wise not to make any sudden moves. I cannot guarantee your safety if it begins to consider you prey. Is that clear?"

Cliona nodded. In the legends, pretty much all humans looked like prey to dragons, but she held her questions, suspecting there would be no easy answers. There was something more happening here, something Damion wasn't telling them. She looked forward to deciphering what it was.

Damion looked over to Zachary. "That means if you're going to fall on the hands and knees when you see it, perhaps it would be wise to remain here."

Zachary tensed, and Cliona worried she would soon have an argument on her hands. She prepared to jump between them.

But then Zachary smiled. "Thank you for the advice."

Damion grunted and then led them the rest of the way.

As they neared the opening, Cliona's breath came faster, though they didn't gain any additional elevation. The tips of her fingers tingled and her heart thumped loudly in her chest. Like the kolma, dragons were largely considered extinct, or a metaphor for something the ancients did not understand. Until today, Cliona had been willing to entertain the possibility of their existence, but had been skeptical.

But now she stood with Damion, who threatened to turn everything she thought she knew about the world on its head.

There had to be a dragon on the other side of the tunnel. Why else would Damion go to all this trouble? Why do all of this for any other reason?

She clenched her fists as they approached the last dozen steps toward the exit.

Then she stepped out into the open, finding herself on a small stone balcony. The wind blew even harder here, the air sharp against her cheek. It pulled at her hair, causing it to snap behind her like a flag in a gale, but she barely noticed.

Because there it was.

From their balcony, they could actually look down on it as it soared through the mountain valleys.

It was, if anything, even larger than she would have thought possible. She knew the legends as well as any other child in the six states, and perhaps even better. The dragon possessed wide wings that, through the movement of both air and teho, kept the enormous body aloft. A muscular, sinuous torso moved through the air in a way that reminded her of a snake in the grass. It had razor-sharp teeth and claws, capable of cutting through stone easier than she could tear paper. Twin horns rose from its head, looking like old gnarled trees.

The dragon below her was everything the legends claimed, and was still somehow more. Even from a distance, there was a power emanating from that creature that could not be denied.

She didn't know how long she stood there, mouth agape, as the creature flew below them. But she could not look anywhere else, afraid that if she pulled her eyes away even for a moment that it would vanish and she would realize this was all a dream. No matter how long she watched it, she couldn't quite believe it wasn't a figment of her imagination.

Beside her, Zachary was stunned into an equivalent speechlessness.

The dragon passed beneath them and then, with a sudden explosion of power, rose straight into the air, ascending faster than any bird could dream to fly. In less than a heartbeat it had gone from being below them to several hundred feet above.

Cliona despaired then. She had never felt such power. She had never even imagined such strength was possible. Of course the wild possessed mysteries of which she knew little, but this was the first moment in her life when she truly understood how audacious of a goal conquering the wild would be.

Against this, humans had no chance.

The dragon dove toward them, teeth bared and claws outstretched. Cliona's breath caught in her throat. Beside her, she felt, more than saw, Zachary take a step back.

She remembered Damion's words and held her ground. On her other side, Damion didn't so much as flinch.

The dragon roared, a sound beyond imagination. In Cliona's mind, it shook the earth, causing the mountains to bow.

But the roar also awakened the teho within her. Strength filled her limbs. She was dimly aware of something similar happening to both Zachary and Damion, their abilities responding to the dragon at a level beyond human control.

The dragon altered its path, and Cleona swore that it turned slightly and aimed itself directly at her. It grew larger and larger. She'd known it was enormous at first glance, but as it neared, she realized she'd still underestimated it.

At the last moment, it angled even more sharply downward, passing in front of them with a rush of wind powerful enough to drive them each back a step or two. Then, before Cliona or the others could even lean over the edge of the balcony to track the dragon's path, it rose before them, held aloft by a barely understandable power.

This time, there could be no doubt. Its gaze was firmly fixed upon Cliona. Her body responded, teho swirling within her limbs like a barely contained storm. Before she knew what she was doing, she was reaching out to touch the creature. It felt as though she and the dragon were the only two creatures alive on the planet.

No more than a foot separated her hand from its jaws, and yet she felt no fear.

And then the dragon roared again.

21

Hakon's mood took a dark turn as they made their way toward the village.

He had never considered himself a man of peace. There was too much blood on his hands for that belief to be anything but a wishful lie. Theirs was a violent world, and violence was necessary to survive. Someday, far in the future, he hoped that might not be true, that his descendants might someday live a life free of the fears that had defined his existence. But that day was not today, and it would not be tomorrow, either. For now, a pacifist in the wild was nothing more than a meal.

All the same, Hakon detested senseless killing. He only hunted when he needed meat, and he liked to believe that any violence he visited upon his fellow humans had been just.

There was nothing worthwhile to find in the blood he had just spilled. They had been criminals, true. But a criminal was just a fool who believed there was a shortcut to survival. Some believed it easier to fight their fellow humans than the wild. In some cases, they were right.

Ari, knowing Hakon well, said little. He would recognize the storm clouds crossing his friend's face, and knew there was nothing to do but wait for the rain and thunder to pass. They each drove a cart, each with several horses tied to it. They'd be returned to the town they'd been taken from.

But when the town came into view, Hakon realized that their efforts had been for naught. The town was a ruin. Even from a distance, he suspected he would find no living soul within.

Truthfully, though, he felt nothing for those who had once lived here. He'd seen devastated towns before, and even after hundreds of years, his soul remained numb. All he hoped was that his guesses were wrong, and that Cliona had never been here.

Ari pulled to a stop beside him. They studied the devastation together. Once, this town might have been the jewel of the area, although that wasn't saying much. There were dozens of homes and a few larger buildings that had likely been businesses. Though it was currently too far west to be a popular destination, the six states expanded ever outward. And there would always be people like Hakon, who did not feel at ease in the city. One day, perhaps, this could have become a thriving town.

No longer.

Humans were superstitious, and now they would avoid the site of the disaster.

He nodded to Ari, and the two of them continued on.

There was no chance Cliona had been here.

He had to believe that.

A breeze rose in the west, and with it, they caught their first scents of decaying flesh. Whatever had happened here had occurred a few days ago, if the smell was to be believed. By the time they entered the town, the wind had picked up even further, and clouds slowly gathered off in the distance. The wind whistled through broken shutters, sounding like the high-pitched whispers of angry ghosts.

They dismounted, and after a quick debate, freed the horses. Both of them preferred to travel by foot, and it seemed likely no one here would require the beasts.

They began their examination of the town, going from house to house.

One fact was quickly obvious. Hakon nodded toward the four parallel marks slashed into a wall. They were deep enough to almost collapse the entire structure. "I haven't seen marks like that in many, many years."

Ari grunted. "I thought we'd driven all the dragons far to the west."

"Not far enough. Or perhaps this one didn't get the message."

They crossed another block, every building showing signs of damage. Parts of bodies lay everywhere. Hakon found them in the shadows of broken doorways, in the middle of the square, and in one case, embedded into a hole in the stone.

He was no stranger to the aftermath of violence, but this sickened him all the same. The endless scenes of tragedy struck with a force he didn't expect. He almost didn't have the courage to ask the question he most needed answered. "Do you see anyone you recognize?"

Ari had seen both Agnesse and Zachary at the academy, and he never forgot a face. The assassin shook his head, then his frown deepened as they came upon even more devastation. "This doesn't feel right."

Hakon guessed Ari wasn't just referring to the loss of lives.

"Have you ever seen a dragon attack like this?" Ari asked.

Hakon looked around the area again. Slowly, Ari's observation dawned on him. "Unless this whole town was filled with tehoin, you're right."

Ari's smile was grim. "I can guarantee that this town was not filled with tehoin. I would have heard of that." He looked around the town again. "It almost seems as though this dragon was angry. This all reeks of rage."

Hakon agreed. But what could they learn from that? It wasn't that dragons were friendly. But neither were they malevolent. Hakon had always considered them to be more similar to the forces of nature. They were indifferent to humans, except for those who dared to use teho.

Those they tended to hunt to the ends of the planet.

"You think they finally got tired of us?"

"I hope not," Ari said. "I'm not sure the strength exists in humanity to defeat them anymore."

They went through the rest of the town, but as expected, they found no survivors. Perhaps the dragon hadn't killed everyone immediately, but it had been several days since the attack, and Hakon and Ari had come too late to save anyone.

Their last stop was a two-story building, whose shattered front sign declared that it had been an inn. They entered the main door, and Hakon covered his face with a cloth. Death had visited many people here. It looked like a group had tried to make a stand in this room. Tables and chairs had been stacked in the corner farthest from the front door to create an additional layer of protection. But from the looks of it, a single swipe from the dragon had destroyed the makeshift barricade and the people behind it. Viscera was scattered everywhere and blank eyes stared, uncomprehending, into the gate of death.

Here, there was nothing to be done.

Ari led the way upstairs. They went from room to room,

searching for clues. Hakon thought it a little strange that they found no bodies on this floor. Nor were the rooms damaged. No humans had been up here when the dragon attacked, nor did anyone attempt to hide up here.

They did, however, come upon a room with a writing desk full of books. Hakon's heart froze. With every house they checked and every face they saw that wasn't his daughter's, he had begun to hope once again.

Ari stepped forward and picked up a few books. Then he went to the chest and opened it, revealing the clothes within. "This was Agnesse's room," he said.

Hakon suddenly found it difficult to breathe. He tried to keep his voice even. "They were here?"

He couldn't remember ever seeing Ari regretful, but he did now. "It looks that way. I'm sorry, friend."

Hakon's knees buckled, and he fell to one knee before he caught himself. His heart and lungs felt like they were going to explode, drenching the room in his grief. His breath came short and fast through his mouth, and in his mind's eye all he saw was the face of his daughter smiling at him, the composite of a thousand past smiles.

The smile he might never see again.

He couldn't.

It couldn't be true. He had shaped this world with his own two hands, carving a legacy written in blood. Teho flowed down his arms and into his fingers, and as he clenched his fists the wooden floor cracked and splintered as his fingers clawed through it.

"No." He stood up and wiped the back of his hand across his eyes with one violent motion. "Not until I see her."

He saw the doubt and skepticism on Ari's face, but his old friend just nodded. "Of course."

They searched the rest of the rooms but came up empty. Agnesse had been here. Of that much Ari was certain.

But they knew nothing else. When their search of the inn was complete, Ari met Hakon's gaze. "Agnesse was here for a reason. Let's find it."

Hakon nodded. Reason had abandoned him. Cliona had been here. He imagined he could feel her presence.

He could think of nothing besides her, but he trusted his friend, and so he followed. They walked to the outskirts of town and began circling it. Hakon focused only on his friend's back. Before long, Ari found a trail he claimed had been used frequently, and recently. They followed it, Hakon's mind stuck far in the past.

The trail traveled up and over rolling hills and wide fields of grassland. Soon, they found an unusual sight. Holes had clearly been dug throughout one part of the country-side. And now they had all been filled in. Fresh dirt marked the locations. Hakon just stared, uncomprehending, but Ari could reason for both of them. "This is it. They were digging for Marjaana's home."

Ari led them to one hole, muttering as he did. "And if they were successful, it stands to reason it would've been the largest hole."

Ari looked over at Hakon, and when he received no response, he shrugged and began digging. He fashioned a large scoop out of teho and began scraping enormous quantities of dirt from the ground. Though his work was efficient, Hakon could see the care that he took.

Hakon watched. Even had he been so inclined, there was little he could do to help. Unlike every other tehoin, he could not manipulate teho externally. In this task, he was no more effective than an average laborer. And there wasn't a shovel to be seen.

He sat down, his mind running in circles and always returning to that same smile.

After a few minutes, Ari stopped. The horrified expression on his face penetrated even Hakon's daze.

His heart broke, fearing the news, but needing to know anyway. "What is it?"

Ari didn't answer at first, but when he did, he was quiet. His words barely carried to Hakon's ears.

"Bodies. Lots of bodies."

22

The dragon's roar was the most beautiful sound Cliona had ever heard. It sounded nothing like the earth-shattering roar from before. Now, it filled her with joy and energy. The teho storming within her body didn't vanish, but it calmed, becoming like the current of a powerful river carving its way through a valley.

Cliona leaned forward, and the dragon brought its head down.

Her hand, small and frail, touched its snout.

The world dissolved. One by one, her senses fled, replaced by an overwhelming sense of unity. Teho flowed from the tips of her fingers and into the dragon. But the current flowed both ways, and in unequal proportion. The constant trickle of teho leaving her body was nothing compared to what returned. Teho filled her as if she stood under a waterfall, mouth open to drink.

Though her limits were far surpassed, she felt no pain.

There was no beauty in the world that compared.

A dark and angry burst of teho slashed between her and

the dragon. For a moment she imagined a hook, tearing into the dragon's side.

What had been one was now two, and separation brought agony. Every muscle felt like it was on fire, and she couldn't control her limbs.

The dragon roared again, but there was no beauty in it. The force of it knocked her back, and someone caught her body as it fell. A great gust of air buffeted the balcony.

Cliona blinked and focused. Zachary was above her, and she was in his arms. His attention wasn't on her, though, but on something she couldn't see.

Her thoughts were sluggish, as though she'd just been woken rudely from a deep sleep.

A wave of tension ran through her body, causing all her muscles to seize up at once. Zachary held her tighter, protecting her from herself.

Then she saw Damion, and she swore she saw his expression change as he looked at her.

He was enraged.

He reached down and grabbed Zachary by the shoulder. And then they were gone.

Cliona blinked at the bright sun now in her eyes. The air was warmer here, and the sun caressed her skin. She wasn't sure where they were, exactly, but they were safe.

But it was still one adventure too many. Another seizure started in her feet and ran up her legs and spine, and this time, her world went black.

She woke in the room that Damion had provided for her in his fortress. Several lanterns were dimmed, and she heard a soft snoring from the corner of her room. She groaned softly and sat up, her entire body aching. Zachary was sitting in a chair in the corner, his head slumped back against the wall.

He mustn't have been sleeping deeply, though, as her movement caused him to wake. His snore abruptly cut off and he blinked rapidly. When he saw Cliona awake, a smile grew on his face. "You had me worried there for a bit."

"What happened?"

"I was hoping you would tell me." He rubbed at his eyes. "All I know is that I got transported to some high mountain peak, where I met a creature that I didn't think existed. Then you touched the creature as though it were a pet. For a moment, it was like you weren't there anymore. And then the dragon got truly angry. I thought for sure I was going to visit the gate."

Zachary's recounting of the events brought a smile to her face.

Not because of what had happened, but because of him. She'd put his life in danger and he wasn't even angry at her. He wanted to understand. Perhaps he was more of a scholar than he admitted, even to himself.

"Something in me called to the dragon. Or something in the dragon called to me. But I felt drawn to it." She shuddered. "It was like I wasn't myself."

"What was it like?"

She struggled to find an answer that did justice to the experience. "It felt like all the boundaries in the world had dissolved away." She paused, the memory bittersweet. "It was one of the best moments in my life."

"Why did it get so angry, then?"

"Something got between us. Teho. You?"

Zachary frowned and shook his head. "Embarrassed as I might be to admit it, I spent the entire experience focused on not soiling my pants."

Cliona laughed. "It takes true courage to admit as much."

"I'm glad you think so. Truthfully, though, I've never been so terrified of anything in my life. The teho emanating from that thing makes even Damion look weak."

That attack of teho had been different from what she was used to. It had carried so much emotion with it, so much anger. She thought of Damion's look right after the connection was severed. Had it been real, or something she imagined?

Zachary stood up. "How are you feeling?"

Cliona experimentally moved one limb at a time. Her muscles ached, but in much the same way they did after a strenuous day of work. Otherwise, she felt fine.

Zachary went to the door. "Damion asked me to speak to him when you woke up. Is there anything you want me to tell him?"

She thought for a moment, then shook her head. She didn't trust her memory, not after such an extreme experience.

"I'll be back as soon as I can," Zachary said. Cliona smiled.

After Zachary left, the room felt strangely empty.

Cliona laid her head back on the pillows and closed her eyes. If not for the ache throughout her body, she might have thought the whole episode a dream.

Dragons were real.

And were more than even the legends claimed.

What did it mean?

If dragons existed, did that mean that other legends were true? Legends she had dismissed because they didn't fit her view of the world. She stared at the ceiling. Her world crumbled around her like old paper exposed to the elements.

For so long, she'd been so certain about so many things.

Now, even her most basic beliefs had turned to sand.

All she had left were questions.

Fortunately, Zachary saved her from herself. He knocked on the door and entered, only a few minutes after he left, carrying an enormous pile of books. "I thought Damion wanted to know when you woke because he was concerned," he said as he carefully laid the books on the table. "But it turns out he only wanted us to get started on translations."

The sight of all the books gave her a measure of courage. If she had questions, at least some of the answers might be in those tomes. She recognized them as being from Marjaana's home.

"He was clear about one thing. He doesn't want full translations. He only wants to know the location of Ava's grave."

"Ava? Really?"

Cliona didn't know much about Ava, but that was because no one did. She was one of the earliest stamfar, but little had been written about her. Or, Cliona thought as she looked at the stack of books, they hadn't found anything written about her. It was said that she had died young. The only reason Cliona knew of Ava at all was an obscure reference in a history book few scholars had any respect for.

They dove into the task, figuring out a system in short order. Cliona kept one piece of paper nearby to jot notes to herself, but mostly, she spoke her translations out loud and let Zachary transcribe them.

It didn't take long to lose herself in the work. Every book Zachary brought was a treasure. The first book was a journal, written in a small, neat hand. It was of a stamfar who had fought against the wilds to begin a working farm.

The journal was a revelation. Cliona recognized some of the traditions farmers used today within the pages, but here the author wrote them down as though they were new and untested. He'd tried many ways before finding the methods that were now known to work.

With a grimace, she put the book aside. She longed to know the secrets within, but a greater responsibility called. The second book was a collection of stories, or myths, of the stamfar. Again, Cliona wanted nothing more than to dive deep into the waters of the book, but she set it in the pile of books to be translated later. She wouldn't find anything about Ava within.

The third book, though, had much more potential. It was the story of a governor of the early stamfar, filled with legendary names.

As Cliona translated, her mind fell into a trance. The translation turned into a never-ending puzzle. She would solve one sentence only to be confronted by the next, and then the one after that. But each was a fresh challenge she loved.

It took her several moments to realize Zachary was tapping her on the shoulder. She startled.

"Sorry," he said, "but my hand is starting to cramp up, and I'm pretty sure we've been at this for hours. Mind if we take a break and go for a walk?"

She almost said no. There was too much left to learn. But then she saw the stack of papers next to Zachary and realized how much progress had been made. She stood and her muscles complained.

Perhaps a break would be good for her.

Together, they left her room and walked outside. Cliona blinked at the bright sunlight.

"Where does your passion for the language of the stamfar come from?" Zachary asked.

"That's a long and not very exciting story."

"I'd still like to hear it."

"It comes from my parents," she began. "When I was little, my father loved to tell me stories of the past. I loved those stories as a little girl. But as I got older, my feeling about the stories changed. I don't know how to explain it, but I sometimes got the sense that my father's stories were more real to him than we were."

Zachary listened without interrupting.

"I sat and listened to his stories long after most other children had outgrown such entertainments. When he told them, they felt so real. The more he told them, the more I wanted to know if they were true."

Cliona smiled. "And that's something I inherited from my mother. She was an herbalist, and knew more about plants and how they could be used than anyone. Her skill was a result of her curiosity, I think. She was always asking questions, and encouraged me to do the same."

They turned a corner and saw a small overlook. Zachary led them there.

"So I suppose it was a natural thing. My father provided the inspiration, and my mother provided the aptitude."

"Was your father a scholar, too?" Zachary asked.

Cliona laughed at the thought. Her laughter died quickly, though. "To tell the truth, I'm not sure what he is."

Zachary frowned.

"He's never worked, as far as I know, but he always has plenty of money. He knows almost as much about the world as any person I've ever met, but he is no scholar. And he's one of the strongest people I've ever known."

"He is?"

"You wouldn't stand a chance against him," Cliona said.

"You know I studied the sword for years," Zachary said. "And I can form a teho blade."

"All the same," Cliona replied. "It isn't that I don't think you're strong. I've seen you fight. But my father is something else yet."

Zachary looked like he wasn't sure if he believed her, but he said nothing. Cliona, not wanting to think of her past, or of her father, changed the subject. "What about you?" she asked. "We know I'll study the legends of the stamfar until I'm old and gray. But if you had your freedom, what would you do with it?"

He didn't answer at first, content to look out at the valley below. Cliona feared she'd asked something too personal.

"Promise you won't laugh?"

"I'll try."

"Someday, I want to be the governor of one of the six states."

Cliona tilted her head as she studied Zachary more closely. "I've always gotten the impression that you hate politics."

He shook his head. "Not politics, but the politicians who twist reality in a bid for power. The governors of the six states are great people, doing all they can to serve their people. But there is a rot growing among the magistrates." He sighed. "Unfortunately, my father is one of the worst offenders."

"Why?"

"I think it is because he grew up in Mioska. The concerns within a city are different, and it twists a person's perspective. My father doesn't believe the wilds are a danger anymore, and doesn't see why the governors spend so much to protect our frontiers. It's made him bitter, and the others around him are no different."

Zachary gestured at nothing in particular. "It's all empty. I grew up in a world where everyone said one thing and did another. My father once said that honesty was the quickest way to an early grave. It's hard to find meaning in such a world, and I've always hated him for that."

Cliona shivered, and for a moment she thought a cloud had passed overhead, but when she looked up, the sky was clear and blue. "Father and I fell out after my mother died," Cliona admitted. "He and she had gone out together, and I blamed him for not protecting her. I know it's not rational, but I can't look at him without having that thought lurking in the back of my mind. But at the same time, I've always known he'd do anything for me. Even as I've distanced myself from him."

"He's a good man?"

"He is." Cliona looked up again at the sky. She made a promise to herself that when she saw Father again, she would make things right between them.

"My father isn't," Zachary admitted. "Do you want to know why I'm at the academy?"

That focused her attention. "It's something I've been wondering since I've gotten to know you better."

"My own mother died long ago from disease. I'm the oldest of three siblings, with one brother just a year younger than me, and a sister three years younger."

Cliona leaned closer. Zachary had never spoken of his family before.

"My father had little time for us, which made me, whether I liked it or not, the head of the household. I raised them both as well as I could, even though my younger brother began to practically worship Father. But my sister and I are close. Then, two years ago, Father arranged her marriage to another magistrate he wanted to ally with."

Zachary's voice turned hard. "I learned, though, that the man was a demon in disguise. He abused those closest to him, and there were even worse rumors. I argued with my father, but the alliance was too important to him."

Zachary paused.

"So I killed him. My father's lack of morals actually protected me from close scrutiny. Because my father had so much to gain from the alliance, it was assumed he had nothing to do with the killing. If anything, Father's enemies in court were actually the prime suspects. But no one ever learned the truth."

He relaxed, as though he'd shrugged off a burden. "Father couldn't prove anything, but he guessed well enough. My actions forced him into a corner. So now I'm exiled, and I'm sure within a year or two he'll try to say I've forsaken my claim to his position in favor of scholarship, and my younger brother will become his heir. But my sister is safe, and for now, that's all that matters."

Cliona looked at Zachary with new eyes. "I think you might make a pretty decent governor."

Zachary smiled, but only for a moment. "Perhaps. But I have a lot to learn before I'm ready to lead."

There was a pain there she didn't understand. She almost reached out to him then. But again, she was afraid he wouldn't welcome the gesture. She leaned in closer, though.

Someone cleared their throat behind them.

Cliona spun, startled, and saw a messenger. The young woman held out a letter to Cliona. She took it and read it, aware the messenger waited for her reply.

She nodded. "I'll be there."

The messenger scampered off, and when Cliona turned back to Zachary, the moment had passed. He was smiling again and gave her a quizzical look. "What was that?"

"Damion. He and I are having a private dinner tonight."

23

———

Hakon wished Ari could dig faster, but the assassin was methodical by nature. And he was being careful not to slice through the bodies with his teho scoop. As Ari dug the bodies up, Hakon pulled them out.

He laid down a shorter man who weighed so much Hakon thought he'd been made from bricks. The man was a bit older than most of the bodies he'd pulled free, and there was something about his expression that made him seem separate from the others. Hakon guessed he'd been a foreman.

The cause of death was easy enough to see. They'd been murdered. By someone with plenty of teho to spare. There were almost no signs of struggle. To kill so many so quickly they couldn't fight back required both power and skill.

So far, almost all the bodies had been young, and Hakon assumed they were members of the digging crew. Damion had them fill in the holes, then buried them in the last remaining one.

And then a dragon had visited the town.

Hakon still didn't understand that part, but he would. Nothing would stop him.

Ari stopped digging. His teho scoop vanished. "There's a ward here," he said.

"And?"

Ari crouched down to get a closer look. He examined the hole for a few moments before he spoke. "If I break it, someone will know we're here."

"Then break it, and we can ask them our questions."

Ari grimaced. "You never understood finesse."

"My daughter's body might be down there. We're not stopping."

Ari held up a hand, silently pleading for a few moments to think. Hakon's rage started to bubble. Sometimes, Ari made life much more difficult than it had to be. The assassin considered the straightforward approach the method of choice for fools only. Why face a problem directly when you could stab it in the back?

Hakon kept his anger in check.

Barely.

Ari nodded. "Just keep your sword close."

He returned to work. A few moments later, Hakon felt the ward shatter as Ari dug through it. The release of teho was powerful. He looked up, half-expecting company immediately.

No one arrived.

They would, though. The only reason to place a ward so far underground was to know if your burial site had been discovered. Whoever had done their work wanted it kept quiet.

Their roles changed. Hakon watched the horizons, alert for new visitors. Ari handled the digging alone, using the gentle maneuvering of his teho shovel to bring bodies out and to the surface. Hakon brushed off each one, checking to see if they were his daughter.

The last body Ari pulled from the hole was an older woman with gray hair and a severe look on her face. Ari crawled out of the hole, covered in dirt. "That's Agnesse," he said.

"You're sure there are no more bodies?"

Ari nodded, and hope bloomed once again in Hakon's chest.

They hadn't found any of Cliona's things, nor had they found Cliona. She wasn't here.

And if she wasn't here, Hakon was sure she was alive.

Ari gestured down to the hole. "I found Marjaana's home, too, if you care."

Hakon stepped easily toward the hole, his steps lighter now. And there it was. "Mind if I check it out?"

"I'll come with you."

They dropped down the hole. Hakon opened the door with teho and they stepped inside. Remembering other stamfar structures, he put his hand to the walls and turned on the lights.

It was clear the place had been sacked. The rooms and walls were bare, and the floor was filthy with the tracks of people walking in and out. Even so, there was no denying this had been the home of a stamfar. The design was familiar, dredging up some of Hakon's ancient memories.

Damion's work had been thorough, though. The two warriors went from room to room, but nothing remained. One door, standing open and filled with teho, had protected what appeared to be an enormous library. Hakon imagined the empty shelves lined with books, and couldn't help but smile as he thought of his daughter here.

It would have been one of the greatest joys of her life.

Ari came into the library. "What do you think?"

"I think Damion found what he's looking for. And I think my daughter is with him."

At Ari's doubtful look, Hakon explained. "This library had to be what he was after. And that door requires at least a kolma to open. So he was here. And knowing Marjaana, we can assume this library was full of books. Books that Damion now needs translated."

Ari understood. "She's in Aysgarth?"

"So it would seem."

"Even I wouldn't dare to go near that place," Ari said.

"Why not?"

"Besides Damion's strength? He's got more tehoin than anyone has seen in one place since the rebellion. Powerful ones, too. As you experienced, even his nelja can be a threat. It's a stamfar building, constructed into the side of a mountain, with only one path to approach it by. Not to mention he's got the place under more wards than I can count. If you're thinking of going there to get your daughter, you're going to need an army." Ari gestured to the door. "Let's get out of here. I'd like to rebury most of the bodies and return Agnesse to the academy."

It was a surprisingly generous offer, coming from Ari. The assassin usually thought nothing of leaving bodies out to feed the wild. Hakon had been thinking along the same lines, though, so he quickly agreed.

The turmoil that rocked him earlier had faded. Cliona had to be alive, and even if she was in the heart of Damion's growing web, he would find a way to her.

They went to work placing the bodies respectfully in the hole. Once all but Agnesse had been laid to rest, they covered up the hole with enormous piles of loose earth.

It wasn't what the dead deserved, but it was the best they could reasonably offer.

Ari was shoveling one of the last scoops of earth on the grave when teho burst a few hundred feet away.

Three warriors, dressed in the familiar black of Damion's uniforms, stood hand in hand. Hakon drew his massive sword as the three leaped into movement. Two of the warriors came for him, while the last angled toward Ari.

A young woman formed a beautiful teho blade. There was a gleam in her eye as she raced toward Hakon. She saw his enormous sword and was confident in her victory.

He strengthened his sword and his body with teho, waiting for her to come close. She was making the same mistake the others had earlier. But he supposed it was to be expected. Word of his arrival apparently hadn't spread.

Hakon raised his sword overhead and snapped it down as the woman came close. The woman raised her teho blade to block the strike. She expected that she would slice cleanly through his sword and take his head with the next cut.

Unfortunately for her, that wasn't what happened. The teho that encased his sword met her teho blade. And in this contest, strength mattered. Hakon guessed she was nelja, among the most powerful and skilled warriors the world now had to offer.

But he was from the past, and she wasn't enough.

His sword sliced through her teho blade and her, slicing through bone, muscle, and organ with ease. His cut opened her up from her left shoulder to right hip.

Hakon stepped past her as she died, focusing on his next opponent, a young man who had kept his distance through the short fight. When Hakon stepped toward him, he formed a small ball of teho in his hands.

Though he'd seen his companion die with one cut, the

young man didn't seem worried in the least, which concerned Hakon.

But what could he do with a ball of teho?

Hakon soon found out.

The ball burst from his hands, straight at Hakon's face.

Hakon shifted to the side, expecting the ball to fly past him.

But the ball changed angles faster than Hakon could move. It drilled into his stomach. Even with teho strengthening his limbs, the blow knocked the wind out of him. He doubled over and the ball shot straight up into his chin, snapping his head back and sending him falling onto his rear.

Hakon coughed, feeling the bruises already beginning to form. Though the ball wasn't a sharp object, both of those blows had hit hard enough to kill an ahula.

He shook his head to clear the stars, just in time to see the ball streak toward him again. This time, it caught him high in the right arm, and even with teho, Hakon feared that his arm would break. The force of the attack brought him crashing to his side.

Despite the pain, he pushed himself to his feet. His opponent offered no quarter, and twice more the ball almost knocked him over. Bruises formed from head to toe.

Hakon tried to cut at the ball with his sword, but it was too quick to hit.

Against most teho attacks, Hakon had little to fear. But not this one. He could withstand more than any other human on the planet, but even he would eventually succumb to blunt force. And Damion's lackey wasn't giving him the time to mount an effective response.

The ball came again, crashing into the back of his left

calf. It kicked his leg into the air, then came back and hit him in his chest, sending him back onto his rear again.

It took Hakon a moment to catch his breath, but when he did, he saw the ball streaking at him faster than ever, this time straight at his face.

Hakon got his arms up in time, but the ball hit hard enough that he feared a bone would break. It knocked him flat on his back, and he rolled out of the way of the next blow. He stumbled to his feet, only to see the teho ball a moment before it struck him on the left side.

Somehow, he kept his feet, though he swayed like a man who had drunk far too much wine.

The ball came again.

Hakon swore. For such a simple attack, he had no idea how to defend against it. If he had the ability to manipulate teho externally, it would have been no problem at all. He was stronger. But it didn't matter. He braced himself for another hit.

A handful of teho darts flashed in front of him, knocking the ball off its brutal course.

Hakon dared to take his eyes off the ball for a precious second. Ari was running from his enemy, who watched, bemused, from a distance. Blood trickled from what appeared to be a half dozen thin cuts. Neither of them, it seemed, had been the victor of their matches.

"Switch," Ari yelled.

Hakon turned further, studying Ari's opponent more carefully. A young man with light hair, and it didn't look like Ari had even managed to scratch him.

Hakon groaned. Every part of his body hurt. What was Ari expecting from him?

He trusted Ari, though. So he found his balance and stumbled forward. His opponent was almost short enough to be a child. Hakon raised his sword, wondering what skill the man would possess.

Razor-thin threads of teho bloomed from the young man's hands.

Hakon swore.

Not wanting to be cut, Hakon reversed his direction and gave up ground as the threads lashed at him. They filled the air around the man, spinning and dancing like marionette strings pulled by a madman. Hakon had little doubt that anything thrown into that space would quickly be cut apart. No wonder Ari had such trouble. Just as the man with the ball had exploited Hakon's weakness, this warrior seemed particularly suited to killing Ari.

Coincidence or planned?

The warrior didn't seem worried that Ari and Hakon had switched, so Hakon guessed coincidence. Ari would have little problem against Hakon's first opponent, and Hakon believed he could beat this man.

But it would hurt.

Hakon watched the threads for a moment more, but there was no pattern to their motion.

The short man expected him to attack with his sword.

But Hakon couldn't cut so many threads. His sword would destroy some, but others would lash out at him. He saw how it all would play out, and he saw the misplaced confidence in the young man's eyes. These two didn't know who they fought, and this one didn't know that his attack would be useless against Hakon.

His blood boiled and he attacked, leading the way with his sword, just as would be expected.

Hakon sliced through several of the threads before others managed to wrap around his hand and the blade. The smile on the short man's face grew wide as he pulled

Hakon deeper into his trap. Razor-thin wires of teho reached around, snapping tightly across Hakon's chest, back, and limbs.

Had Hakon been anyone else, the attack would have sliced through his body at multiple angles, leaving him as nothing more than a pile of pieces in the empty grasslands. An appetizer for the creatures of the wild that roamed the night.

But teho ran through Hakon's limbs, and the wires did nothing but scratch the surface of his skin. They cut deep enough to draw plenty of blood, but nothing that came close to being fatal.

His assailant frowned, but he didn't yet understand the problem he faced.

New threads whipped at Hakon as the ones already wrapped around him pulled him closer to his opponent. Cuts appeared over his arms, legs, and chest. Blood dripped from a dozen wounds, but still there was nothing fatal.

The young man shifted tactics. He created even more wires. They wrapped around Hakon's arms and legs, trying to hold him in place. Hakon felt the man's impressive strength fight against his advance.

But Hakon was several times the man's size, and teho made him stronger than any human could achieve through muscle alone. He fought against the wires, grimacing as they cut deeper into his skin. Would he reach his enemy before the wires cut something vital?

Hakon believed he would. He kept as much teho flowing through his body as possible.

His advance was inexorable, and with every step, the expression on the short man's face changed.

First concern, then worry, and finally, panic.

Damion's assassin lashed at him with everything he

could. Dozens of threads wrapped around his legs and arms, pulling and sawing at his joints.

Hakon felt the attempts but ignored them. He'd let his body forget what it meant to fight, but pieces of the knowledge returned with every duel. Despite the pain of the wires, his focus was clear. These wires couldn't kill him. A familiar rage had taken hold of him, an anger he thought he'd let go of when he'd been released from his prison of nightmares.

Anger brought clarity.

Hakon raised his sword overhead, both hands reaching up to grasp the hilt. The assassin's final efforts became a frenzy as he fought with all his power against this hulking death.

It did him no good.

Hakon brought his sword down, ignoring everything the man tried. His sword sliced clean through the man, barely slowing. He fell in two parts, and the wires of teho vanished, as though they'd been no more than a bad dream.

His opponent destroyed, Hakon's strength finally fled him. His injuries from his first opponent screamed for attention, and he took a few steps back and sat down, staring at his handiwork.

Before long, there was movement beside him, and Ari sat down next to him. The distance the assassin had kept through the entire journey had disappeared, and it felt like old times.

It felt good.

"I haven't seen anything like that since I was woken," Ari said.

Hakon grunted.

"Solveig thought you didn't have it in you anymore. That you'd surrendered your rage for good."

"I had hoped to."

"This is what you are, Hakon. It always has been."

Hakon didn't respond. He wanted to be more than he had been. But he feared his friend was right. Ari's words struck close to his heart.

"You're planning on going to Aysgarth, aren't you?"

Hakon nodded.

"You're going to need help. Those three were surprisingly skilled, and I suspect they weren't even that important to Damion."

Hakon nodded again. He'd been thinking the same, and there was only one place to turn for such help. "You said taking Aysgarth would require an army. But perhaps you'd settle for a band?"

24

Cliona followed her escort through the labyrinthine walls of Aysgarth. Had she more attention to spare, she would have kept track of the twists and turns they made, but her mind couldn't be bothered. It held onto thoughts of Damion.

The kolma unsettled her in ways she struggled to define. At times, she admired him more than anyone else she'd met. His conviction, strength, and purpose brought her closer to him. And yet, those same qualities came with a sharp edge.

But wasn't that edge necessary for what he hoped to achieve?

A certain amount of ruthlessness was needed to change the world.

Both Zachary and Damion wanted to change the world. Both wanted to create a world where humans could thrive.

If she had to bet on one, though, it was Damion.

The longer she spent in Aysgarth, the more she became convinced his desire wasn't an empty dream. He had the strength and the administrative skills to make his future a reality. Those who lived here worked hard, and in exchange, they were rewarded with a safety unheard of anywhere in the six states.

Zachary had nothing but hopes. Noble, perhaps, but without resources and the will to move mountains, what did those hopes amount to?

The escort stopped in front of a door protected by two more guards. They all greeted one another, and after a quick knock, the door was opened.

Cliona didn't even have time to prepare herself. The transition from the hallway to the dining room happened too quickly.

Damion was already seated.

Everything about the room felt intimate. A little fireplace kept the room warm, and the only furniture of note was a small, round oak table and two chairs. The table was currently covered by papers that Damion studied with the same intensity he did all things. He gestured her over. "Apologies. I was just finishing up and lost track of time."

Cliona let herself enjoy the sight of this ruler bent over papers, much the same way she spent much of her time. She *wanted* to trust him. She just needed to put her fears to rest.

Damion finished his work and organized the papers into a tall stack. She felt an expression of teho, and a few moments later an aide came in to take the papers. Damion gestured for her to sit. As she did, cups of wine were brought. She took a sip, and her eyes widened.

Damion smiled. "Do you like it?"

"It's easily the best wine I've ever tasted."

"It's among my favorites, too. It's grown on the slopes not far from here." He swirled the dark liquid and took another sip. "How go the translations?"

"Well enough." Cliona forced herself to put the wine down. She loved wine, and she hadn't lied. It was the best she'd ever tasted. If she wasn't careful, soon she'd be tripping over her own feet, and she needed a clear head. "It's a unique challenge to be translating so many different works while looking for one specific piece of information. I still haven't figured out the best way to go about it."

"I understand, and I wanted to thank you, again, for coming here on such short notice. I've read a few of your translations, and I'm impressed by how fast you've worked."

Blood rushed to Cliona's cheeks and she looked down. It was a kind compliment, but she wasn't one to blush. As always, Damion left her stumbling, unable to find the balance she typically enjoyed.

She was saved by the arrival of the meal, which was nothing like what she expected. If she had to guess, it was the same meal being served in the kitchens throughout the fortress. Damion noticed her look.

"I'm not terribly interested in lavish meals," he said. "The food served for everyone else is good enough for me."

They ate their meals, and Damion questioned her about the work of the translations. Over the course of the meal Cliona relaxed. Damion knew more about the stamfar than most people she had met, and his questions were insightful. They often made her pause and look at her assumptions in a new light.

But all the same, she felt as if the meal were a prelude to what he was really curious about.

She finished her last bite, comfortably full, and took another sip of wine. She was nearing the bottom of the cup and enjoying it immensely. But she didn't ask for a refill, even though Damion did.

There was a natural lull in the conversation, and she took the opportunity to ask the question that had most been on her mind. "When you were leading us up to the dragon, you said that you and it had an agreement. What did you mean by that?"

Damion took another sip of his wine. "I wondered how long it would take you to ask about that." He put down his cup and his smile faded. "The agreement is not something that I created. It's something I inherited. To tell the truth, I inherited all of this." He extended his hand to encompass the whole fortress. "I lost my family when I was young, but I was raised by a stamfar."

Cliona blinked.

From anyone else, such a claim would have been madness. Even from Damion, it seemed too much to be true.

She shook her head, and he smiled. "It's fine if you don't believe. Few know the truth, and I'd be concerned if you weren't skeptical. Nevertheless, I was. And from him, I inherited the dragon. It's not that I can control it, but that I can, at times, persuade it to do as I ask."

Cliona still shook her head. It was impossible. "The last of the stamfar died hundreds of years ago."

Damion leaned closer to her. "What if I told you they didn't? What if I told you at least one still lived?"

She leaned away from him, her heart pounding in her chest. "No. I'm willing to believe that there are still kolma. What I've seen from you has no other easy explanation. But not stamfar. We'd know."

Damion shrugged. "Would you?"

He let the question hang for a moment before continuing. "It is of no matter to me whether or not you believe me. But I answered your question honestly. And now I'd like you to do the same. Where did you learn to manipulate teho as you do?"

Off-balance as she was from his most recent claim, she

still noticed how sharply he looked at her. This was the question he'd wanted to know the answer to, the reason why he'd asked her here. But with thoughts of stamfar still in her head, she blurted out the answer before she was even sure she wanted to. "My father."

His eyes narrowed. "It's an exceedingly rare technique. What is your father's name?"

"Hakon."

Damion took another sip of his wine, then leaned back and studied her. Again, she felt uncomfortable under his gaze, though he did nothing that was overtly threatening. He finished off his wine with one long gulp, then put his cup down.

"Now, that *is* interesting."

25

"I had really hoped that my days of doing this were far in the past," Solveig said. She looked worn from the healings she had just administered.

Ari offered her half a smile that was utterly unconvincing. "They started it."

She wasn't amused. "All those years between you two, and you still have the combined sense of an immature six-year-old."

Hakon knew that she spoke at least half in jest, but his blood still hadn't cooled from the battle. Anger roiled beneath the surface, waiting for an excuse to burst forth.

He hadn't felt like this for a very long time.

Once, it had been all too familiar. "The risks were worth it," he said, sharper than he intended.

"You could have asked for help. With enough time, we could have disabled the ward instead of letting Damion know that we're poking around in his excavations."

"Cliona is missing, and you didn't see that town." He glared at her. "I had to know."

Solveig held up her hand in a gesture of peace. "I understand. But there are other ways. You push ahead no matter the consequences, the same as you always do." She directed her anger at Hakon. "It's exactly what happened last time, and now you're playing with fire again."

Hakon clenched his fists but held back his retort. Solveig was one of the few people who wouldn't back down from an argument with him, especially if she believed she had the right of it.

And she probably did today.

But he'd had to know.

Solveig finished the last of her healing on Ari. "Would you leave us?" she asked him.

Ari looked between the two of them and nodded. He put his tunic back on and left the room. Hakon and Solveig glared at each other for a long minute.

"You're thinking of gathering the band?" Solveig asked.

Neither he nor Ari had said anything to her yet, but it was no surprise she had guessed. She was the most observant of them. If she wasn't also a warrior and healer of unmatched skill, he would argue that academics should have been her home long ago.

"Have you really thought this through?" She sat down across from him, so close that their knees were almost touching.

"He has my daughter."

"Most likely as a translator. *She* doesn't even know who she is. It's unlikely that he'll discover her identity. She's a scholar, and she'll be safe."

"Agnesse would probably have a pretty strong argument against that."

She looked like she'd been slapped. "I'm not saying she's not in danger. She is. I'm saying you have more options than assembling everyone and charging in."

Hakon kept his voice even through a heroic effort. "Such as?"

"I have people in Aysgarth. Give me time to get a message to them, and maybe we can figure out a way to transport her out."

Hakon fixed her with a hard stare. "Given what I've learned about Damion, such an attempt seems unlikely to succeed."

"It's better than risking his wrath for a plan that is no more likely to succeed. This isn't just about your daughter. If he thinks he's in danger, he could attack before the six states are ready."

Hakon lost his temper then. "Is that what this is about? You're afraid that he might attack the states? He has my daughter!"

She didn't even bat an eye at his anger. "Grow up, Hakon. This world is always one crisis away from a season of bloodshed that could even put the rebellion to shame. Ari and I do all we can to keep the balance. To keep people alive. I like Cliona, and I want to help her if I can. But not at the cost of a war."

"And that's where we disagree," Hakon growled.

Solveig's eyes widened for a fraction of a second. She spoke softly, freezing the room with her tone. "Do you truly believe that?"

The question finally succeeded in cooling his anger. It still burned, but now within control. He lowered his voice. "No. I don't." He swallowed to keep his voice from cracking. "But I can't lose her."

Solveig hesitated for the first time in their argument. "There's more to it than you understand."

"What?"

He saw her flex her hands, the way she did before she

formed her teho blades. Whatever she was about to say, she was worried it might anger him enough to attack her. But she remained unarmed.

"I've been watching you," she admitted, "ever since you were released."

"What?"

"One of the conditions of our early release was that I keep an eye on you throughout the years. Isira wasn't certain what you would do, and wanted assurances that something —something exactly like this—would never come to pass."

"You've been spying on me?"

It wasn't the fact that she had been watching him that bothered him. Especially given the conditions, he understood that well enough. But she hadn't approached him, even in the darkest moments before Sera had come into his life.

The moments he'd thought about ending it all.

All she had done was watch.

"Yes."

Minutes slowly passed as Hakon mastered his anger. "Why tell me now?"

Solveig held up two fingers. "First, because you need to know Isira is watching. If you re-form the band, she might even act."

Hakon's heart twisted at the thought. Few people in the world terrified him.

But just the mention of Isira's name made his knees shake.

Solveig put down one of her fingers. "Second, as I watched you, I saw a side of you I didn't think existed. I saw the man you became. I've watched you with your daughter, and once, I even spoke with Sera. She was so proud of you."

Solveig paused. "Now I see you here, and I see the anger

that drives you. We're arguing just as we did in the rebellion. I fear that if you continue down this path, even if we save Cliona's life, you'll lose your daughter for good. I know the years since Sera's passing have been hard, but you've raised an amazing daughter. Cliona is a wonderful woman. But if she sees this," Solveig gestured at Hakon, still covered both with his blood and the blood of his enemies, "will she let you back into her life?"

He was ashamed to admit he'd never considered the question.

Solveig was the only one who could sometimes convince him of the error of his ways. He looked down at his hands. He'd enjoyed traveling with Ari, and feeling like he was part of the band again. But he loved Cliona more.

"Fine," he said. "We'll try your way first, but if it doesn't work, will you join me?"

"Of course."

"I'm still going to reach out to the others. If the time comes that I need them, I want them to be ready right away."

Solveig grimaced but nodded. "You better start with Irric."

"That bad?"

"And then some," she said. "If you go to her first you'll have your entrails spilled throughout the local bar before you even say hello. Besides, Meshell will never say yes unless Irric agrees."

"Well," Hakon said with a forced smile, "apparently I know what I need to do next. Where is he?"

Solveig grinned. "Same place he always is. In the middle of the battlefield."

26

Cliona translated the first line of yet another paragraph, dictating the passage to Zachary, whose practiced hand wrote with quick and firm strokes.

She glanced over at him, head down, eyes focused on his work. While his presence did assist her considerably, she still felt a pang of guilt. He'd come to Aysgarth for her, and in exchange for his generosity she asked him to sit at a desk for hours on end, writing her words on paper. If not for her, he'd probably already be close to returning to the academy, where he'd be among his friends, and among women who didn't use him as nothing more than a scribe.

Knowing his dreams for his future made it worse. This wasn't what he wanted from his life, and she felt as though she was holding him back.

He hadn't complained once, though.

To speed up their search through Marjaana's library, Cliona had decided to translate limited portions of each book. Usually she did the first few pages. If those proved promising, she then translated the first paragraph or two of each chapter. And if the chapter seemed promising, she'd translate the first line of each paragraph.

At the first hint the book didn't hold the secrets she sought, she put it off to the side to be translated later.

The work grated against her nature. She took pride in finishing what she started. No matter how many hours went into the project, their methods prevented her from feeling closure on any book.

But there was so much left to do. Though Damion claimed he had other translators, he made none available for the task. What she produced in a day would have awed most scholars.

Here, it barely felt like progress.

Zachary's writing stopped, and Cliona realized her thoughts had run away with her again.

There were moments where the task ahead of her felt impossible. In the past weeks, they'd gone through dozens of books, and they still weren't through the collection of histories Marjaana had. Which comprised only a fraction of the full number of books.

The risk to Cliona's method, and the worry that sometimes kept her up at night, was that by skimming across the surface of these books like she was, she might very well have had the answer in hand and passed over it.

Zachary stood up from his writing desk and stretched. He came around behind her, put his strong hands on her shoulders, and began massaging her back with his thumbs.

A few weeks ago, such a gesture would have caused her to tense up.

No more.

She felt her shoulders physically drop as Zachary rubbed the knots loose from her back. She leaned her cheek against his hand.

"You're doing good work," he said. "No one else could do better, and most would do quite a bit worse."

"It would be nice to know that we're at least heading the right direction," she said. "Maybe we shouldn't even be looking in the histories."

Zachary was silent for a few moments, but his hands never stopped. "It pains me to say it, but perhaps you need to speak again with Damion."

In their weeks at Aysgarth, Zachary's opinion of their host hadn't changed much. But Damion, much to Zachary's delight, wasn't the type of ruler who spent much time at home. Though Cliona didn't keep too close track of him, it seemed he was gone far more often than he was around. They'd only seen him a few times since the night Cliona had dined with him, and then usually only in passing. Most of the time, Damion barely seemed interested in them.

Zachary approved.

But he was also right, now. Cliona could understand Damion's secrecy when he'd first given her the assignment. Surely they'd earned some measure of trust by now.

It was time to learn what they were really looking for.

Two guards were stationed outside the room, and Cliona let them know she would like to meet with Damion whenever he was next free. Unlike the orders Agnesse had given the guards outside Marjaana's home, these two were only present to guard the books. There were no awkward searches here. Cliona and Zachary were welcome to take whatever they wanted in and out of the room.

Just the thought of Agnesse made Cliona's blood start to boil.

She forced herself to think of happier things. She was the one chosen by Damion. Agnesse had to endure a long and very bumpy ride back to the academy with a broken leg.

There was no reason to give the woman much more thought.

As had become their custom, Cliona and Zachary ended their day of work by taking a walk around the walls of Aysgarth.

Her initial impressions of the place hadn't changed much since their first visit. In many ways, she thought of it more as a military fortress than a town, although in reality it felt as though it existed somewhere between the two.

There was plenty to be impressed by. Those who lived and worked here enjoyed plenty of food and shelter, and there were no beggars on the streets. It was the most competently administered town she'd seen.

At the same time, it lacked something vital. There were taverns and gambling halls, but after a couple of attempts at patronizing them in the evening, Cliona and Zachary had decided the places weren't for them. They were too quiet, the other patrons too controlled.

Aysgarth had discipline to spare. But it was short of fun and frivolity.

What Cliona had come to appreciate, perhaps more than anything, were the views. This was the first time she'd spent considerable time living in the mountains, and the vistas never got old. For those alone, the trip might have been worth it.

In the end, though, Aysgarth seemed a mirror of Damion's character. Admirable in many ways, but something about it clashed against Cliona's sensibilities.

That night, a summons came for her.

She followed her escort deeper into Aysgarth, to chambers Cliona had never been to. Damion welcomed her into a small study. Several bookshelves lined the walls, filled with leather-bound journals.

"You wanted to see me?" Damion asked.

Cliona sat down across the desk from him. "I did. Although we've made decent progress over the past few weeks, I feel like I could be more useful if I had a better idea what I was looking for."

Damion sat in his chair silently for a moment. "You're not sure you have enough to work with?"

There was a challenge in the question, but Cliona didn't retreat. She shook her head. "No. All that I know is that you want to find Ava's grave. But there are hundreds of books to go through, and I don't even know if I'm starting in the right place. If you have any more context, it might be really useful in finding the answer you're looking for."

Damion thought for a moment longer, then stood up and went to the bookshelf behind him. He pulled out a leather journal and returned to his desk. He opened the journal to a bookmarked page. Then he spun it around for her to look at. One passage stood out.

Ava's power grew in the west, faster than any of us expected. The council only captured her through a single act of betrayal. Now, the secret of her strength lies buried with her.

Cliona looked up from the book. "What's this?"

"Notes from my master," Damion replied. "Taken when he was young."

"*This* is the basis for your search? It's only three lines!" Cliona leaned back. Back at the academy, a scholar needed dozens of pieces of evidence to do something as mundane as request a book from the restricted archives.

Damion took the book back, as though he was afraid to leave it in her hands for too long. "It's enough. There's something buried with Ava that provided enough strength for her to threaten the stamfar council. My master believed it at the end of his life, and he was rarely wrong."

The lines raised more questions than they answered. "Why do you think Marjaana knew the location of Ava's burial?"

"She was one of the council. Their record-keeper, in fact. If there is a written record, only Marjaana would have had it. My master spent the last years of his life looking for Marjaana's library."

Cliona lowered her head in thought. She'd come here looking for context, and Damion had given her more. The lack of legends about Ava weren't due to the passage of time, but the intentional efforts of her peers. They'd betrayed her, then erased her from history.

Which also meant she'd been looking in the wrong books. If Marjaana kept any written record, it was in her own journals.

It was something, at least.

Cliona's curiosity overcame her sense of decorum. "You speak fondly of your master. Who was he?"

A hint of a smile played upon Damion's face. "Torsten."

"*The* Torsten?"

"The very one."

Shards of the mystery that was Damion melded into a story. Torsten had been the last of the imperialists. A man rumored to be invincible both on the battlefield and in politics. Though the band had eventually broken the back of the empire, Torsten had been the one who negotiated the treaty that formed the six states. Even in defeat, his legacy lived on through the treaty he had forged.

And then he had disappeared. Most historians assumed he'd retired to a quiet life somewhere and died alone.

But that had been over 150 years ago. And Damion couldn't be much older than thirty.

She shook her head. "That's impossible."

Damion shrugged. "The truth doesn't require your belief, but I've never lied to you."

"What happened to him?"

Damion gave her a curious look then, one she didn't understand. His fingers tapped lightly against the journal. Then he answered her question.

"He was murdered."

27

Cheers rose from the crowd like waves cresting and crashing over rocks, the sound a physical force that disoriented Hakon. If not for Solveig's firm grip on his wrist, he would have been lost among the tides of people.

If walking the streets of Vispeda had been a trial, this might as well have been an execution. The scents of roasting meat and fragrant wine mixed with the stench of unwashed humanity. Vendors shouted for his attention, his size making him an easy target. Bodies jostled against him, unconcerned by either his size or the weapon he carried on his back.

More than once, he saw bystanders eyeing him up as though he were cattle at an auction.

They thought him another hopeful, here to make his name and his fortune.

"When you told me Irric was on a battlefield, this wasn't what I imagined." He had to shout to be heard.

Solveig pulled on his wrist, dragging him like a stunned fish against the current of spectators leaving the arena.

They entered the arena through one of the many open gates, finding a bench near the back. The old wood creaked under Hakon's weight as he sat down. The previous fight had just ended, and for a short while, the entertainment was beyond the high walls of the fighting pit. Only the true fans remained, filling the benches near the front in preparation for the battle to come.

Before long the benches began to fill again. Spectators carried armfuls of meat, wine, and ale, many of them stumbling and spilling their sustenance on fellow fans. Hakon pressed his hands into his thighs to prevent himself from clenching them into fists. Farmers and ranchers still fought against the wilds for that food, and its waste was an affront to their efforts. But they were outside of Taunka, one of the few cities that made Vispeda feel like a village.

Beside him, Solveig had either grown used to such decadence or controlled her emotions better. Likely, Hakon suspected, both were true.

Then the subject of their search stepped out into the arena, and Hakon couldn't help but chuckle.

Irric was nearly as tall as him, with blond hair almost as light. Hakon, though, was still nearly twice the weight as the wiry warrior. And as Irric stepped onto the sands of the fighting pit, he gave the crowd a smile and a wave that brought the spectators to their feet. Hakon swore he saw a group of women swoon in the front rows.

Some things never changed.

"I take it he's something of a favorite?" Hakon asked.

"To say the least," replied Solveig.

A few minutes later, another man appeared on the other side of the arena. He shared Irric's lean build, but stood considerably shorter. Both men used wooden weapons.

Solveig answered his questioning glance. "We finally

learned we shouldn't let our best fighters die for our amusement. Fighting with steel is now illegal. Doesn't mean it doesn't happen, but not in the larger arenas."

Perhaps humanity did change. Slowly, and never as fast as one wanted, but it crawled forward one painfully slow step at a time. The last time he'd been to a fight, there'd been no armor and the weapons were all the various styles of sharpened steel a warrior might prefer.

A judge announced the contenders and the fight commenced. Hakon leaned forward, eager to see his friend's skills after so long apart.

The first exchange was a light one, both contestants measuring the reach and speed of their opponent. Irric looked as competent as always, but his opponent was fast, and his blows were strong.

"Both men are in the hunt for a duel with the local champion," Solveig explained. "The winner of this match wins the opportunity."

Hakon glanced over at her. "You follow this?"

She showed no sign of embarrassment. "I follow everything the band does."

The second exchange was no test. Wooden swords clacked together, the moves impressive. It ended with Irric being forced to retreat.

Hakon's eyes narrowed.

The third exchange lasted longest of all. The contestants struck and retreated. The echo of the swords filled the arena, and the crowd was surprisingly silent. Just when Irric looked completely lost, he found an opening and scored a definitive strike against the shorter man. The judge called out the point as the crowd rose to their feet.

Hakon joined them, but without enthusiasm. "He's playing."

"He is," Solveig said. "But with reason." She gestured at the crowd. "Everyone believes they are here for the fight. But Irric understands that what they really want is the story, written in the blood and sweat of the fighters. He could rise through the ranks, destroying everyone he fought, but to what end? He's won and lost dozens of times, and each time he rises a little higher. There's a reason why this crowd leaps to its feet for him. He inspires them because he never gives up."

Hakon looked at his friend down in the pit. He couldn't imagine anything being more like Irric.

Fight and inspire.

Never give up.

If Solveig had been the mind of the band and Hakon the muscle, Irric had been the heart, rousing them onward even in their darkest moments.

He recognized the jealousy in his heart and acknowledged it.

Distracted as he was, Hakon didn't sit when the rest of the crowd settled for the second point. In that moment, Irric saw him, and their eyes met.

Irric's eyes hardened, but then he saw Solveig. Some unspoken communication passed between them, and he gave her a small nod.

The match was best of seven rounds. And even Hakon had to admit he was entertained. Irric made every round a battle, and in time the match was tied at three rounds apiece. Irric swayed in his corner, as though exhausted from the fight.

Hakon almost laughed at the sight. A hundred and fifty years ago, he'd watched Irric carve through entire armies without breaking a sweat. When he looked around the arena, though, he saw how the audience bought the act.

Spectators sat perched on the edge of their benches, their meat getting cool and their ale warm. Several were praying to Gunnhildur, the stamfar of war and battle.

Hakon wondered how Irric would allow the fight to end.

The final round lasted five long passes, and the swordplay was impressive. Without the aid of teho, either would have beaten Hakon easily.

And Irric was barely trying.

The fight ended with one decisive cut, and Irric on the ground, clutching his side.

The crowd went wild. Some were ecstatic to see such a fight. Others were fans of the opponent and cheered the victory. But many yelled their displeasure at the result.

After the fight, both contestants were allowed a brief window of time to speak. Irric went first, complimenting his opponent's skill. He then told them he would return to training and healing, and when the audience saw him next, he would be healthy and stronger than ever before. He would never stop fighting.

They devoured his words like children who had played all day without a meal.

Irric bowed to the crowd, gave a pained wave, and shuffled out of the arena.

His opponent spoke well of Irric, and promised an excellent fight against the champion.

Then the spectators started to disperse.

"Let's get some food first," Solveig said. "It will be a while before he is free of fans who wish to speak with him. He always makes time for them."

When they finished their meal, they stood and stretched. Most of the crowd had departed, and most of the shops were closing. Only a nearby tavern seemed to be doing a brisk business.

Solveig led the way around the arena to a camp. Perhaps a dozen tents were arranged around an open fire pit, and a group of fighters were gathered. From the bits of conversation Hakon overheard, it sounded as though they were discussing the day's fights.

Irric sat quietly in the circle, allowing the man he'd fought to enjoy most of the attention. When he saw the two of them approach, he stood and met them at the edge of the camp. Any trace of his injury was gone.

Irric and Solveig embraced, then Irric squared up against Hakon. The look in his friend's eye made Hakon want to grab teho to protect himself.

But not against a friend.

Then Irric's face cracked into a grin, and he swept the larger man into a hug that threatened to crack Hakon's ribs. "It's good to see you, friend!"

Hakon coughed and caught his breath when Irric put him down. Slight as Irric appeared, he was all muscle under his loose clothing. "You too," he wheezed. He put his hands on his knees.

Irric caught him by surprise again when he took a step back and launched a powerful kick at his chin. Hakon only had time to blink, and then the warrior's boot connected with his face, and his world went black.

28

Slim as Damion's help had been, it focused Cliona's search. She put aside all the history books and made straight for Marjaana's journals. The stamfar's orderly mind made the process considerably easier than it could have been. All her entries were dated, and at the bottom of every entry was a list of topics covered in that entry. Cliona spent the first half day of her new search looking for an index. But if one had ever existed, it wasn't among the books they'd recovered.

All Cliona had to do was translate the topics to see if the entry needed further attention.

At times, during their breaks, she had to pinch herself. Damion's arrival had changed not just the course of her life, but her thoughts. She still didn't believe half the myths told about the stamfar. They were no gods, though their power might have rivaled a deity's. But perhaps the myths were far closer to the truth than she once believed.

The work was still some of the most challenging of Cliona's life. Marjaana had one of the most extensive vocabularies she had ever encountered, and as many of the labels weren't more than a word or two, there was often precious little context to use for translation. Many years had passed since Cliona had encountered so many unknown words in one place. Often, she had to translate the entry above to make her best guess at what the topic word meant.

Day bled into day. Zachary, though a useful aide, lacked the zeal for the work. He took long breaks at least twice a day to stretch his legs. Cliona let him go on his own. As the days passed, she sensed his frustration building, and as it did, so did her guilt. He never should have come with her.

In the evenings they walked around Aysgarth together, although the walks didn't feel as intimate as they once had.

They stopped at one of their favorite overlooks.

Off in the distance, she believed she could feel the dragon.

At least, she thought it was the dragon. Ever since her experience on the mountain, she felt like there was another presence lurking in the back of her mind. At night, as she fell through the space between waking and dreams, she thought she could even feel its emotions. It wanted to be near her, but whenever it approached too close, that hook of cold teho pulled it back.

She blinked, focusing on Zachary and his problems.

"You don't have to remain," she said. "There's no danger here, and this task will take time. For all I know, it could be months or years before I find what Damion is looking for." She smiled, hoping to soften her dismissal. "Certainly there are more interesting women waiting desperately for you to arrive back in Vispeda."

He shook his head and pursed his lips. "Do you know you're always being watched?"

"What?"

Zachary tilted his head, a small gesture aimed behind them and off to the side. Cliona looked out of the corner of her eye. There were guards there, which wasn't unusual. But now that he'd pointed it out, she did notice that they were paying close attention to the couple. Still, she and Zachary were outsiders here, and she didn't understand Zachary's worry.

When she said as much, his frown deepened and he shifted his weight from one side to the other, his agitation apparent. "I know you won't agree with me, but I really think you should leave. I don't think this place is as safe as you believe."

"Perhaps." Cliona didn't see the danger Zachary did, but she didn't want to argue. "You know why I need to stay, and I will. But you need not. You should ask to leave."

"Do you really believe he'll let me?"

"He's given his word that he would allow us to return at any time, so yes."

"I—" Zachary shook his head. Something was on the tip of his tongue, but he refused to speak it. She'd never seen him so torn about anything. He retreated two steps from her. "I'll talk to you later."

Cliona watched him leave but made no move to stop him. She wasn't blind to the risks she took. But from where she stood, the benefit was worth the risk. Here, they fought the wild, and the wild retreated. She wanted to be a part of that.

She watched the sun as it set on the horizon, then returned to her own rooms.

The next morning, when she went to the library where the books were being stored, Zachary wasn't there. Nor did he show up at any point that morning. Cliona translated alone, and she missed his help and his company.

There was no point in complaining, though. If leaving was what would make him happy, he should go.

In time, Zachary fell from her mind. The work, as it always did, consumed her.

She didn't see him that night at supper, and she almost went to his room to check on him. This was the longest she'd gone in weeks without seeing him. But she didn't. Perhaps it was easier this way. He could return to Vispeda and forget her.

The thought hurt more than she expected.

That night, to forget him, she worked on a journal until the language of the stamfar swam in her vision.

Cliona woke late the next morning, but Zachary still wasn't in the library when she arrived.

He must have left without even saying goodbye.

The thought left her feeling empty inside. After everything, she thought they would at least remain friends.

It took several pages of translating to push him out of her mind.

When someone touched her shoulder, she nearly jumped out of her skin. She looked up to see Zachary standing beside her.

She surprised herself by leaping up, almost embracing him before catching herself. The hint of a grin on his face let her know he'd noticed, though. It quickly disappeared. "Can we go someplace private?" he asked.

She looked around the library, which was empty except for the two of them. But she was so pleased to see him, she nodded.

They left the library and Zachary led them to his chambers. It was the first time Cliona had been within them, and she was surprised by how neat he kept them. She'd always imagined him as more disorganized.

Zachary gestured for her to sit down, and she did.

"I'm sorry I left the way I did," he began. "I needed time, but I shouldn't have left you wondering."

He cut her off before she could tell him it was fine.

"That isn't why I wanted to speak to you, though. I just spoke with someone in the fortress, someone who claims they have a message from Solveig. Apparently, this person has been trying to reach you for a while, but they never had a chance when you were unguarded. They gave me this." He held out a letter.

Cliona took the letter and examined it. It had Solveig's seal, and as she ran her fingers over the seal, she felt the teho wrapped around it. Had the letter been tampered with, it would have caught on fire.

The letter raised countless questions. How did Solveig know she was here already? How did Solveig know she was tehoin?

Maybe the letter held the answers. She unraveled the ward, then broke the seal. The handwriting within certainly looked like Solveig's. Cliona read, her eyes growing wider and wider. When she finished, she read the whole letter again.

Then, to ward off Zachary's questions, she gave him the letter to read.

As he did, he became more and more agitated.

Though she sat in a room of stone, Cliona felt the world shifting like sand beneath her feet. She couldn't tell anymore what was real and what was a lie.

Cliona held her head in her hands. Her mind needed something steady to hold onto, something she could believe in. The past few months had chipped away her certainties about the nature of the world, but this was the final, devastating blow from the chisel. Her thoughts shattered.

Not only did she not know what was real anymore, she realized for the first time the danger she'd put herself in. A harsh wind of self-recrimination blew the shards of her psyche away, leaving her empty inside.

Zachary's hand grasped her own, and she clutched it tighter than she had any right to.

He served as the anchor she needed. Unlikely as it was, this man who had so little in common with her was the one constant in her life. She could depend on him. She leaned against him, taking comfort in the slow rise and fall of his chest.

Slowly, the pieces that were her re-formed.

"What do we do?" he asked.

"The only thing we can. We stay."

29

Hakon woke up feeling like he'd been kicked in the face, although it felt like a horse had done the kicking instead of a human. He groaned.

"Slowly," a familiar voice said. "I've healed you, again, but you really ought to stop getting beaten by everyone you cross paths with."

Hakon opened his eyes to see Solveig and Irric bent over a small board, playing a game with small wooden pieces.

Irric glanced over. "Sorry," he said. "Didn't think that would land quite as hard as it did."

Hakon rubbed at his jaw. It was sore, and there was still bruising around the bone, but he'd suffered far worse, even recently.

"Of course," Irric said, "I also didn't think I'd ever see you knocked flat with one blow."

Hakon waved away the apology. "It's deserved. Maybe some warning next time?"

Irric chuckled. "Wouldn't be half as fun."

Hakon rolled into a sitting position and scooted toward them. From his brief glance at the pieces, it looked as though Solveig was destroying Irric's position. But that was no surprise. She and Ari had always been the strongest players in the band.

"Solveig tells me your daughter's gone missing, and that Damion's likely involved." Irric spoke as he examined his board and carefully moved a piece.

Hakon nodded. "Will you help?"

"Of course." Irric didn't even hesitate as he watched Solveig move a piece.

"Truly?" It seemed too easy.

"Truly." Irric moved another piece, scowling as Solveig captured it and took it off the board. "I bear you no more ill will over what you did." He smiled. "At least not after this afternoon. You've paid for your crime. Besides, fighting here is only interesting for so long. As usual, you promise more excitement."

Hakon had spent most of his time on the way here thinking about what he might say to convince Irric.

All his arguments proved unnecessary. He bowed his head toward his friend. "Thank you."

"Don't thank me yet," Irric said. "I told Solveig that I wanted to be there when you meet Meshell again. Part of the deal."

Hakon glanced over to Solveig, who shrugged. "Ari wants to watch, too, and I have to admit that even I'm interested."

Hakon rubbed at his sore jaw. "You three have a pool, don't you?"

"Told you he'd figure it out," Solveig said to Irric.

"What are my odds?" Hakon asked.

Irric resigned the game and stood up. He moved quickly around his tent, packing his goods. "Let's just say none of us have it going well for you. It's more a question of how bad it will get before she ends it or we're forced to intervene."

"Your concern is touching."

Irric collected the last of his gear and Hakon and Solveig waited as he said his farewells to the other competitors.

They walked away from the arena together. Solveig and Irric dropped into the conversation of old friends who hadn't seen each other for some time. They shared news of mutual acquaintances, and of the events of the day. Hakon listened for a while, but eventually his attention drifted. On the way here, he'd been so focused on convincing Irric to join them there'd been little time for anything else.

Ironically, it was Irric's old familiarity that pushed Hakon to the edge of another mental cliff. He watched as Irric sidled up next to Solveig and threw his arm around her. Smiled as Solveig batted his arm away. This moment could have been any moment from their past lives, when they had wandered the whole of the empire and more together.

But it wasn't.

Despite appearances, Hakon had ripped them apart, and he'd gone on to start a new life. In his mind, he'd always considered the choice the start of a new chapter.

Watching the two of them, Hakon wasn't so sure.

Their stories had continued without him.

His had ended, and he'd started a new book, alone.

A story of a lost soul finding something that felt like redemption. Guided by Sera's strong and compassionate hand. And Cliona.

In the centuries of his life, he had loved several women. But none like his daughter. She'd cracked something in his heart and wormed her way deep inside.

Hakon had loved Sera. But even that paled in comparison to what he felt for Cliona. Calling it mere love seemed to diminish it somehow.

And, he thought now, it was Cliona's birth that had truly started his story anew. All the others of the band had found a new way forward, a way to use their gifts to continue influencing the world.

He'd retreated from it all to raise a family.

Two visions of the future wrestled for control of his heart. In one, he was one of the band once again. As he watched Irric and Solveig, he knew he was welcome. They'd been closer than blood once. Perhaps, in time, they could be again. It was the life he knew best, the one he had missed the past forty years. It felt right, like it was the path he was supposed to follow.

In the other future, he remained apart. He settled for being Cliona's father and nothing more. And that was good, too. Perhaps it didn't satisfy him in quite the same way, but a man could die happy knowing he'd raised a good daughter.

The two books that could be his future could never be made one story. They were too different.

Despite the temptation the vision of the band offered, he couldn't travel down that path. He loved them all, but not like Cliona.

They came to a small clearing and found Ari waiting for them. He was stretched out in the grass, enjoying the last rays of the falling sun. He stood up and embraced Irric. They exchanged pleasant greetings, and Hakon felt the pull of the band stronger than ever before. Four of them were together now, and he could feel the energy in the air.

It was the same energy that had once brought down an empire.

It called to him.

"Did you find Meshell?" Solveig asked.

"Close enough," Ari replied. "I was able to track her work pretty easily. After talking with a few informants, I think I can guess what she's up to."

"And?" Solveig pressed.

Ari smiled. "I think she's planning on assassinating a magistrate."

30

Cliona put the paper in the fire and watched as the flames devoured it. It wouldn't do to have Damion finding it lying around.

"We should leave," Zachary said.

"The answers are too close."

"They aren't worth our lives."

She turned on her heel and he took a step back. "But they are. If Damion's right, Ava might be buried with an artifact that could save thousands of lives. Ours are a pittance in comparison."

"So we just stay?"

"We finish what we came here to do. Once we know where the artifact is, we decide what to do."

Zachary paced the room quickly. "The longer we wait, the more likely it is he finds out we know."

It was a risk. After reading that letter, Cliona knew she would struggle to look at Damion the same way. And he was observant enough to notice.

But progress had a cost. And she was willing to pay it so others could reap the benefit. "Are you staying with me?"

Zachary paced for a few more moments, then stopped and stood straighter. "I'm with you."

A part of her was surprised how easily her opinion of Damion changed. It made her wonder if she'd been deluding herself about him all this time.

They took the rest of the day off, but returned to the stack of journals the next morning.

Cliona worked as quickly as she could. Time had become an enemy.

Their break came out of nowhere.

Two days after the letter, she found references to Ava's rise in the west. The entries even had Ava's name as a topic. Cliona laughed to herself. After all that work, even Zachary could have been trained to find the entries in question.

After a brief hesitation, she began translating the entire series of entries. Zachary dutifully wrote the translation down.

Eventually, though, he stopped. When the familiar scratch of his handwriting faded, she turned to him.

"I'm not sure this should be written down," he said.

She considered his point. She liked writing, because it meant she didn't have to trust her memory. But with this, he might be right. Any secret known by more than one person was no longer secret. And when something was written, there was no telling where it might end up.

She returned to her work, no longer reading aloud. She read the pages slowly, translating as she went, forcing herself to settle for an imperfect record. Zachary, not having anything to do, quickly became bored. He stood and stretched, then began pacing the room.

Cliona kept half an eye on him as she worked her way through the passages. Marjaana hadn't left a cryptic clue. She'd written an entire account of the event. Within an hour, Cliona knew more about Ava's rise and fall than Damion.

For once, she knew something he did not.

When Cliona saw Zachary step toward the door to the library, she stopped him. "Damion's watching us," she reminded him. "Best to stay close, for now."

Zachary stopped short of the door, sighed, then turned away. He paced for a while longer, then lay down on the floor and laced his fingers behind his head. He closed his eyes. "Let me know if you need anything."

But Cliona was already lost in the journal entries.

Though the entries were concise summations of the events of Marjaana's life, Cliona's imagination had no problem filling in the details.

Ava's rise had been unexpected. Among the stamfar, she hadn't seemed to be anything special. Of the woman's early life, Marjaana admitted to knowing little. When Ava had first appeared as someone of notice, it had been with a small group of supremely devoted followers.

More than once, Marjaana referenced the odd beliefs Ava's followers possessed, but she never explicitly wrote down what those beliefs were.

In time, Ava's following grew, until the point where she was considered a threat by some of the leading stamfar of the time.

Though Marjaana's account was dry and sorely lacking in detail, Cliona painted a vivid image of the events.

She imagined a movement, growing in power as it attracted people from all over the land. She saw the debates in amphitheaters between Ava and the ruling class.

Heated words were soon replaced by cold steel.

At some point, Ava's rise had gone from a matter of concern to a problem to be dealt with.

Marjaana wrote extensively of the council meeting in which Ava's fate was decided.

And again she was there, around a table with figures who were now legends, debating whether one of their own needed to be killed. The decision didn't come easy, but it was made.

The others joined forces, and a battle raged.

Of the war, Marjaana spoke little. Such was not her domain, and all she wrote was that the casualties were high, and that Ava's followers fought with a zeal the council's forces couldn't match. Though the price was higher than anyone had expected, the movement died when Ava herself was captured and chained by the council.

Then there was only one further entry.

The debate of the council as to what to do with Ava.

Marjaana's final words on the matter were frustrating. *She is to be buried in the old temple, as per her wishes.*

After that, nothing.

Marjaana went on with her daily notes. She continued her experiments, seeking to better understand their world. Cliona quickly flipped through the rest of the journal and the next, simply looking at the topics of each entry to see if Ava was ever mentioned again.

She wasn't.

Cliona returned to the entry that provided the tantalizing clue. The old temple.

Where did gods worship?

And then she knew.

She stood up, almost knocking her chair over. Her sudden movement caught Zachary's attention and caused him to sit up. He rubbed his eyes.

"I think I know where it is," Cliona whispered, as though

the very mention of the secret would summon Damion into the room.

"Where?"

Cliona shook her head, and Zachary's face fell. "It's not that I don't trust you, but for now, it's safer if I'm the only one who knows anything."

He acknowledged the point, though the hurt remained. Then his features hardened. "What will you do?"

The question anchored her to reality.

If she told Damion, it wouldn't take long for them to reach the destination. Though the location was on the other side of the continent, she suspected his ability to transport would get them there quickly.

And then there would have to be another excavation. Though Cliona knew the approximate location, she couldn't point to it exactly. But eventually, Damion would possess the artifact. It was only a matter of time.

The question, which up until that moment had been academic, now had very real consequences.

She paced the room, walking the same route Zachary had earlier.

Then she stopped and looked at him. "I can't ask you to take this risk with me."

He stepped toward her. "You know you don't have to. I'm with you."

She'd expected as much. Like her, he was already entwined in this problem, and the risk to him worried her. All the same, she was glad for his company.

"Then it's time for us to figure out how to escape Aysgarth," she said.

31

The four of the band appeared in a land far different than the one they had left. Hakon, who hadn't asked about their destination, groaned. The air was heavy with moisture and sweat formed on his forehead even as he stood still. Though Ari had transported them to a clearing, thick jungle surrounded them. Hakon slapped at his bare arms as mosquitos went for his blood.

"Of course she'd be in Garor," he growled.

Of the six states, Garor was by far his least favorite. It occupied a large swath of land on the southeast corner of the continent. It was hot, humid, and filled with insects. Hakon detested all three things.

"It appears that several of the magistrates here have decided that they are tyrants rather than servants," Ari said. "Meshell seeks to remind them of the error in their thinking."

Such had always been their fear when they decided to topple the empire. It made no difference to humanity if all they accomplished was replacing one large empire with six smaller ones. But because they'd been removed from the flow of time, they never had a chance to guide the development of the six states. Hakon's crime prevented them from truly finishing the work they had started.

The other four, it seemed, had found ways to pick up where they had left off.

"How close are we to the magistrate Meshell is interested in?" Solveig asked.

"Maybe two days," Ari said.

"Then we camp tonight. Early rise tomorrow followed by a full day." She glanced at Hakon. "Unless you want to go ahead of us?"

With teho, he could travel the fastest of them all. But he didn't think encountering Meshell alone was wise.

"I'll travel with you."

Their course decided, Ari established a perimeter. He moved with practiced ease. Hakon watched with interest, noting how Ari wove his traps of teho together to make a beautiful interlocking perimeter. Once Ari finished, they were probably safer inside his wards than inside a fortress built of stone.

Not only that, but the barrier had the added benefit of deterring mosquitos.

Hakon almost embraced Ari for that, but worried that Solveig might become jealous.

He was the last to fall asleep. As he looked around at the sleeping forms of his companions, it almost felt as though he were home. He'd been gone for a long time.

As Solveig promised, they were up and moving early the next day, before the sun rose. Hakon was grateful. In Garor, even the autumn heat was unpleasant, and Hakon predicted a miserable day ahead.

They moved fast, the miles passing underfoot. By noon, sweat covered every bit of Hakon's body, and his feet were soaked from walking through standing water. Almost all of Ari's transport locations were in quiet places where he could come and go unobserved. Here, though, it meant a slog before they reached anything that could be called a road.

By afternoon they'd found one and the traveling became easier.

They walked until well after the sun fell, long after every other traveler had sought the shelter of roadside inns.

Several creatures approached them, thinking them prey, but a teho dart from Ari was usually enough to convince them otherwise.

Solveig called a halt after the sun had set, and they rested once again.

The next day, the mood of the group had lightened. Despite their long absence from one another, old habits and mannerisms quickly returned. Irric flirted with Solveig. Ari scouted ahead. Only Meshell was missing.

The woman who had once been his most constant companion.

He would see her today.

The thought made his sweat turn cold.

The band's good humor died when they turned a bend in the road and came upon a dozen corpses.

Hakon drew his sword as the others prepared for battle.

But there was no one left to fight. They relaxed and examined the scene.

Most of the dead wore dull cloaks of green and brown that blended well with the trees and the mud. Guards of some sort.

He could guess the murderer well enough, though. Short gashes across major blood vessels had killed most of the soldiers, although a few had met more brutal and unpleasant ends. Up close, the dead looked like they had been hard men and women in life. Most possessed a fair number of scars.

Their experience had done them little good. None of their weapons remained, but Hakon couldn't see many wounds on the corpses. Most only had one, and that one had killed them. If they had fought for their lives, they hadn't done a very good job of it.

Up ahead, Ari confirmed Hakon's guess. He stared at a body that was separate from the others. "Nice clothes," he grunted. "Probably the magistrate."

"They were transporting something," Solveig said, pointing to wheel tracks in the dirt. "Heavy, too."

"Food and grain, most likely," Ari said. "He was hoarding it, according to what I've heard."

Hakon looked around at his three friends. "Are none of you worried?"

Solveig shook her head. "Isira doesn't care about this."

It seemed odd, but Hakon trusted them. "So where is she now?"

Ari stretched. "Same place she always is after her work is done. These corpses are still warm."

Irric slapped Hakon on the back so hard it hurt. "I hope you're thirsty, friend."

AT THE NEXT INN, Hakon noticed several sacks of grain in the corner, and a celebration was already underway. Solveig spoke with a few patrons and then reported her findings. "She's probably in the next village. There's a tavern known for its cheap ale."

"Just like old times," Irric said.

"Maybe we should wait until morning," Hakon suggested.

Solveig arched an eyebrow at the suggestion. "Would you rather deal with her drunk or hungover?"

Hakon grimaced. "Good point."

"Besides," Solveig added, "by tomorrow she'll be gone again, and we'll have to start the whole process over."

Hakon looked at his friends. "You're enjoying this, aren't you?"

Irric laughed. "Of course we are."

Hakon grumbled under his breath, but they made their way to the next village.

The tavern was just as Hakon imagined it. The walls looked like they might collapse inward at any moment, and the only sign that it was a tavern was the sounds of revelry coming from within. Solveig shook her head at the sight. "Some things never change."

For a moment they all stood outside, until Hakon realized they expected him to lead the way in. He searched their faces, feeling like a man walking to the gallows. "This would go easier if one of you went in first."

Irric pushed him halfway to the door. "We know."

Hakon stared at the door, as though sizing up a legendary opponent. Then he took a deep breath and opened the door before he talked himself out of it.

Nearly a dozen faces turned his way, more curious than anything. But only one caught his attention.

Meshell was as beautiful as ever. Tonight her dark hair was unbound, resting between her shoulder blades. She wore no jewelry. Her clothing was as dark as the uniforms favored by Damion's soldiers, except her garments had been tailored specifically for her. Their eyes met, and as hers narrowed, Hakon summoned teho and strengthened his body.

He made it three steps toward her before she launched herself at him.

He'd forgotten how fast she could move. Teho knives were in her hands, and she drove them into Hakon's chest.

He didn't fight back, but raised his hands above his head. "I'm just here to talk!"

Throughout the tavern, patrons were rising to their feet. And because this was a tavern Meshell had chosen, they weren't running. Instead, they were drawing their own knives. None of them looked kindly at Hakon. He suspected Meshell had been paying for the drinks. It was her preferred method of making new friends.

Meshell growled and drove her knives into him again, their points digging further into his flesh.

Out of the corner of his eye, he saw the rest of the band enter the tavern and walk up to the bar. Ari ordered three drinks.

Meshell, frustrated her knives weren't having their desired effect, kicked at him, her boot landing square in his chest.

He flew backward, a table collapsing under him.

One of the patrons, in his effort to escape, rammed into another patron. It was the spark that sent the entire room into a fight.

Meshell leaped on top of him, knife ready to strike.

Hakon had endured enough. He grabbed her and threw her off him. She landed on her feet. Hakon stood and punched a patron who charged at him, sword upraised. He pulled the punch considerably, but it still folded the man over his fist.

Then Meshell was at him again, knives quick as lightning, and almost as unpredictable.

She broke his guard and pummeled him with every weapon she had. He staggered under the onslaught.

She let him have a moment to catch his breath. He looked behind her, where the other three had turned around to watch. Solveig and Ari looked like they had a running commentary, and Irric was lazily keeping the fight away from the group with the length of his sword while sipping from a mug of ale with the other hand.

He had missed them.

He never even saw the blow that knocked him unconscious.

HAKON WOKE up on the floor of the tavern, staring at the ceiling. His head hurt, and his vision swam as he sat up.

Most of the patrons were still present, but the fight had ended while he'd been out. He looked around. The broken tables and chairs were piled high in one corner of the tavern. The remaining tables were full now, the patrons forced into proximity by the lack of seating. Hakon saw plenty of bruises and cuts, but no injuries worth concern. His awakening earned a few glares from others, but there was no further reaction.

Meshell was gone, but the rest of the band sat at the bar, drinking ale and speaking in quiet tones. They turned when he stood up.

"Satisfied?" he asked.

"Delighted," Irric replied.

Hakon looked around the tavern again.

"Outside," Solveig said.

He left the tavern.

The village was quiet, and Meshell was easy enough to

find. She stood on the outskirts, looking out into the wild, a mug of ale in hand. Hakon joined her.

"You told me it was over," she said. Her voice was cold and distant.

Explanations were pointless. She understood him, better than anyone else. And she hated him for it. "I did, and I'm sorry."

She took a long drink from her mug. "You think your apology means anything?"

He shook his head.

"She'll come," Meshell said, "when she hears we're all together again. And I won't go back. I'll never suffer that again."

Hakon didn't know what to tell her. The risk was real.

Meshell finished off her mug with one long pull. "Why didn't you look for me, after?"

He heard the tiniest crack in her voice, the last vulnerability she possessed. It drove a dagger deeper into his heart than any of the teho blades she'd used in their fight.

How many nights had he tormented himself, asking some variation of the same question? She had once been his whole world. He mourned the loss of the band, but losing her had almost broken him completely. If not for Sera, it very well might have.

"Because I knew you wouldn't forgive me."

Something moved in the marshland outside the village. It gave off a sound Hakon couldn't identify. Whatever it was, it was either desperate or brave to approach this close to the village.

"Coward," Meshell said.

He had no argument in his defense.

He couldn't bring himself to ask the only question he had left.

She answered it anyway. "I'll help. Not because of you or your daughter, but because I want to kill Damion and finally finish what we started."

Hakon nodded. "Thank you."

As he turned from her, he realized he had wanted more. Not forgiveness, exactly, but a chance at it. The others had held that future out as a tantalizing possibility. Only Meshell had closed the door. Of them all, though, it was hers he craved most.

He made it a couple of steps before she called softly to him. "Why her?"

That had been the other question he dreaded. But he wouldn't lie to her. Never again.

"I made the decision, once I met her, that I would never again be the man I had been. And she—"

"Was as different from me as possible?"

Hakon nodded. Something in Meshell's voice gave her away. "You met her, too?"

"Couldn't stand her."

He laughed at that. "No, you wouldn't."

"Did it work?"

"What?"

"Becoming a new man?"

Hakon thought for a moment, of the years he'd spent raising a family. And of how he felt more at home now, among his friends after a bar fight, than he ever had in the house he'd built for Sera. "I don't think so."

She let him go, and he returned to the tavern. Irric ordered him an ale and together they drank until Meshell returned. "What next?" she asked the group.

"Vispeda," Solveig answered. "There is a small chance that Cliona has gotten in touch. If nothing else, it's a place to prepare. Damion's fortifications have been extensive, and if we're going to breach them, it's going to require both materials and planning."

"Are you thinking a direct assault on Aysgarth?" Meshell asked.

"I'd prefer not to," Solveig answered, "but if there are no other options, yes."

Meshell bobbed her head toward Hakon. "You won't have a chance unless he learns how to fight again."

"We were actually just discussing that," Solveig said. "You want to train him while I gather information?"

Meshell ordered another ale. Hakon swore he could see her imagining several days of beating him senseless in the name of training. She smiled. "I'd be honored."

None of the band seemed to be in any hurry to leave, and Hakon's thoughts drifted away as the others caught up on Meshell's last few years. To Hakon, the details didn't matter. She'd gone and done what she was best at, protecting their creation in the ways she could.

His feeling of being caught between two worlds intensified. What would Cliona think of him, bruised and drinking in a tavern where a fight barely interrupted the night?

That answer was easy enough.

It would just be one more piece of evidence she would use to curse him. She was too kind to ever say so out loud, but he saw it in her eyes, in the way she said, "I love you," without any emotion behind the words.

He didn't even blame her.

He had failed to protect Sera. And she had never quite forgiven him.

She would hate him if she saw him here.

And maybe that was as it should be.

But he loved his daughter, and he would protect her, whether she thanked him for it or not.

32

Cliona examined her pack one last time. Books, clothes, and the supplies they would need to survive the wild were packed in tightly. Most of what she'd brought in her traveling chest would be left behind. As it was, when she threw the pack onto her back and over her shoulders, the straps dug deep into her skin.

She foresaw little comfort in her life over the next few weeks.

Zachary sat in a chair across the room from her, eyes closed, waiting for her word.

They were both dressed in their darkest clothing. It wouldn't pass as a uniform on even the most cursory inspection, but any little bit of confusion or doubt might make a difference.

Three days had passed since she had discovered the location of Ava's tomb.

Three days of pretending to work, certain that one moment she would turn around and find Damion looking over her shoulder, a knowing smile on his face. Long nights of restless sleep, debating the wisdom of everything they planned.

Zachary had pulled his weight and more. He had a gift for slipping in and out of places he probably wasn't supposed to be, a skill he claimed he had honed as a child in his parents' estate. Every evening, he had more supplies procured for their escape.

The moment had come. It was a cloudy night, obscuring the sliver of moon that hung in the sky. They had all that they could carry, and there was no reason to delay.

Cliona tied her pack shut for the third time that night.

Her plan for escape was anything but certain. She almost didn't believe the idea had been hers in the first place. But Aysgarth, it turned out, wasn't an easy place to leave. They couldn't just stroll out through the front gates. Not if what Solveig had written was true.

They had done all they could. Zachary had passed along a note to the one who had given him Solveig's message. It spoke in very general terms of what Cliona had found, but she believed that if something happened to her, Solveig would be able to decipher it.

"It's time," she said.

Zachary's eyes opened and he leaned forward. "Do you need anything from me?"

"Just watch for trouble."

She sat on the edge of the bed and closed her eyes.

At the very least, if the key piece of her plan failed, no one would know except Zachary.

She felt it, just as she had been the last few weeks, calling for her.

She reached for it. In her mind, her hand touched its snout, and something shifted inside of her, like the last brick being fitted into place. "Please come," she whispered.

And it did.

She opened her eyes. "Let's go."

Zachary opened the door, stepped through, and punched the first guard hard in the stomach.

Cliona let teho flow through her body, and she delivered a kick straight to the second guard's groin. As he collapsed, she delivered an uppercut that caused his eyes to roll up in his head as he fell to the stone floor, limp.

Zachary wrestled with the first guard, who had recovered quickly. Zachary stood behind the man, with his arm around the guard's throat. But the guard summoned a teho knife in a reverse grip, prepared to drive it into Zachary's leg.

Two quick blows from Cliona caused the guard to lose focus. He collapsed next to his partner, and she and Zachary dragged them into Cliona's room, where they were quickly bound and gagged. Hopefully, by the time they were discovered, this would all be over.

Zachary led the way. He'd taken the opportunity to explore more of Aysgarth while she translated, and his knowledge proved useful now. Zachary took every turn in the maze of stone with the confidence of a man who was certain he knew where he was going.

Cliona really hoped he knew where he was going.

They came out on the lowest wall of the fortress. It was lightly guarded, as the only access to it was from a long series of mountain switchbacks that led to the fields below. Cliona and Zachary squeezed into an alcove and waited.

As they waited, Cliona reached out and grabbed Zachary's hand. He squeezed it in return.

The night remained silent, and Cliona feared her efforts had been meaningless.

She closed her eyes and listened.

It was close, but it flew far overhead, wary of the lines of teho below. Aysgath's protections were far greater than its remote location and thick walls. Damion's wards worried even the ancient creature.

"Please, help us," Cliona asked.

The dragon hesitated, torn between a deep desire Cliona couldn't understand and its wish for self-preservation, which she did.

Then it folded its wings and dove toward them.

Cliona heard shouts a few moments before the creature struck. The whole fortress rumbled, and the quiet night came alive. Soldiers rushed past them as they ran to the higher levels to deal with the threat.

Zachary glanced out, and when it was clear, he gestured her forward.

Above them, chaos erupted. Stone crumbled and people screamed, and power vibrated the very air. Teho bloomed from dozens of warriors in response, but none held a candle to the fire that burned in the center of the dragon.

Cliona feared to even turn around to watch as they fled down the switchbacks. This close, the pull of the dragon was almost irresistible, a desire that made her mouth water and her body ache.

When she slowed, Zachary grabbed her hand and pulled. His touch anchored her.

There was no need for stealth. Every eye was turned to the battle above, and they ran as fast as Zachary's legs could carry him.

When they neared the bottom, a violent explosion of teho erupted above them. The gelid touch of Damion's teho asserted its dominance over the dragon. In the back of her mind, Cliona felt the battle between the dragon's will and Damion's.

The dragon was losing.

Cliona slid to a stop. They were still too far from the final defensive wall at the mouth of the valley. The dragon needed to distract the defenders a while longer.

"What are you doing?" Zachary yelled.

"Go!" she shouted. "I can catch up to you, but I need to do this."

He shook his head and stepped toward her. "No. We stay together."

There was no time for an argument. The dragon quickly lost the last of its will to fight. She pulled Zachary in and kissed him full on the lips.

After a moment of surprise, she pushed him, hard enough that he stumbled several steps back. He looked lost.

"I will catch up," she said. "But I need you to go, now. You're too slow for this to work otherwise."

He still hesitated, but then turned and ran, his legs running even faster, as though to prove Cliona wrong.

Cliona closed her eyes, and the dragon was there, as though an extension of her body. It hurt, and it felt as though its lungs were being crushed. The teho that gave it such enormous strength was blocked, forced to circulate in uneven whirlpools within the creature.

It felt nothing but pain.

Cliona breathed out slowly, remembering the lessons her father had taught her.

Through their connection, she eased the dragon's breath, and the teho began to flow easily again. The pain eased, and Damion's control slipped.

Above, the dragon roared.

The kolma fought back, his hooks in the dragon deep. Cliona could slow him down, but not defeat him. Not without more time. It was best to retreat.

The dragon swiped at one last building, its claws tearing through the stone with ease.

She looked down at the wall, and with a smile, asked one last favor of the dragon.

It accepted, and flew straight into the air, disappearing above the clouds.

Cliona let her connection fade into the back of her mind. She couldn't even see Zachary in the darkness, but she trusted he was somewhere ahead of her. Teho filled her limbs and she ran.

Her feet barely touched the ground.

She hadn't truly run since leaving home for Vispeda. Long ago, as a child, she and her father had run through the woods freely, and the memory brought a smile to her face. The wind whipped through her hair.

The dragon broke through the clouds in a full dive.

Its wings snapped open just above the ground, and it raced across the freshly harvested fields, the power of its passing flattening everything beneath it.

It crashed into the wall at speed, breaking through the thick stone as if it were a thin piece of wood.

Then it rose one last time and disappeared out of sight.

"Thank you," Cliona said.

A long, satisfied roar answered her, echoing in the night.

She caught up to Zachary as he neared the wall. She put her back to the wall and intertwined her fingers. "Come on," she said.

He looked more than skeptical.

"We don't have time for this. Hurry."

He shrugged, looking for all the world as though he expected her to drop him. But he stepped on her hands, and she hefted him easily to the top of the wall.

He swore in surprise as he grabbed the wall and pulled himself up.

Before he could reach down to help her, she had leaped to the top on her own.

This section was empty. The guards on the wall rushed to where it had been breached.

They ran across to the other side, and Zachary looked to her. "Are you going to catch me on the other side?"

She frowned. "No. You can find your own way down." Then she jumped.

Behind her, Zachary scrambled over the wall, hanging from the edge and dropping roughly to the ground.

A moment after he had found his feet, Cliona felt the blast of teho that came from Damion transporting. He had come to investigate the wall, and it wouldn't take him long to understand what had happened. She let her teho fade so he wouldn't sense her. From here, they were on foot.

Then together they ran into the wild, the first part of their very dangerous journey complete.

33

Hakon stared up at the blue sky, rubbing his jaw where Meshell had hit him. He and the ground were becoming well acquainted, and it was getting old.

But if he was getting frustrated, it was nothing compared to Meshell's exasperation. "Get up," she said.

Hakon pushed himself to his feet and rolled his shoulders back.

Perhaps hitting people wasn't the most civilized way of dealing with frustration.

But it sounded terribly appealing.

He sprinted at Meshell, the teho in his legs giving him speed others could only dream of.

Meshell slid away from his first punch, unimpressed by anything Hakon threw at her. Hakon kept up his advance, enduring the blows she landed in exchange for forward momentum. He hoped that if he could keep her retreating, she would make a mistake.

She didn't.

Despite his effort, he couldn't land a single meaningful

blow. Meshell's blows wore him down, and his advance slowed. Almost before he realized it had happened, he was giving up ground, and a few moments after that, he was flat on his back staring up at the blue sky again. He swore.

Meshell sat down next to him. "There's no point."

"You've gotten so much stronger."

"True," she said. "But so have you, even though you don't notice it. If anything, all I've managed to do is close the gap between us a bit. You still control more teho, and your technique is almost as good as it was during the rebellion."

Hakon frowned. "Then why can't I hit you?"

"It wouldn't mean anything for me to tell you," she said. "It's the sort of thing you need to figure out on your own."

"No more today, then?"

Meshell shook her head. "No. And I'm getting hungry. I think Irric is cooking tonight."

As they neared their camp, it certainly smelled as though Irric was cooking. All of the band could make an edible meal, but Irric prepared feasts. The scents coming from the campfire made Hakon's mouth water.

They'd been camped outside Vispeda for a few days now. Solveig had gone into town to be seen and to check for any messages from Cliona. Ari did Ari things, transporting all over the land seeking more information. When he wasn't gone, he stayed at the camp, which was safer than hiding in town. Irric, Meshell, and Hakon were the three permanent residents of the camp, and they spent their days training and talking.

The wall Hakon had built between them wasn't down yet, but every day it crumbled a little more.

When they reached the camp, Hakon was surprised to find Solveig sitting at the cook fire next to Ari. He'd felt no burst of teho, which meant she had walked from Vispeda.

She had news, then.

Hakon hurried the rest of the way, and she held up her hand. "We've got word from her," she said. "For now, she's alive and well."

"What does she say?"

Solveig closed her eyes and recited from memory. "Tonight we run. Ava is at the temple."

Hakon blinked. "What does any of that mean?"

"Plenty," Solveig said. "It means that we know she was at Aysgarth, so the assumptions we had made were correct. By 'we,' I assume she means Zachary, whose body was also missing from the dig site. He's tehoin."

"Who is Ava?"

Solveig grimaced. "I had to turn to other scholars to find out. Our best guess is that Ava was a stamfar. The name appears on some of the earliest lists we've found. But we know nothing else about her. If Cliona believed it was important enough to tell us about, though, it means it's important."

"And the temple? Where's that?"

"The stamfar only ever had one temple we know of. In Husavik. No one alive has seen it, but it's mentioned in several texts."

Irric and Meshell swore together, and Hakon felt his stomach sink. Perhaps there were worse places to travel, but none came immediately to mind.

"Is that where we need to go?"

Solveig shook her head. "Put yourself in your daughter's place. They must understand Damion's power and intent if they planned to run. They'll have no ability to transport. Husavik is unreachable. Besides, she responded to my message, so she knows we're aware of her plight. They'll run for Vispeda. It's the closest place they know."

"Can they make it?"

Meshell answered that question. "No. The wilds around Aysgarth are too dangerous, even if they weren't being chased by Damion."

To Hakon, the answer seemed easy. "So we rescue them, then. If we can't breach Aysgarth, we can at least meet them on the way."

"That was my thought, too," Solveig said.

Before they could begin discussing the particulars of their plan, Hakon felt a powerful and familiar expression of teho behind him. His stomach twisted and he wiped his suddenly damp palms on his pants. They all stood and met their visitor.

She looked like a child, aged maybe sixteen or seventeen years old. In some ways, she reminded Hakon of Cliona. His daughter, too, had possessed an intense gaze at that age.

Isira took them all in with a single glance. "I did not think I would ever see the five of you plotting together again."

Hakon stepped forward, ready to shoulder the responsibility of their actions. They were all here for him, after all.

He ran into a solid wall of teho, and his whole body was held immobile. He couldn't so much as move his jaw. Instinctively, he fought for control of his body, but he quickly surrendered that fight. Defeating Isira was as easy as drinking an ocean. He forced himself to relax.

Isira's glare froze the blood in his body. "You're fortunate I don't kill you where you stand." The world's only remaining stamfar turned her attention to Solveig. "Explain."

"His daughter is in trouble. We've agreed to help him."

Isira hardly looked placated. If anything, Hakon swore

her grip on him tightened. "What trouble possibly requires all five of you?"

"Damion," Solveig said.

"Ahh." Isira thought for a moment. "What is Torsten's pupil up to now? I've felt his power growing in the west. He hoards tehoin the way a moneylender does gold."

"We don't know," Solveig explained. "Eventually, I expect he will fight against the six states, but for now he is seeking Ava's grave. Hakon's daughter is one of the scholars most skilled at translating stamfar texts. Damion has enlisted her help, and we doubt it was willingly."

"Who is Ava?"

"I'd hoped you might know. An early stamfar, is all we know."

Isira shook her head. "I've never heard of her."

Solveig bit her lip, clearly debating whether her next question was appropriate. "Would you intervene? If Damion hopes to continue Torsten's plans, much blood will be spilled."

"You know my answer. It is the same as it has always been."

Solveig looked as though she was about to argue, then thought better of it.

Isira looked around the group. Hakon wished he could turn his head so that he could see what was happening. But Isira's control over his body was nearly absolute. She wasn't even thinking about him, but he couldn't fight her in the least.

The stamfar sighed. "What do you intend?"

"Rescue Hakon's daughter, for now," Solveig answered. "We haven't thought past that."

"Will you kill Damion?"

"It's possible. He will try to stop us, and we would rather not see more innocent blood spilled."

Isira's laugh was bitter, more bitter than anyone who looked so young should be able to make. "You already bathe in rivers of blood. What's a little more?"

There was no answer to that, and no one dared try.

Isira shook her head. "I should just kill you all and be done with it."

Then, as suddenly as she arrived, Isira vanished. Hakon collapsed, the strength drained from his body.

Silently, they all returned to their spots around the cook fire, each lost in their own thoughts. A few minutes later, it was Irric who broke the tension. He chuckled to himself, and when Meshell glared at him, he smiled.

"I don't think she likes us very much," he said.

34

Their first night beyond the wall of Aysgarth was a living nightmare. Sharp trees sliced at her clothes and pack. Jagged stones, half buried under dead pine needles, tripped her as she ran. She didn't dare sprint more than a few steps before twisting her head to check behind her, certain that Damion would be right there.

He never was, but it never stopped her from looking again a few steps later.

Fear gave her a stamina she didn't know she possessed. They ran through the night into the coming of dawn, and only then did they slow to a walk.

There was a single road that led to and from Aysgarth.

They didn't take it, certain it would be searched. They followed game trails, never certain where any one would lead. Time and time again they came to an obstacle that couldn't be passed. When they did, they would backtrack and choose again.

Ever so slowly, they traveled east.

Toward civilization. Toward help.

She guessed it was sometime after noon when she called

for their first real rest. The constant fear of discovery had faded, leaving only exhaustion.

Zachary could barely keep his eyes open. But they darted at every sound. She asked him to ward a resting site for them, which he did. She prepared a bit of food, but he fell asleep before eating.

She smiled at his soft snores. But the expression soon faded as the reality of their situation set in. Who knew how far they were from help? Father had taught her how to survive the wilds around their home, but these lands were harsher than the ones she'd grown up in.

For a moment, she missed Father.

Most days, he barely crossed her mind. But whenever she had been in the wilds with him, she'd felt safe, as though there was no danger that could touch her.

She let Zachary sleep for a few hours, then woke him. Despite her fear of the wild, and of discovery, she fell asleep within moments of closing her eyes.

It seemed like no time at all had passed when Zachary shook her awake. From the position of the sun, though, it looked like he'd let her sleep a little longer than he should have.

They ate in silence and shouldered their packs. Cliona's shoulders and back protested against the weight, but there was nothing for it. They resumed their journey.

Night soon fell, the high peaks blocking the sun early. They found a path that traveled along a stream, providing them their longest uninterrupted progress so far.

Cliona kept glancing behind them, never convinced they were alone. Birds flew overhead, and occasionally they would startle another animal, but the trip was otherwise quiet. Zachary's breath came hard, and she worried about him. But he never complained.

Eventually, her paranoia earned a reaction from Zachary. "Could you stop? You're making me nervous."

"Sorry. But don't you think that was too easy?"

Zachary laughed. "You had to summon a dragon for us to escape. No, I don't think that was too easy at all."

She supposed he had a point, but something felt wrong. Damion wanted Ava's grave too badly. He should be burning down the forest behind them in pursuit.

But as the night passed and Damion refused to appear, she began to wonder if maybe she wasn't the one being irrational.

The moon rose high in the sky. Despite her daily walks with Zachary, Cliona could tell she hadn't been spending enough time moving the past few weeks. Her continual focus on translation meant she spent far more hours hunched over old books than she did walking, climbing, and running. Muscles, weak from disuse, complained at the sudden demands placed on them. The backs of her legs and shoulders, in particular, burned from the effort.

She reminded herself that every step brought her closer to Vispeda, and to people who could help. Every step was one farther away from Damion.

Her focus narrowed the farther they walked. Soon, Zachary's back and the ground in front of her were all that she was aware of. At times, it felt like she was moving through a dream.

She was still the first to notice that something was wrong. A discrepancy tickled her awareness, just beyond her ability to identify. She stopped and let her focus expand once again, berating herself for becoming careless.

The forest they walked through was quiet. The only sound she heard was the rustling of tree leaves off in the distance. Zachary noticed she had stopped and turned around, a question on his face. She held up her hand to silence him. The hairs on the back of her neck stood up.

Her perspective shifted and she swore, summoning teho into her limbs.

It wasn't a presence, but an absence that she had noticed.

Songbirds, whose songs had been a nearly constant companion on their escape, no longer sang.

The rustle in the trees grew louder, and it was only then Cliona realized she felt no breeze. The air was perfectly still, and behind her, no tree swayed in the wind.

"Zachary, a shield!"

She looked up just in time to see a shadow moving in the trees. It was fast, even with teho aiding her sight.

Zachary frowned, and the moment of confusion cost them what safety they might have found under his teho.

The shadow dropped from the tree, crashing into Zachary's back. His eyes went wide as he was flung to the ground. As he fell, the shadow leaped at her.

It was too slow, though. Teho filled her from crown to toe, and she tracked the shadow, catching her first real glimpse of it in the moonlight.

She'd never seen anything like it. Had it been standing, she imagined it would have come to about her waist. It had a long torso with even longer arms. Its hands spread wide, with three fingers and one opposable thumb. Though it kept its legs tucked in close to its body, she'd seen the power and speed they'd hit Zachary with.

Unsure of how to defend herself, she settled for dodging to the side. The creature swiped at her with its long arms as it passed, but she leaned back in time to let it pass in front of her face.

The creature landed with a bounding gate, becoming

quadrupedal for a moment before launching itself back into the trees. It wrapped its hands around a branch and swung higher into the canopy, disappearing from sight as quickly as it had appeared.

She turned to see Zachary returning to his feet. He looked dazed but otherwise unharmed. "What was that?" he asked.

His inexperience showed. His eyes were focused on where the creature had disappeared, not on the trees around him.

Sometimes she forgot that he'd been raised the son of a magistrate, sheltered by all the protections of a city. He was strong, but he didn't know how to survive out here.

Another shadow dropped from the trees, again landing on Zachary's back. Again he fell, his face buried in the roots and twigs near the path.

This creature was the same as the first, but larger. It stood, balanced on Zachary's back, and could almost look Cliona in the eye. It grinned, exposing a set of sharp teeth suitable both for tearing into flesh and scaring children.

As it looked at her, it made an enormous fist and punched down at the back of Zachary's unprotected skull.

35

____

Hakon checked the edge of his sword one last time. For years, he'd kept it hidden in a safe place underneath his home. When he and Sera had first married, he'd retrieved it every few months when she was out gathering her supplies. He'd felt vulnerable without it.

Eventually, the feeling faded. By the time Cliona was born, Hakon rarely even thought of his blade.

Fortunately, the sword had endured the years of neglect well. The edge was still sharp, and now that Hakon was using teho again, the edge meant less. His true edge was the mysterious power that ran through his body, that allowed him to strengthen his blade and cut what no other could.

The others in the camp did much the same. It had been dark here for a time, but they were traveling far enough west that the sun set later. For this work, they wanted the cover of darkness.

He watched the band. Solveig danced her forms in the moonlight, her thin teho blade carving patterns in the air. Had her sword been steel, it would have snapped in combat.

But Solveig's teho didn't break. Beside her, Ari was perfectly motionless, almost invisible in the darkness.

On the other side of camp, Irric and Meshell dueled. Irric was a swordsman, through and through. He'd mastered steel long before he mastered teho, and it showed in his movements. He used few of the tricks teho blademasters typically employed, but he was good enough he didn't have to.

Meshell was almost the opposite, and like Solveig, wholly unique in her fighting style. She preferred her two long teho knives, but she was comfortable changing their length with a thought. Most tehoin were taught to fight with a blade of constant length, so that they grew comfortable with it and knew how not to cut themselves.

Meshell didn't need to worry. Long ago, Hakon had taught her some of his techniques, and she was the only one before Cliona who had been able to use teho the same as him. She alone could use the power both as an external weapon and an internal one.

It made her the most dangerous of the band, especially now. Once, Hakon's strength and skill had been enough to best her, but their training had revealed how far he'd fallen behind her.

In time, the duel ended and the band gathered.

Solveig gave each of them a long look. She left Hakon for last. "I want you taking the rear."

He started, but she gave him no time to protest.

"Of us, you're the greatest liability. Likewise, if we do encounter trouble and your daughter is involved, I expect your judgment will be the least dependable." Her words were harsh, but her tone was not. She spoke truth, but without malice. "You'll take the rear."

He couldn't argue against her reasoning. Especially

when he thought of how much they were all risking for him. He swallowed his pride and nodded.

The others took up their usual positions. Ari, with the best senses, took point. Meshell took Hakon's normal place, followed by Irric and Solveig. They all joined hands, and Solveig examined them one last time.

Hakon's heart beat faster, though they couldn't get too close to Aysgarth.

This was it.

Finally, a chance to save Cliona.

Solveig nodded to Ari, and when Hakon blinked again, he found himself in a mountain valley.

The band spread apart without speaking, and Hakon easily slipped into the routines that had once been his entire life. One by one, the band disappeared down the trail, and Hakon took the rear, watching behind them for any form of danger.

Ari's closest transport spot had been three days from the walls of Aysgarth. Any closer and he worried that the use of teho would trip one of Damion's wards. From here, they walked.

None of them believed for a moment they could surprise Damion. But they could give him as little time to prepare as possible.

The forest they walked through was old, bounded to the north and the south by imposing mountains. Hakon heard the flow of a stream somewhere to the south, though he saw nothing. Ari's transport location, as it usually was, was near no human trail. They followed game trails steadily west, and Hakon listened to the sound of two birds singing to one another up ahead.

This was a rich land, but one few humans had reached.

After an hour of walking, the group met to discuss their

options. The undergrowth here was thick, and they'd made little progress.

Ari summed up the decision quickly enough. "We can take the path, which risks discovery, or we can stay on the trails, and make miserable progress."

"The longer we're out here, the more likely it is something goes wrong," Irric said. "We always knew we were going to be discovered. I vote for the road."

The others agreed. Even Ari, who typically avoided roads as though he might catch the plague by stepping on one. They angled north, and eventually came to the road to Aysgarth.

Road was a generous term. Two rutted wheel tracks fought against the wild, and from the looks of it, the wild was winning. At the very least, Hakon felt sorry for any wagon that attempted this route. He suspected very few returned.

They followed it for an hour.

At a signal from Ari, the band dispersed into the woods. Hakon didn't have long to wait before discovering what had alarmed the assassin.

He saw a patrol, and better trained than most. A group of four men and women, moving down the path as silent as ghosts. This was no routine assignment. No patrol moved so quietly, nor focused so diligently on their surroundings. They were hunting.

Hakon let them pass, his large body pressed to the ground behind a thick bush. When they were well down the trail, Ari and the others emerged.

"You think they know we're here?" Irric asked.

"It's possible." Ari frowned. "But if we've already been spotted, I have no idea how."

"Should we kill them?" Hakon asked. Any soldiers they

fought now would be soldiers they wouldn't have to fight later.

Solveig dismissed the idea. "We're still days away from the walls. Better if we can remain unseen for now."

They made it another mile before the hair on the back of Hakon's neck stood up. Behind them, the birds had stopped singing. He signaled a stop, and once again the band retreated into the shadows.

Not a moment too soon, either.

Just as Hakon settled into a place to hide, the same group of soldiers they had seen before made another appearance. Again, they moved like wraiths, but this time, they were paying even closer attention to the ground.

Hunters indeed.

Hakon recognized skilled trackers when he saw them. And they'd noticed the band's passage.

Hakon made himself small, but prepared for the worst. If this group was so skilled they had noticed the band's tracks, they would also notice the tracks ended here.

The only option was to fight.

He held himself back. He no longer led the band. It was Solveig's decision.

A lance of teho took the lead tracker in the head. From formation to throw couldn't have been more than a heartbeat.

The others reacted quickly. One threw up a shield of teho while another threw darts in the direction the spear had come from. Hakon heard the darts tear through the underbrush, but he didn't worry for his friends. Damion's warriors might be skilled trackers, but they were still only vilda. They had no chance.

He pushed himself from his prone position, drawing his blade as he approached the last of the patrol. From Solveig's ambush to his cut couldn't have been more than a few seconds.

But it was still too slow.

The woman made no effort to defend herself. She wove teho into a ball and launched it straight into the air. As Hakon cut down, slicing her in two, the ball of teho burst, warning any tehoin within miles of the nearby danger.

Horns answered the burst immediately, echoing from higher up the valley.

A lot of horns.

The other two trackers fell beneath the blades of the band, but Hakon barely noticed.

Only a few hours into their rescue, and they'd already been discovered.

The battle for his daughter was about to begin.

36

Cliona launched herself forward, leading with her fist. Thanks to the teho flowing through her limbs, her punch hit before the creature's blow killed Zachary. She held back, but it still knocked the creature off her friend.

It bellowed in pain and anger, and the forest above them erupted in a cacophony. There had to be at least a dozen of the beasts lurking in the canopy. Cliona kept one eye on the leader and one on the trees as she spoke. "You planning on getting up anytime soon?"

Zachary groaned and pushed himself to his feet. He looked around, but his motions were slow. Either that last hit had dazed him, or he still didn't realize the extent of the danger they were in.

"We could use that shield," she said.

The creatures attacked before Zachary responded. When two jumped at her from the trees at the same time, her mercy came to an end. In retrospect, it had probably been a mistake to let the leader live. Her time at the academy had made her soft.

She swung a fist at one, breaking through the protective bone of the ribs to the soft organs underneath. The creature coughed once, a deep expulsion of air as Cliona collapsed its lungs. She pulled her hand out, but not before the second creature landed on her, tearing at her neck with its razor-sharp teeth.

Cliona found a hold on the second creature and ripped it from her shoulders. She twisted and threw the creature at yet another one that jumped down at her from the trees. The crack of bones could be heard even over the screeches of the remaining animals.

Apparently, seeing her in danger was enough to convince Zachary to join the fight. A teho blade appeared in his hands in time to slice through a creature charging at him from the underbrush. It was a bit of a sloppy cut, but with a teho blade, it didn't matter.

"Shield!" she yelled.

"I can't make a shield!"

The confession froze her for a precious second. He could form a blade but not a shield?

There was no further consideration of the matter when two more of the creatures caught her from behind. One wrapped itself around her legs while the other scrambled onto her shoulders. The strength in their long arms and enormous hands almost brought her down.

Zachary attempted to rush to her aid, but his hands were full with more of the creatures. There might have been more of them than she thought.

But if there were three left or three dozen, her response was the same. She reached back, trying to grab the wild animal, but it had learned from the mistakes of its predecessors. It avoided her grasp, and her balance wobbled as the other restricted her movement.

A third beast jumped on her, pinning her arms to her torso. All three were biting her, their jaws gnawing against her hardened skin. So far, they had failed to draw blood, but it was only a matter of time before her focus was broken.

Panic began to set in. She struggled, but her efforts earned her nothing. More of the creatures were descending from the trees. She watched as they swung gracefully from limb to limb, eyes focused on the fresh meal that had walked into their lands.

They appeared familiar with teho blades. A ring slowly formed around Zachary, each of them screeching, disorienting him with quick motions and loud noises. One would dart in, and when Zachary turned, would quickly dart back. Before long, he would fall under a coordinated rush.

A moment before Cliona surrendered to panic, she heard Father's voice, deep and steady.

"Breathe," he said, "nice and slow."

She was a child again, out on a hunt. They'd been pursuing their quarry for the afternoon, and Cliona had the bowstring pulled taut on her first shot. She'd begun breathing too fast.

She breathed, deep and slow, from her diaphragm. The first form Father had ever taught her. The teho within her calmed, flowing steadily to every limb of her body.

As she calmed, she felt a sense of disorientation. She'd been doing this practice in one form or another for most of her life. But this time, it was different. The power within her was greater than before. Before she had thought of it like wading into a calm pool of water, but now it felt more like a lake.

She embraced teho, letting it flow through her.

She spread her legs and arms, and the creatures trying

to hold her surrendered their grip. They screeched, but there was nothing they could do against her new strength.

She caught the one that had pinned her arms before it could escape. She spun once, gaining momentum before she threw the creature as hard as she could at the circle now completed around Zachary. The animal hit its fellows with a surprising crunch, sending several to the ground.

The others seized the opportunity to attack, but Cliona rushed to Zachary's aid. Every blow she landed was fatal, and it only took a few moments for the creatures to realize this was one feast they would never enjoy.

The creatures broke, and a few moments later, the woods were quiet once again. If not for the corpses that littered the surrounding area, it was as if nothing had happened.

Off in the distance there was a burst of teho in the air.

Moments later, horns echoed down the valley.

"Is that for us?" Zachary asked.

"I don't think so," Cliona answered. "That's almost a mile away. I can't imagine our fight attracted that much attention."

"We should find a place to hide, then. Wait for it to pass us by."

Cliona shook her head. "Whatever's happening, Damion is worried about it. He's got other enemies, and it might be worth investigating. Perhaps there will be people there who can help us."

Zachary just stared at her for a moment, clearly skeptical.

She patted him on the cheek as she walked past him.

"Don't worry. If things get too dangerous, I'll keep you safe."

37

Solveig looked to Irric. "Advance or defend?"

The last of the horns faded, leaving an eerie silence behind. The forest around them had gone unnaturally quiet.

Irric looked up the valley, though there was little to see but a mass of trees. "Any significant changes in the terrain?"

Ari shook his head. "More of the same. Gets a bit steeper near the wall, and they keep several hundred feet cleared, but this is mostly it."

Hakon bit down on his tongue. They needed to advance. Cliona was somewhere up there. But there was a reason Solveig had asked Irric and not him.

"We move up until we find a place we can defend," Irric decided. "He'll come with numbers, and we'll want every advantage we can get."

For a moment, Hakon considered leaving the band behind. It was foolish, but none of them understood. Cliona was close. He felt it in the marrow of his bones. If it came to a fight, he feared they would retreat.

And Cliona would never know how close her father had come to saving her.

The band didn't lack strength or skill, but they did lack resolve.

Solveig glanced at him, but he kept his face as still as stone. "Very well," she said. "Ari, find us a spot."

The assassin nodded and disappeared up the path.

Hakon followed the others.

For now.

He didn't know what he would decide if forced to choose between Cliona and the band. For now, the best hope of saving her meant remaining with his friends, but his patience was nearly at an end.

They hadn't gone far before they stopped. Ari had chosen well. The forest farther west was particularly thick, naturally funneling any advance into the small gap the road followed. Beyond the chokepoint, where Hakon and the others currently stood, there was a small clearing which provided clear lines of attack.

They took up positions behind cover and waited.

Hakon's mind raced as his body became still. Cliona was close, and he was standing still. The urge to run up the valley was almost unbearable.

Far off to his side, in the direction of the stream, he heard something moving through the trees. Branches rustled in a way no wind could cause. He listened for a moment, but the sound came no closer to him. Whatever it was, it was moving farther down the valley.

Damion's forces didn't make them wait long.

Hakon heard them long before he saw them. Whoever advanced, they didn't possess the same stealth of the first group. Twigs cracked underfoot and bushes rustled as they neared. Hakon tensed, and less than a minute later the first soldier stepped through the chokepoint into the clearing.

He was young, but tehoin, his dark blade held before him, walking with unearned swagger.

The band waited until more of the soldiers stepped through the gap. When as many were in the clearing as there would ever be, Solveig once again signaled the attack with one of her spears.

The first soldiers didn't have any time to react. Solveig formed the teho spear in her hand even as she threw it, a feat of remarkable control that left no time for defense. Ari and Meshell weren't far behind, darts filling the clearing.

The soldiers were cut down, but the success was short-lived. Teho exploded from higher up the valley. The amount of it froze Hakon in place. Alone, each burst was like a single candle, but all together, they released the heat of a raging inferno. Hakon couldn't recall ever sensing so many tehoin in one place. Not even during the rebellion.

The rulers of the six states were right to fear Damion's efforts. Against such a force, many of the states' armies would have little hope. Dozens, then hundreds, of teho darts were launched into the air, all of them aimed for the clearing and the surrounding area.

Hakon watched for a moment and shook his head.

So many tehoin, and coordinated as well.

The others took cover behind shields, and Hakon ensured that his body was filled with teho.

The darts landed, tearing through trees and branches as though they were paper. None of the darts came close to breaking Hakon's skin. The shields of his friends also held. The barrage had been an impressive display, but against the band, ultimately futile.

When Damion's tehoin advanced, it was more of a

cautious march than a charge. The tehoin in the front led with shields, and behind them, another volley of teho darts arced into the air.

Hakon watched, fascinated.

He'd never thought he would live to see the day so many tehoin would fight with such cohesion.

Trees fell as their trunks were weakened by the barrage of teho darts. Hakon and the others were still uninjured, but the same could not be said for the wilds.

How did one fight against such an advance?

Each of the band responded in their own way. Solveig threw a few spears, each strong enough to break the shields that advanced toward them, and in a few instances, strike the men and women hiding behind them. Ari and Meshell flitted around the edges of the battlefield, dancing in and out of danger, too mobile for the tehoin to surround and attack.

Irric charged into the heart of the enemy formation, his teho blade and shield working together to crack the enemy advance. Hakon joined him.

Hakon hollered, the frustration and anger from the past weeks boiling into a pure rage. All he wanted was to hurt those who had stood against him. Reason abandoned him as he charged gleefully against the enemy.

His sword rose and fell, cutting a bloody path through the formation. The blades that came against him could neither cut him nor stop his own massive sword. Across the clearing, Irric enjoyed no such protection against the weapons, but his technique kept him safe enough.

Slowly the two warriors neared one another, becoming a two-person wedge the advance broke on.

Hakon grinned wildly as he stood shoulder to shoulder with Irric. His heart pounded, firm and steady in his chest, and teho flowed through him like a calm river. Not since the rebellion had he felt so alive, so whole.

It ended too soon.

No more soldiers opposed them. Off in the distance, more tehoin gathered, but they took a moment to regroup and plan their next tactics.

Whatever they tried, they would have no further success. Not against the band.

Off to the side, not too far from where he had launched his ambush, there was a rustle of undergrowth. Two figures emerged, and Hakon could barely believe his eyes.

Cliona had found them.

38

Cliona wasn't usually the type of person to charge into danger. Though she felt comfortable enough defending herself if the situation required it, she'd never been inclined, as some of her childhood friends had been, to seek out risk.

The world was dangerous enough already.

Running toward the exchange of teho down the valley easily ranked as the most dangerous journey she'd ever undertaken. She saw the volley of teho launched into the air, falling down and decimating a section of the forest. Trees fell as their trunks were destroyed, and Cliona hoped that whoever was the target of that attack survived.

They were her best hope.

There was another exchange of teho, the sums of the energy exchanged incredible. Cliona had guessed at the number of tehoin under Damion's command, but her best estimate had been far too low. The fact anyone survived the volleys to fight was a testament to their strength.

But who could fight against that? No tehoin Cliona had ever met would survive such an onslaught.

The battle still waged, though, so they lived.

Zachary followed behind her, holding back but not quite letting her out of his sight. He didn't want to be anywhere near that fight, and was rightfully cautious.

They came to a small overhang of granite, a ledge about ten feet high. From it, Cliona saw a clearing where dark figures clashed with a small group. She hid behind a tree and watched.

The battle was as one-sided as she expected. The only surprise was which side had the advantage. For all the dark figures swarming in the clearing, none seemed to be much of a threat to the group that fought there. As Cliona watched, her eyes adjusted to the shadows, and she saw more clearly. She saw one swordsman of incredible skill holding off three enemies at once. Two figures moved around the edge of the clearing, never still long enough for her to form a lasting impression of either.

Another man stood in the center of the clearing, even larger than Zachary. He had long blond hair and carried a sword that looked big enough to cut a horse in half. Though it must have weighed as much as two or three normal swords, the man swung it as lightly as some swung daggers. He cut through people with single swings. Steel, bone, and flesh seemed as nothing to him.

The battle ended just as Cliona understood its contours. Damion's soldiers retreated for the moment, but the fight was far from over. An ocean of teho gathered above them, held back by these warriors alone. If she wanted help, the time was now.

Zachary had just reached her position as she jumped from the ledge. His curse followed her as she fell. She landed softly and approached the clearing, her hands above her head so that she wouldn't be considered a threat.

When she entered the clearing, five warriors stood there. One woman, in particular, looked very familiar. Cliona blinked, unable to believe what she saw.

It was Solveig.

But instead of the books Cliona typically saw her with, she carried a thin teho blade. Blood marred her traveling clothes, which already looked out of place on the older scholar.

Cliona opened her mouth, but the words died as her breath was stolen from her.

The warrior with the giant sword turned, and she recognized him as well, though she hadn't seen him for almost a year now.

Her thoughts froze solid as her jaw hung open.

His eyes went wide and he said something, though her ears rang so loudly she heard nothing. He moved toward her and the sword dropped to the ground, forgotten. His arms opened wide to embrace her.

But he was covered in blood and he shouldn't be here and he wasn't a warrior and this was all wrong.

Wrong.

She took a half step back.

That small gesture froze him in place the way his appearance had frozen her thoughts. The joy on his face vanished, and in that moment, she knew what it looked like to break a heart.

She wanted to take the moment back, but the moment was gone.

Zachary finally showed up behind her, putting his hand on her shoulder, shattering the reunion between Father and her. "Cliona, what's wrong?" Then Zachary got his first glimpse at the group of warriors. "Solveig?"

The scholar stepped forward and took control of the

situation. Slowly, Cliona's mind began working. Father was here with Solveig and these others. That meant they were here to save them. For this moment, that was all she needed to know. Those were enough facts for her to work from.

Solveig spoke. "Are you two injured?"

They both shook their heads.

"Good. Ari," she called, apparently to the small man in dark clothing that almost looked like the uniform of Damion's men. "It's time to transport us."

Damion's warriors didn't give them that chance. All seven heads in the group turned to the west as the largest volley of teho yet arced into the sky. At the same time, a yell echoed from the nearby woods as another charge gathered. Solveig threw up a shield around both Zachary and Cliona as the sharpened teho rained around them. The others followed suit, and Zachary positioned himself so his body was between the incoming teho and her.

With Solveig's shield protecting them, the gesture was useless.

But Cliona appreciated it.

Only Father stood in the clearing without a shield. But the teho bounced off him harmlessly, even as it sliced into the stone at their feet.

The five warriors met the next charge with terrifying calm. Cliona watched Solveig, a scholar she admired, dance nimbly between teho blades as her own never seemed to miss a heart. The others were no less skilled, felling enemies almost as quickly as they appeared.

For the most part, though, her eyes remained locked on the fifth member of the group.

The man who wore Father's face.

But it was not the man she knew.

He cut through enemies with the same ease as the

others, his blade somehow slicing through teho, although that should be impossible. She'd known Father had considerable martial skill. He'd trained her.

But not this.

This man was a master of the blade.

Then it was strangely quiet, and once again only the seven of them remained in the clearing. Zachary looked left and right, and he was the only one with a sword still in hand.

She put her hand on his arm. "Zachary."

She brought him back to the present, and he saw this battle was over. He dropped the sword, a sheepish look on his face.

Before they could speak, a new power bloomed to the west, this one more powerful. One Cliona had felt before. "Damion."

Solveig wasted no time. "Everyone, together. Ari?"

The small man nodded, and everyone held hands.

Then Cliona blinked, and she was no longer a captive in Damion's lands.

39

Ari transported them to the camp outside Vispeda. They would be safe here, at least for a while. Hakon clenched and relaxed his hands, easing the pounding of his heart.

Cliona was safe.

So why did he suddenly feel so empty inside?

He looked up from his hands and at his daughter, who was staring at him as though he were a stranger.

Maybe he was.

The band drifted apart, each dealing with the stress of combat in their own way. Solveig and Ari spoke quietly for a moment, and then Solveig approached Hakon. "Take some time with Cliona. But then we all need to talk. Damion will know it was us."

Hakon nodded, and Solveig let him be. The boy and Cliona stood alone. He swallowed the lump in his throat and went to them.

He stopped and stood in front of them awkwardly. He wanted to embrace his daughter, but her posture warned him against it. With so much to say, he didn't know where to start. He took the easy way out, turning to the boy. "You must be Zachary. Solveig told me a bit about you." He thought of the way the boy had thrown his body between the teho attack and his daughter. "I'm Hakon, Cliona's father. Thank you for everything you've done."

Zachary grimaced. "Truthfully, she probably did more to save me than I her."

Hakon liked him. He was big and lean, and although Cliona was stronger, he'd still risked his safety to protect her on the battlefield.

Cliona, however, wasn't interested in the two of them getting to know each other. She spoke to Zachary. "Would you give us some time? I'm sure Solveig will help you get settled."

Zachary looked between the two of them and nodded, turning and beating a hasty retreat.

Cliona's glare fixed on Hakon, rooting him in place. She asked no questions, but there was no need. Hakon's knees felt suddenly weak.

He'd taken down an empire. But he didn't have the strength to face his daughter.

And he still didn't know what to say. Everything sounded foolish, but he had to say something.

"I'm glad you're safe," he said.

"Me too, and I'm grateful you came." He saw that she, too, was struggling to find the right words.

"Where would you like me to start?"

"The beginning is good."

He almost asked her which one, but knew the joke would be lost on her. "There's more to my past than we ever told you."

"You don't say."

He supposed there was no better place to begin than

with the largest secret. "I'm kolma." He gestured to the tent and to the rest of the band. "As are they."

She accepted the news with surprising aplomb. In response to his look, she shrugged. "Damion told me he was as well, and provided enough evidence to prove it. I've gotten rather used to impossible claims over the past few weeks."

Hakon summoned as much teho into his body as he could, and he reached out his hand to her. "Feel for yourself."

She hesitated for a moment, then took his hand. Her eyes widened slightly as she sensed the teho within him, but her surprise was less than his.

Her own power had grown, far deeper than Hakon would have believed possible. She was nearly kolma herself.

She released his hand, and he let the teho fade. For now, the focus was on him. He continued his explanation. "These are friends of mine from a long time ago. When I learned that you'd gone missing, and that Damion was involved, we joined together to search for you."

"Did Mother know?"

The question stopped his explanation cold. He nodded, suddenly afraid.

"Why did you lie to me?"

Had his rescue snapped the last tenuous thread of trust she had in him? "We both wanted for me to put my past behind me and start something new. We wanted you to live your life unburdened by my history." She nodded, but tears formed in the corners of her eyes. "Cliona, I—"

She cut him off with a sharp gesture. "I need some time." When he didn't move, she added, "Alone."

He nodded and took a step back. "I love you, Cliona."

When she didn't respond, he turned and walked away.

.   .   .

He was sitting on a small rise in the land, looking up at the stars, when she approached.

Meshell sat down next to him, so close their arms were touching. She offered him a flask and he took a long pull. It burned from the moment it touched his tongue, but he welcomed it.

"Didn't go so well?" she asked.

Hakon's chuckle was grim. "To say the least."

She snatched the flask from him, took a drink, then handed it back. He took another drink, and suddenly remembered it had been some time since he'd eaten. The liquor would hit him hard, and soon.

"Am I a fool?" he asked.

"Of course."

Strangely, Meshell's affirmation of his fear made him feel better. In Hakon's long memory, Meshell had never lied to him, nor had she ever softened her opinions for him. At the moment, it was just what he needed. "I'm worried I'm going to lose her."

"She's not yours."

"What?"

Meshell took another long drink. "I don't know why parents are incapable of seeing such an obvious truth. She's a person, not a possession. You can't lose what you never owned."

"I'm afraid she'll never speak to me again, once all this is over."

Meshell sighed in frustration. "When you married Sera, you knew she would grow old and die, and you would have to watch. You even had a child, knowing the same. Why?"

"Because I believed the time together was worth the pain

that would come."

Meshell gestured to the tents. "It's the same now, even if you don't see it. When you bring a child into this world, you're giving birth to something that will die. We hope it will be after we go to the gate ourselves, but one way or another, we all eventually say goodbye. She might never speak to you again, but if so, that will be no more than the fulfillment of a bargain you made when she was born."

Hakon grunted. "I can see why you never wanted children."

He suspected she'd been drinking before she came over, because her reply was surprisingly unguarded. "True. I never wanted to bear that pain."

"It's not a very optimistic view."

Meshell swore softly at him. "You're not listening. I'm telling you that one way or another, someday you'll say goodbye to Cliona, and it will be for good. Which means you need to treasure the moments you have with her while you have them. Stop worrying about the days you may or may not have, and focus on the time you have with her now."

Hakon glanced over at Meshell. Whatever vulnerability she'd let show was gone, and she glared at the stars as though she could force them to wink out of existence through her will alone. They'd been in similar circumstances dozens of times, and he knew that anything he said would slide off her armor.

But she was right.

He was a fool, in more ways than one.

"Thanks," he said.

She grunted and passed him the flask, and together they watched the last of the stars fade from the night sky, fleeing before the approach of the sun.

fter her conversation with Father, Cliona found Solveig. She and Ari were sitting by the fire, close enough to one another for Cliona to understand their relationship. Solveig looked up and gestured for her to join them. Cliona squatted down a few feet away and warmed her hands by the flame.

Strange. Solveig had been a part of the same lie Father had told, but her anger didn't extend to the scholar.

She was far too tired to figure out the answer to that puzzle.

"How are you?" Solveig asked.

Cliona didn't know. Too many thoughts warred within her mind. "Tired."

Solveig thought for a moment, her gaze taking in the whole camp. Then she gestured to a tent. "There's a place for you there. It's not much, but it should be good for rest. We can talk in the morning." Then she saw the light of the sun on the horizon and smiled. "Later in the morning."

Cliona nodded. A bed of needles would probably be comfortable enough for her right now. "Zachary?"

"He's fine. He went to sleep a little while ago."

"Thank you, both for your message and for coming for us."

"You're welcome. And Cliona…" Solveig hesitated. "I don't know if it matters at all, but I'm sorry that I helped hide the truth from you."

Cliona had no answer for Solveig, no forgiveness to offer. Not yet—not until she had time and space to think. She turned and went to the tent, asleep almost before her head hit the pillow.

When she woke, the sun had already warmed the tent enough that her hair was damp against the pillow. Soft voices filtered through the fabric of the tent. She spotted everyone quickly. Father and the woman she didn't know were off, sparring with one another, their movement too quick for her eye to follow. Solveig and Ari were sitting in the center of the tents, speaking with one another. Zachary was with the tall swordsman, apparently taking lessons.

She considered speaking with Father, but that was a conversation she wasn't ready for. Instead, she broke her fast as the others completed their activities and trickled toward the center of the camp. They'd been waiting for her.

Once her meal was finished, Solveig led the conversation.

Zachary and Cliona shared their experiences, starting with the dig and the discovery of Marjaana's home. Cliona did most of the talking, but she was grateful for Zachary, who added any important details she skipped over. She saw the skeptical looks of the others when she spoke of their experiences in the mountains, but for the moment, they let her speak without having to answer their questions.

When Cliona finished, Solveig spoke briefly, telling of

how the band, as they called themselves, had come back together to search for her after a long time apart.

Cliona looked around the circle, finally making the connection she'd missed. "You're *the* band, aren't you?" The legendary group of warriors who'd brought down an empire.

And Father was one.

Their silence was answer enough.

Cliona sat there for several minutes, mute with shock.

Eventually, Solveig continued. She confirmed that the information from her message was true. Vinko and Agnesse and all the others had been murdered, and the town destroyed by the dragon.

Cliona mourned most for Vinko. They never would have that meeting in Vispeda he'd promised her.

As Solveig spoke, Cliona stole glances at Father.

At this man she'd never truly known.

Once, when she'd been younger, perhaps nine or ten years old, she'd gotten lost in the woods around her house. She'd been inattentive and foolish, out on one of her first pickings alone, flush with the unearned pride of having completed the task once with minimal supervision.

Night had fallen by the time Father found her, and Mother later told her he had been searching without fail for hours.

His determination and his love for her weren't in question. Even in her darkest moments, she never doubted that. Damion was more powerful than any governor, and Father had risked his wrath without a second thought.

Perhaps even more impressively, he'd convinced his friends to join as well.

When Solveig was done, and they were all caught up,

Irric raised his hand. "Sorry, but I'm not sure I heard right. Did you say you touched a dragon?"

Meshell chimed in a moment later. "And then asked it to help you escape?"

Cliona nodded.

Irric scratched at his chin. "Right. Care to explain any of that in more detail? I'm a bit confused on that whole part."

"It's tough to explain," Cliona said. "Up in the mountains, when we first met, I felt it interact with my teho."

"I felt that, too," Zachary said.

"It's not uncommon, particularly among older dragons," Ari said. "We know dragons can cause a teho reaction. But I've never heard of anyone getting so close to a dragon and living to tell the tale."

Cliona shrugged. "All I can tell you is that when I touched it, it felt like I was joined to something much wider and deeper than me."

"Which is when Damion interrupted," Zachary concluded.

Solveig looked to Father. "Have you ever had any similar experience? You came across quite a few dragons back in the day."

Father shook his head. "Never. But, to be fair, I never let them get that close either. If they did, I was usually swinging a sword at them."

Solveig switched the topic. "It's an interesting problem, but one we'll have to solve later. For now, we have more pressing concerns. What are we going to do about Damion?"

Meshell spoke first. "He's not going to stop until he has whatever artifact is buried with Ava. And if he knows the five of us are involved, it's about the same as declaring war."

The silence around the circle acknowledged her point. Cliona looked at this group, wondering who they were to speak of Damion and his plans so casually. She thought of the battle in the clearing, and suddenly felt an edge of fear.

"I'd hoped to return home after making sure Cliona was safe," Father said, "but I get the feeling that none of us will be safe until this is put behind us."

Irric stood up. "So, we're going to Husavik, then?"

No one argued with him.

Zachary sputtered as he realized what was being discussed. "You want to go into *the wastes*?"

"You don't have to join us," Irric pointed out.

"Yes, he does," Ari said. "He knows where we're going, and if Damion finds him, then he'll be able to find us." He flashed an insincere smile at Zachary. "Sorry. But it's still better than being buried next to Marjaana's home."

Zachary didn't look convinced, but the others all accepted the decision with less discussion than Cliona and her friends needed to decide where to eat in Vispeda. "Just like that, you're going to go?"

"Ari's got a transport spot a week or so away from Husavik," Solveig said. "It won't be our first time in the wastes."

Cliona looked at her father. *No one* went into the wastes. They were called that for a reason. Nothing but windblown sand as far as the eye could see.

Solveig issued orders, and the group began their preparations for the trip.

Father checked in on her, and she assured him, once again, that she was fine. He wanted more from her, but there was nothing else she could offer at the moment. She didn't know what to think of her father's hidden past, and it didn't look like she would have much time to decide. The currents of fate had picked her up and pulled her downstream. All she could do was fight to keep her head above water.

Later, Zachary found her and pulled her aside, out of earshot of the others.

"Are you sure about this?" he whispered.

She shook her head. "But I don't think we have any other choice. I agree with them that Damion won't stop until he has Ava's artifact. The only way for us to be safe is to find it first. And anyway," she added, "aren't you curious?"

"Not so much that I want to risk my life," he admitted. "We're safe now! And there's one thing we could do they aren't thinking of. We could run and hide. Those five have strength to challenge Damion. We don't. But we could hide. The world is too big for him to find us if we're careful."

She stopped her packing and looked up at him. "You wouldn't be free. You would never have a chance to go home and see your father. You'd give up your dreams, including someday being a governor."

"Not all of them," he said. "Not if I was with you."

She started at that, realizing what he meant. "Truly?"

He nodded, and she believed him.

For the first time, she doubted. She didn't want to live a life in hiding. But perhaps with Zachary, it would be bearable.

It would mean sacrificing the answers to their past. And giving up any hope of influencing the future.

She leaned forward and their lips met. She reached around to the back of his head and pulled him closer, not caring who saw.

After a long, lingering moment, she broke it off. For a moment, he hoped, but then looked into her eyes and saw her answer even before she spoke it.

"I'm sorry, Zachary. I need to know the truth, too."

41

The wind kicked up, scooping up loose sand and whipping it across the band and their companions. Even with the light cloth wrapped around his face, the sand stung Hakon's eyes.

Lifetimes had passed since he'd last been in the wastes, and many more could have come and gone before he would have felt the slightest desire to return. Countless miles of sand and stone, sharp and hot, was all the wastes had to offer. No one settled here, and for good reason.

Still, the wilds found a way to survive even when humans could not. Insects crawled through the sand, burying themselves when danger approached. Here and there, sharp, pointed plants grew, though how they found the water necessary for life, Hakon had no idea.

It hadn't always been so. There were ruins here, majestic and barren structures of the stamfar, beyond any skill of current builders. At times, the sand would blow in such a way as to reveal long stretches of flat and smooth road, made of a material Hakon couldn't name. Once, there had been a reason to live here.

Something had happened.

A story, now perhaps only to be found in the books Cliona could read.

He smiled at the thought.

She was among the very best in the world at what she did. Wasn't that all a father could ask for?

Hakon knew the stamfar weren't gods, despite the religion that had grown up around them. They were humans, gifted both with a power and knowledge that no longer existed.

Cliona might change that.

With her pen and her mind, she might do more to change the course of humanity than he ever had with his bloody sword.

That was a good thing.

A very good thing.

The wind died down, and Hakon unwrapped the fabric from around his face. He wanted her to see him well. Meshell's advice from the night stuck with him.

Cliona walked ahead, Zachary by her side, as he usually was. Hakon increased his pace until he, too, walked beside her. "I'm proud of you, you know."

She looked at him and rolled her eyes. The familiar gesture transported him back to a different time, when she had given him that same look at least once a day. She was a grown woman now, but some habits remained. "Why?"

"I was thinking about the wastes, and the stamfar, and how you might be the one who helps us to finally understand our past."

They walked in silence for almost a minute before she responded. "You don't understand the stamfar any better than we do, do you?"

Hakon grimaced. He didn't like how she classified herself

as different than him. Kolma or not, they were all still human. But he understood. For most of her life, she'd lived in a world where kolma and stamfar were mostly legend. That didn't change overnight, even if she now traveled in their company. "I might know some facts about the stamfar you do not, but you are right. Even knowing them personally, I do not understand them. Nor do I understand what they had once built."

Cliona stopped. "You said 'knowing.' Present tense. Do the stamfar still live?"

"Just one."

Cliona's eyes widened, and he knew there would be a volley of questions. He held up his hand to prevent them.

"Her name is Isira, and she was one of the last stamfar born. Teho had already begun to fade in humans, though kolma were plentiful. But she has survived these long years, mostly by remaining out of sight."

"You know her?"

Hakon gestured to the band behind them. "We all do."

"What is she like?"

"She's a good woman. We don't agree on much, but I believe she has the interests of humanity at heart." Hakon felt his hands begin to sweat, and it wasn't due to the heat. Once again, he was evading telling the full truth. Cliona deserved better. "You should know, she imprisoned me for a very long time."

"How long?"

"In my case, a little over a hundred years."

Cliona stopped. "You were imprisoned for over *a hundred years?*"

Hakon thought of the box Isira had put him in, constructed of a material he didn't recognize. If he'd known what awaited him, he would have killed himself before going in there. Over a hundred years of being trapped motionless with nothing but his sins to think on. Nightmares played endlessly through his mind, his memories distorting until he didn't know what was real or imagined. Despite the heat of the day, he shivered. To this day, he still didn't fully understand the hell he'd lived through.

All he knew was that he would never willingly return.

None of them would.

"What happened then?" Cliona asked.

Hakon didn't care to relive the memories of those days, but Cliona deserved to know. He'd never hide anything from her again.

"I wasn't well for a long time. Our bodies and minds aren't built for the punishment Isira devised, and healing took years. When I was at my weakest, I found your mother. And you know the story from there."

They walked for several minutes in silence. Cliona stared at the ground, in the way she did whenever she was thinking through a particularly hard problem. "Why didn't you tell me, really?"

"I wanted you to live without the burden of knowing my past."

She shook her head. "I don't believe you." When she saw the look on his face, she tried again. "Perhaps that's what you tell yourself, but it's a lie. When we were out in the wild together, you never hid the truth from me like some of the other parents. I knew exactly how dangerous it would be, and I knew what I could risk and what I shouldn't. You trusted me with the truth then, when others wouldn't have. So why not with this?"

Hakon stopped. She was right. Why hadn't he told her? Under the cold light of her reason, his explanations didn't make sense. He'd always trusted her, in all ways but this one. Why not?

The others passed by, giving him curious looks, but he was somewhere else, exploring memories from more than twenty years ago. They continued walking, confident he and Cliona would be safe.

He believed in truth.

So why had he lied?

Cliona's eyes narrowed, a sure sign she'd just pieced something together. "Why were you imprisoned?"

Hakon swallowed the lump in his throat. He suspected Cliona already knew the answer. "The band and I fought for the rebellion. We helped bring down the empire, but after the treaty was signed, I undertook one last task. I killed the last of the enemy generals. I acted alone, but for that crime, Isira imprisoned us all."

Hakon could see Cliona working through the story, putting the unspoken pieces together. She looked up at him. "You killed Torsten!"

Hakon nodded.

"Damion must hate you." Her face paled. "And I told him your name. He knew who I was at the end." She clenched her fists, realizing for the first time just how much danger she had been in at Aysgarth. "If you'd told me who you were, none of that would have happened." She glared hard at him. "So why didn't you tell me?"

It had been to protect her, hadn't it?

But she was right. The truth was always better protection than a lie. If he'd really wanted to protect her, he wouldn't have done as he did.

When understanding struck him, it almost brought him to his knees.

He looked her in the eye. "I lied to you because I wanted to be a father you'd be proud of."

Her eyes watered, and she looked away. "You were, once."

He didn't try to stop her as she turned away from him and rejoined the rest of the group.

42

Journeying with the band made traveling almost comically different than any other trip Cliona had ever taken through the wilds. The wastes' name was well-earned, with nothing but sand and hidden dangers from horizon to horizon. But with the band, she felt no more worried than she did walking the streets of Vispeda at night.

If stamfar were gods, kolmas were demi-gods. And though they seemed plenty human to Cliona, they walked through the world in a different way.

The wilds still tried to kill them. Here, more fiercely and in more creative ways than Cliona was used to. There was the lack of food and water, but the band had come well-prepared on those fronts. The sheer distance of the journey might have killed them, but Ari had transported them far enough into the wastes to ease her fears. Once they found the artifact, he could simply transport them out.

Wild creatures were the only real concern. The wastes were too barren to support large predators, but Cliona quickly learned the small ones were just as dangerous.

Spiders, scorpions, and snakes all called the wastes home, and from the way they behaved, believed they were the kings and queens of their small kingdoms.

The kolmas argued convincingly against the creatures.

She was used to Father's almost preternatural awareness of his surroundings, but when that awareness was multiplied by five, no other predator had a chance. At least once an hour some creature would make an attempt, slithering or crawling through the sand in an attempt to put an early end to their quest.

No creature came within twenty feet before it met its own end at some pointy manifestation of teho, expertly launched.

At night they had no wood for fires, but they still gathered in a small circle and shared their evening meal. Ari and Meshell, both masters at manipulating teho, set wards around the camp each night that put all other wards to shame. Both in strength and thoroughness, she'd never experienced their equal. The smallest spider would die upon contact, and the power flowing through the weaves was enough to deter anything short of a dragon.

And maybe even that.

So what should have been a harrowing adventure turned into a rather mundane walk. She never took for granted the efforts the band went to, but with them, the wastes hardly seemed as terrible as they'd been made out to be.

The only problem with such protection was that it left her too much time with her thoughts. Enough time to have considered the problem of Father from every angle and still gotten no closer to a conclusion.

Though he was never more than a hundred feet from her, it felt as though they were on opposite ends of the continent. She'd been frustrated at him when they last spoke, and although her words had been harsher than she intended, she didn't regret them enough to apologize. Both the sentiment itself and the anger behind it had been true enough.

Several days later, the wastes finally gave her something else to think about.

At first, she thought it was a mirage. The shadows that loomed in the distance seemed too tall to be real. But they were. The band didn't say anything, but she'd become familiar enough with them over the days of travel to understand their body language. Their destination, it seemed, was close.

They reached Husavik the next day.

The buildings on the outskirts of the city were small homes. Though time and the wastes had stripped the buildings of paint, the walls and roofs remained. Cliona didn't know how a material could last so long, but it endured.

Whatever had happened here hadn't been peaceful. There were places where the buildings had been reduced to rubble, evidence of a fight Cliona wondered if anyone had ever written about.

Zachary was the only traveling companion who shared her wonder. The band had been here before, and it bothered Cliona that none of them seemed particularly excited to return. Husavik was inaccessible for most scholars, due simply to the cost and effort required to reach it.

What answers lay hidden within these buildings?

The band didn't seem to care, but Zachary indulged her fascination with pleasure. He stuck close to her as she explored the area, always staying within sight of the band.

They made camp in a larger home, abandoned long before Father had been born.

As night fell, Cliona's anxiety and frustration increased. It was the first time she'd been under the same roof as Father, and the space felt too small for both of them. She wandered up the stairs of the house to a room on the third floor that looked deeper into the ruined city.

A short time later, she heard heavy footsteps on the stairs. She feared it was her father, but was relieved when Zachary appeared in the door. "Mind if I come in?"

She gestured for him to join her at the window. He did, and together they looked into Husavik.

"Want to talk about it?" he asked.

"About what?"

"Your father."

She sighed and gathered her thoughts. "I'm sure he thought he was doing what was best. And there's some part of me that knows it doesn't change everything else he's done for me. But it still feels like I woke up one day to discover that my whole life was a lie."

Zachary laughed bitterly, and she glared at him.

"Sorry," he said, "but I can't help but think about just how different our lives have been. I grew up never knowing what was true."

"What do you mean?"

"My father's only concern in life is to amass more power," Zachary said. "He shares my dream of becoming governor, but I've never understood why he wants the role. He couldn't care less about what happens to the people he serves. I think he just likes having people obey him."

Zachary made a fist. "When I learned the sword, it wasn't because my father wanted me to be able to defend myself. It was because that was what young men in important families did. My whole childhood, he didn't care much what I did, so long as it didn't reflect poorly on him. He only ever told me that he was proud of me in public, where others would see it. At home, behind closed doors, it was different. I could never trust what he said. His actions rarely lined up with his words."

Cliona couldn't imagine such an existence.

"The only reason you're upset is because your father has been so honest with you in everything else." Zachary's quiet words stung like a slap to her face.

A dozen memories and more surfaced, each reinforcing his point. Father had taught her how to control teho. He'd shown her how to stay safe in the wild, and how to confront her fears.

It mattered that he had lied. But maybe not in the way she thought.

She nodded, then reached out and took his hand. "Thank you," she said.

He pulled her closer, and there was nothing more to be said.

43

———

Hakon woke up feeling more uncertain than ever. This place, combined with his lack of progress with Cliona, worked together to twist his insides into a permanent knot. When they broke their fast, he barely ate. He wanted to find whatever artifact was buried with Ava, then return home. Or maybe Vispeda, someplace Cliona would feel more comfortable and willing to talk with him.

He was surprised that Cliona stayed close to him as they left the house. Most days she'd gotten into the habit of maintaining some distance, a constant reminder she wasn't ready to talk.

Today she seemed different, but before Cliona could speak, Solveig began giving directions.

"Ari, I want a better sense of this place. Will you scout for us?"

Ari nodded and vanished.

"While he's doing that," Solveig said, "the rest of us can split up and study the surrounding outskirts. We stay close enough we can help each other if we need to."

Cliona interrupted. "Can I explore with Zachary and Father?"

Solveig thought for a moment, and Hakon could guess well enough the thoughts running through her mind. From a tactical perspective, the grouping wasn't ideal. Meshell was the best choice to accompany the two young scholars. But Solveig was weighing the dangers against Cliona's desires. "That's fine," she finally decided.

The group split in two, with Solveig and the others heading west, and Cliona leading her partners east.

Hakon followed his daughter and Zachary, noting that they were standing closer than usual. He smiled but said nothing. In time, he hoped to know Zachary better, but he seemed a good man. More importantly, he trusted his daughter. If she cared for him, that was enough.

Cliona wasted little time in saying what she'd intended to before Solveig's interruption. "I'm sorry for what I said a few days ago."

"And I'm sorry, again, for not having told you the truth earlier."

She nodded. "Honestly, I'm not sure how I feel about everything yet. But I promise to figure that out, and soon."

Hakon smiled. "We're together now. So take your time. I'll be here."

She returned his smile, and for the first time since seeing her outside of Aysgarth, he felt like he had his daughter back.

They explored the nearby area. To Hakon's eye, there was little to see. It was nothing but building after building, none that looked terribly unique. After hundreds of years of aging, they looked like slight variations on one main design.

Cliona clearly thought differently. The girl had never

been able to resist a mystery, and there were enough here for several lifetimes. She had her mother's eye for detail and a mind that jumped from idea to idea faster than he could follow. She had a theory for everything she saw, often created before he even noticed the detail that had caught her attention.

Eventually he stopped trying to contribute to the discovery of the temple. He settled instead for watching Cliona and Zachary with one eye while watching their surroundings with the other. There was nothing obvious he could point to, but Husavik always made the hair on the back of his neck stand up. Even the wildlife avoided the city.

He wondered what the wilds knew that he hadn't figured out yet.

He felt teho above him, and when he looked for the source, he found Ari on a rooftop above them. The assassin spotted them and vanished, reappearing a moment later next to Hakon. Cliona and Zachary, too entangled in their investigation to notice the teho, jumped in surprise.

"There's a problem," Ari said. "A big one. Where's Solveig?"

"West of last night's campsite. Probably about the same distance away as we are," Hakon answered. "What's wrong?"

"Tehoin, and a lot of them, in a different part of the city."

"Damion, then."

"I fear so, although I didn't dare approach close enough to find out for sure."

"Find Solveig," Hakon said. "We'll meet you back at the camp."

Ari nodded and disappeared, transporting to the roofs to find Solveig as quickly as possible.

Cliona asked the same question that was on Hakon's

mind. "How could he have known? We didn't tell anyone about the translation, nor did we leave any text behind."

"He had other scholars," Zachary reminded them. "Maybe one of them found something we missed."

"How doesn't matter right now," Hakon said. "If Damion is anything like the man who trained him, he's cunning."

Before he could say more, though, teho formed an intricate pattern around Zachary.

Hakon frowned and looked around, wondering if the young scholar had seen something that alarmed him.

Zachary backed away from Hakon, shaking his head. "I'm sorry."

Powerful teho exploded behind Zachary, and Hakon saw a face he hadn't seen in many, many years.

More than a century of living hadn't changed Damion's features one bit. He moved fast, striking Cliona before his daughter even realized the danger she was in. She crumpled to the ground, her features slack.

Hakon roared. He'd just gotten his daughter back. His hand reached for his sword as he sprinted, teho exploding in his legs. He drew the blade and swung in one motion.

Damion barely got his shield up in time. Teho met teho, and the force of the impact knocked Zachary off his feet.

Unfortunately, Damion wasn't so easily defeated.

Hakon remembered Solveig's fears about the mismatch in strength, so he didn't try to break through Damion's shield. He spun, striking at Damion again with all the force he could muster.

Dust blew away from them in all directions as sword met shield.

Damion still stood strong.

Hakon's cuts could have brought down buildings, but Damion's shield hadn't even cracked.

Before Hakon could swing again, Damion hit him with a sphere of teho. The other kolma didn't bother with sharpened forms of the power. He settled for blunt force, and had more than enough of it to spare.

The blow knocked Hakon back twenty feet.

The sphere came at Hakon again, but Hakon batted it away with his sword. Though his sword was reinforced with teho, it still reverberated in his hands.

Hakon dashed forward. Damion let the ball of teho fade as he formed a shield to block Hakon's cut. Torsten's apprentice stopped the sword, but Hakon expected as much. He twisted quickly, lashing out with an elbow. Damion barely got a shield up in time, but Hakon finally caught him off balance. Damion stumbled backward and grimaced as he fell to his knees.

He was up too fast for Hakon to take advantage of. "I forgot how fast you were," he said.

Hakon attacked again. He didn't need to win. He only needed to hold Damion here until the others arrived. Damion's teho would be felt for miles.

Damion didn't give him the opportunity. He dropped his shield and created several balls of teho. They streaked at Hakon, and he couldn't dodge or cut them all.

Three hit him and lifted him off the ground, sending him crashing through the wall of a building.

Hakon shouted and tossed the rubble out of the way.

But too much distance had opened up between them. Damion didn't need to win the fight either.

Zachary scrambled on hands and knees as Damion bent down to pick up Cliona, carrying her in his arms as though she were his child. Zachary grabbed onto Damion's ankle.

In a final, desperate gamble, Hakon threw his sword.

The giant blade spun end over end, aimed perfectly at Damion's head.

Damion smiled, and the sword cut through empty air.

Hakon stumbled forward and fell, now in the street alone.

44

———

Cliona awoke in a dim room, confused. Zachary had done something with teho, and then she remembered feeling more teho, and then nothing. Her head pounded, and when she brought her hand up to her face, she felt the bruising there.

"Sorry about that," a familiar voice said.

It only took her a few seconds to realize what had happened, and when she understood, she growled softly.

Zachary would suffer, and slowly, for this.

As though Damion could read her thoughts, he said, "Don't be too hard on the young man. It's safe to say that I gave him little choice in the matter."

"I'm not going to find Ava's tomb for you."

"You will."

The quiet confidence in Damion's voice only strengthened her resolve.

"You don't believe me?" He genuinely sounded hurt.

"How could I help someone who would destroy an entire town just to keep a secret?"

"Ahh, I see." He paused, thinking for a few moments.

"Would you kill one person to save ten? Or kill one to save a thousand?"

The intimidation and awe she had once felt in his presence was gone. Anger washed it away. She stood up, regretting the decision immediately. Stars exploded in her vision. It only fed her rage. "You've lived as long as you have, and your only argument is that your purpose justifies your actions? I learned better when I was a child."

Damion laughed, the sound bitter and harsh. "From your father?"

Her nostrils flared.

"You really didn't know who he is, did you?" Damion mocked her. "All your life, he deceived you. Perhaps you detest my methods, but I've never once lied to you."

"Father never destroyed a village."

Damion laughed even louder. "Oh, he's destroyed villages. And towns. And empires. Hakon has more blood on his hands than anyone alive today."

Cliona clenched her jaw. She wanted to argue, to claim Damion was a liar. Two weeks ago, she would have, confident in her claim.

But what did she really know about Father? She'd seen him in the clearing below Aysgarth. That man had been capable of anything.

"In a way, all of this is his fault, you know," Damion said. "He's the one who killed my master. And it was my master's death that sent me down this path."

Cliona closed her eyes. Her head seemed to be pounding even worse, every beat of her heart a fresh wave of pain.

Damion continued. "Torsten was never a warrior, never strong with teho. His gift was his mind. After the rebellion shattered the empire beyond repair, my master agreed to peace. They signed a treaty establishing the six states you grew up in. The ink was barely dry when Hakon came."

Damion's eyes were unfocused, reliving his memories in a different time and place. "It was a rainy night when he attacked, all alone. Because his teho is internal, we didn't even know how much danger we were in until it was too late. He carved a bloody path through all of our guards."

He swallowed, fighting to keep his emotion contained. "I had been training for a long time by then, and was more than just a student. I was the head of Torsten's guard, responsible for my master's life. I met Hakon in a courtyard, and he terrified me, dripping with blood and rain. We fought, and although I fought with everything I had, no one could best Hakon in those days. He sent me flying off a cliff, leaving my body broken and mangled on the rocks below. By the time I had healed enough to make my way back to the castle, Torsten was dead and Hakon was gone."

Cliona hated herself for it, but she could imagine the scene.

She couldn't erase the memory of Father cleaving through Damion's soldiers as though they were nothing.

She'd always known Father was capable of violence. A pacifist in the wild was little more than a free meal. But there was a difference between killing a family of forest cats hunting around the perimeter of your property and slicing a man in two.

And this man in front of her seemed to know her father better than she did.

It left her standing there, angry, but with nothing to say.

Damion stood, too. "I didn't come here to argue. You've a sharp mind, and one that would be a great asset. I'd like you to help me without coercion. But you will help me."

"No." The past two weeks had taken both Father and

Zachary away from her. She wouldn't lose her morals, too. Her denial was all that was left to her.

Damion sighed. "You will. Because I'm willing to do more to coerce you than you are willing to lose to stop me." He stepped closer to her, close enough to make her skin crawl. "You're smart. Shall we peer into the future together?"

She clenched her fists, but again said nothing. She hated this feeling of powerlessness.

"First," he said, "I will begin by threatening someone. Your father, perhaps?"

He watched her reaction. "Not your father, then. Probably not Zachary, either. The poor boy is on the verge of committing suicide for what he did, but his betrayal is still too fresh in your mind. How about a small girl, plucked at random from a village? I'll bring her here, and threaten all kinds of unpleasantness."

Cliona's throat tightened. She believed he would, and not even bat an eye. In the pursuit of his vision, he'd lost something, something vital. And he was right. She would give in, though it would tear her apart.

He nodded. "You understand. And of course, you're clever, so you'll look for ways out. Maybe you'll work slowly, or mistranslate something. You'll hope for rescue while devising your own escape. Which will force me to give you ultimatums. Maybe for every hour that passes, the girl will lose a finger or a toe. Or maybe something else. It will depend on my mood. And I do have my other scholars here. They are slower and less accurate, but they'll check your work. Mistakes will cost the poor girl, too. And again, you'll capitulate."

Damion smiled, a sight that made her feel sick. "So, the choice is yours. We can do all of that, or you can accept that we'll end in the same place anyway and just do the work I ask you to."

She silently cursed him, but nothing she said or did would make any difference. In that, at least, he spoke true.

"Fine," she said. "What would you like me to do?"

45

———

Hakon was on his feet moments after Damion disappeared. He gave himself one moment to curse Zachary, then focused on how to rescue Cliona. No doubt she was within Damion's encampment.

Ari knew the general location of the camp.

Hakon let the teho fade from his limbs. Holding onto it for too long drained the body, and he would need all his strength soon enough. He checked himself for any lingering injuries, then ran to the house where they'd spent the night.

He found the rest of the band already there. Meshell and Irric stood as sentries while Ari and Solveig spoke quickly together. The familiar scene made his heart pound. Why weren't they doing anything besides talking?

He charged into the midst of the band.

"Damion took Cliona. Zachary betrayed her." He looked at Ari. "Where's his camp?"

"The northwest corner of the city," Ari said.

"Let's go."

"No." Solveig stepped toward him. "He'll be expecting you, and you'll be walking into whatever he's prepared."

"So we all go. Then it doesn't matter what he does. I know we're stronger than him."

"No," Solveig repeated. "We wait. We make a plan."

Hakon didn't have time for any of this. None of them understood. If they wouldn't come with him, he would go alone. He'd killed Torsten. He could certainly kill Damion.

Fire burned through his thoughts, purifying him of reason or doubts. All that mattered was Cliona.

Without a word, he started marching away.

"Hakon!" Solveig called after him, but made no effort to pursue.

He ignored her.

He'd wondered, for several weeks, who he would choose if forced to decide between the band and his daughter. Now he had no doubt of the answer. His friends were already in the past.

Then Meshell was there, blocking his way.

He growled at her. "Not now."

"Then make me move," she replied.

Long ago, he'd told Cliona legends of famous berserkers, warriors who lost all sense of self-preservation in battle.

She hadn't liked those stories.

She'd never liked heroes who abandoned rationality.

But Hakon knew the rage that led there. Sera had convinced him he had left it in his past life. Now he knew he'd just been hiding from it. He felt it like a burning coal inside him, contained these long centuries. White rimmed the edges of his vision as his heart pounded in his ears. Teho strengthened his limbs, and he was one wrong word from losing control.

He fought to keep from tipping over the edge, but he still swung at Meshell.

She stood between him and Cliona.

He blinked as he hit nothing but air. Then Meshell's uppercut lifted him bodily off the ground, and he went crashing onto his back. He stared dazedly at the sky, and then she was on top of him, a teho knife in hand. She held it to his neck, and it drew blood.

He started.

It drew his blood.

"Get off me!" he roared.

With her open hand, she grabbed his hair, pulled his head up, and then slammed it against the street, hard. She'd moved the knife so as not to cut him deeper, but now stars swam in his vision.

"Get off—"

She repeated the procedure, even harder. His ears rang.

She hissed at him. "Enough!"

He struggled, but her positioning on top of him prevented him from gaining any useful leverage.

She leaned closer. "Do you know what it was like for me? Not just Torsten, but after. What it was like to watch you turn your back on us? *On me*?"

Meshell's voice came close to cracking. "I waited for years, knowing it would take time for you to heal. And then you were with her, and the sword I had forged just for you was buried under your home." She let go of his hair as her words sunk through his thick skull.

Meshell took the knife from his throat. "We owed you *nothing*, yet we all came when you asked. Even I, who swore I'd never see you again. Because we are the band. And we fight together."

The knife vanished into the air and Meshell stood up, driving her knee into his stomach as she did.

"And now you would leave us, again? Just as you did with Torsten?"

Hakon thought he saw her eyes water, but she spun away from him and walked back to where the others stood.

Hakon lay there, staring at the sky, his cheeks flushed with shame.

He didn't want to face the band again.

His tears surprised him. But once they started, they were impossible to stop. A long lifetime of grief found release, his tears watering the dusty street beneath him. Grief for the loss of his daughter, for the loss of Sera, and for the loss of his closest friends.

When the tears ended, he felt lighter, and the feeling of chains tightening around his chest diminished. A shadow fell over him and he saw it was Irric. The swordsman smiled and extended his hand. Hakon took it. Irric pulled Hakon to his feet. He nodded toward the rest of the band. "Come on. Let's figure out how to get your daughter back."

Hakon followed, feeling like a dog with its tail between its legs. "I'm sorry," he said, his voice hoarse. There was so much more he wanted to say, but as he looked from face to face, he knew he'd said enough. Words had always been cheap.

Solveig began as though the whole episode hadn't happened. "The fact that Damion went to all this trouble, not just for Ava, but for Cliona, means she's valuable to him. We can't say he won't harm her, but I suspect she'll be fine, at least until Damion finds whatever he's looking for."

"Can we beat him to it?" Irric asked.

"Without Cliona, I don't see how. He has far more people and the best translator in the six states. We'd have to get awfully lucky."

"He'll be vulnerable when they find it," Meshell said. "It will force them to concentrate their forces in a new place. That transition is when we hit them."

"So we just wait for them to find it?" Hakon asked. His body rebelled against the idea. Cliona needed him now.

But his loyalty to the band kept him in place.

Solveig thought about Meshell's idea, then agreed. "It makes sense. We can use the time to scout out their positions, and figure out some tactics." She looked at Hakon. "I assume you just fought him?"

Hakon nodded.

"Then we need to have some idea of his fighting style. We can start training, and maybe we can figure out a way to use Ari. Damion's not in Aysgarth anymore, so he's more vulnerable than he's been in some time. Let's take advantage of it." She met Hakon's gaze. "We'll do everything we can to get Cliona back safe."

Hakon knew they would. He just hoped it would be enough.

46

Cliona had wondered, for a short time, if the sheer magnitude of the task before them would slow Damion down. The ruins of Husavik stretched for over a mile, and in many places the buildings were packed close together. To find the temple might take days of searching, if not longer.

But this was Damion, and her hope for delay was short-lived.

Instead of sending her throughout the town, he sent groups of soldiers. Each had at least one among them who could draw. Within hours of her arrival, a steady stream of papers trickled into her tent. The quality of the sketches varied widely, but all were good enough. If any buildings had writing on them, the stamfar words were copied with care.

Damion continued to surprise her. She felt as though she was taking a tour of the abandoned city without ever leaving her tent. Seeing so much in so little time gave her a perspective she wasn't sure she would have developed on a more traditional expedition.

One such discovery was about stamfar design. Even in decay, the lines of the buildings were pleasing to the eye. They hadn't been built for efficiency or function alone. They were built to be beautiful. Though the legends said the stamfar struggled against the wild just as they did today, they still put the time and energy into making beautiful buildings.

She'd started to see something similar in Vispeda. In the center of the city, where the wilds hadn't reached in some time, the original buildings were being torn down and replaced with new ones. First came survival, and then beauty.

But how did she find the temple?

She started with assumptions. Her first and biggest assumption was that a stamfar temple would be an uncommon structure. Thus, any building that seemed more or less the same as the others could probably be safely eliminated. That assumption alone eliminated most of the buildings.

Cliona considered delaying the process, but she saw no good way to do so. Damion checked on her every hour and made her explain her work thus far. Every time he appeared it was with a smile on his face, but his presence served only to remind her of the threats he had made.

The sun was setting when Damion made his last check. Then he told her to get some rest.

"Really?" She'd expected to be working through the night.

"My soldiers can't draw enough detail in the dark," he said. "And there's no rush. If Hakon hasn't attacked yet, he won't bother until we find the grave. It's when we'll be the most vulnerable. You'll work better after some rest."

With that, he was gone, taking the papers with him.

Having nothing better to do, Cliona lay down on her bed and waited for sleep to take her.

She heard movement outside her tent a few minutes after Damion left.

"Cliona?"

At the sound of his voice, she leaped to her feet, angry beyond comprehension. She threw aside the flap of her tent and let teho fill her body. She ignored the guards who ringed the tent. Zachary's eyes were just beginning to widen in surprise when she grabbed him by the throat and lifted him into the air.

When her guards realized her intent, they backed off, content to watch the scene play out before them.

Zachary didn't try to fight. His feet dangled limp in the air, and even though he could get no air into his lungs, his body remained relaxed.

He wanted to die.

And that desire was the only fact that saved his life.

Disgusted, she opened her hand and let him drop to the ground. He gasped and choked, but before long was back on his feet.

"I'm sorry," he said. "I'm so sorry."

He took one step closer to her, then hesitated. He opened his mouth, then closed it. Then tried again. This time, the words spilled out of him, so fast she could barely understand him. "He threatened my younger sister. Told me he knew all about her, and I believed him. He told me he could give the order anytime. But it didn't seem to matter. At first, all he wanted was to know how the dig around Marjaana's home was going. It seemed like there wouldn't be any trouble."

Cliona interrupted. "That's how he knew to come so soon after we discovered it."

Zachary kept speaking, as though he hadn't even heard her. His confession spilled from his lips. "Then, at Aysgarth, he wanted to know what progress you were making. Compared to the danger my sister was in, telling him was harmless. I didn't think anything of it."

She hated it, but Cliona believed Zachary. Damion's threats were persuasive, as she knew firsthand. But it didn't excuse him. "You could have warned me."

"I tried! Before we left Marjaana's home I tried to tell you he wasn't someone you should trust. And at the camp outside Vispeda I tried to escape. But you refused to come with me."

Cliona stepped toward him. "You still chose to signal where I was." The accusation crystallized in her mind. "Which meant you even let him know about the escape before it happened. Otherwise he wouldn't have given you something to signal him."

Zachary's face fell. "I couldn't risk my sister's life."

Even if it was true, Cliona didn't find herself in a forgiving mood. "Just leave," she said.

She turned to face her tent.

"If there's anything I can do to make it up to you—" Zachary began. Then he stopped, and Cliona wondered if his words felt as empty to him as they did to her. He had betrayed her. Whether for a good reason or not, the fact remained. It wasn't a mistake she could just forgive. He had lied to her, just like Father.

She stepped into her tent and closed the flap behind her.

After a while, he left.

She slept restlessly that night, her thoughts running in useless circles. She awoke to Damion entering her tent without so much as announcing himself. He set the piles of papers she'd been working on back at her desk, exactly the way they'd been when she had ended her work the night before. Then he gave her a fresh stack of paper with a smile. His soldiers, it seemed, had been busy this morning.

He left her to work.

The sun reached the height of its journey for the day, and Cliona pulled aside the flaps of the tent so that a breeze might come through. She returned to her desk, wondering if she should go out again and ask one of the guards for lunch. Then she absently flipped through a few pages, dismissing several possibilities quickly.

A surprising breeze picked up, blowing a few of the papers off her desk. She weighted the others with small stones, then went to pick up the windswept pages. Her eyes froze on one drawing. Then she sat down heavily in her chair. Staring at it.

There were ways to delay, at least for a while.

She could put it in the bottom of the stack. She could pretend as though she'd never seen it.

It might work.

But when Damion appeared in her tent a few minutes later for his hourly update, she knew she couldn't lie. Not with any success. He saw the look in her eyes, and his grin widened. "Show me," he said.

For the briefest of moments, she considered showing him the wrong one. But he'd know, sooner or later, and an innocent would die.

A few hours wasn't worth it.

She found the paper and handed it to him. "The temple of a thousand suns. I'm guessing it's where Ava is buried."

47

"They found it," Ari reported. "The whole camp is moving toward a building near the northeast corner of the city. Not a building like any I've seen, either. If it's a temple they're after, this seems like the place."

The band had been waiting, taking turns distracting Hakon from worrying about his daughter. He understood Cliona should be safe until her use to Damion had ended. But that knowledge did little to ease his fears. Only Meshell and the others, working together, had prevented him from committing to a useless, suicidal assault.

Ari squatted down in the dust and used his finger to draw a small map of their destination. The temple was large, sprawling across an open square Ari estimated was about five hundred feet to a side. The main building was about two hundred feet wide, and as tall as any building they'd seen. A smaller building stood on each corner of the square, small and blocky. Ari reported Damion's soldiers were taking up positions around the main temple and in the surrounding buildings.

"Do we attack now or wait for Damion to appear with Cliona?" Irric asked.

"We go now," Solveig said. "This isn't just about Cliona. Damion can't reach that grave. If he gets much stronger, the six states won't be able to stop him. We force him to fight before his warriors settle into position."

Together, they formed a plan of attack. Hakon and Meshell would attack to the south while Irric and Solveig advanced north. Their goal was to distract and destroy Damion's forces. Ari would find a place to watch, looking for an opportune moment to strike.

In a perfect world, Ari could kill Damion and transport Cliona out before Damion's warriors even knew what had happened. Ari's role was likely the most dangerous, but there was no hiding the eagerness in his eyes.

Hakon swallowed the lump in his throat. A few months ago, he thought he would die without ever seeing these faces again.

He'd been a fool to let them go so easily. He stood up, squashing the sudden wave of feeling that threatened to burst from his chest. "Then let's go."

They gathered in a circle, each of them putting their hands in. Before Solveig completed the circle, she looked at Hakon. "Any last words?"

He shook his head, emotion once again choking him. "Nothing that wouldn't bore you." He looked from face to face. "Thank you."

Solveig put her hand on top of the others and Ari transported them to the temple square.

The temple distracted Hakon for a precious second. It was a tall building that expanded like a bulb before tapering to a narrow point. It reminded him of a flower about to bloom, but as delicate as it looked, it had endured hundreds of years of neglect.

Damion's soldiers didn't give him time to appreciate the temple's graceful lines. Teho came to life all around him, reminding Hakon of his true purpose. He turned south and took in the challenge that awaited him.

Ari had put them near the center of the square, so most of the space around them was open. Damion had a few squads of soldiers in the square, but most of the teho came from the taller buildings that were across the street. They'd put most of their strength into defending the perimeter.

Those were the buildings that had to fall.

Darts of teho streaked toward him, but he ignored them. They glanced off his hardened flesh. One dart, probably thrown by a nelja, scratched his forearm.

Hakon ran, Meshell at his side. Behind him, Solveig and Irric ran the other way. Two buildings in front of him had more soldiers. He gestured for Meshell to take one while he took the other.

The soldiers within his building were halfway through building a barricade to the main entrance when he reached them. He swung his sword, slicing through the barricade a moment before he ran into it.

The barricade exploded inward, debris flying in every direction.

Half a dozen warriors stood in an open space on the other side of the door. They either covered their faces or dove for cover as wood and stone flew. Hakon gave them no time to recover. He cut through them and ran up the stairs. The second and third floors were empty, and he took the last set of stairs four at a time as he reached the top of the building.

A squad of four soldiers had taken position on the roof, and they were ready for him.

Darts were thrown at his face and two soldiers charged him with teho blades.

Hakon turned his face to protect his eyes from the darts.

Within a moment his building had been cleared. Damion's poor soldiers had no idea who they were fighting.

On the building next to his, Meshell burst onto the roof. She frowned when she saw him, and Hakon guessed she was disappointed he had cleared his building faster than she had hers.

His blood began to boil. He wanted a fight. Damion's soldiers were tehoin, and a fearsome force against one of the six states, but they were little challenge for Hakon. He wanted Damion before him, where they could settle this feud once and for all.

Across the square, Irric and Solveig cleared their buildings almost as easily as Hakon and Meshell. But it had been too easy. There hadn't been that many soldiers in the square, and Damion was no fool. He had his own strategy, but what was it?

Hakon looked around, wondering what they had missed.

He figured it out a few moments later.

A roar, impossibly loud, echoed over the empty lands.

Hakon spun and looked behind him, to the south.

He saw the shadow in the sky, one he'd hoped never to see again. Long wings stretched out, visible even from a distance. Another roar caused the building under Hakon's feet to rumble.

And it was still miles away.

They should have known. Cliona had warned them, but they hadn't taken her seriously enough.

Meshell leaped across the gap between their buildings and landed next to him. She was grinning from ear to ear. He wondered if maybe her own imprisonment had broken her in a way she hadn't healed from. He appreciated a good fight as much as the next person, but not this.

Hakon twirled his sword and rolled his shoulders.

Whether he liked it or not, Cliona's safety was through that dragon.

The momentum of the battle changed in a heartbeat. As the band had their eyes to the south, Damion and a group of his best warriors transported into the middle of the temple square, almost exactly in the same spot the band had shown up a few minutes prior. Hakon risked a quick glance back. Cliona and Zachary were with him.

He longed to run to his daughter. She was right there, only a few hundred feet away.

But the dragon came, and seemed to be increasing its speed.

He didn't have the time to save her.

Besides, he and Meshell were the two best suited to fight the dragon. Killing it might be impossible, but they might be able to drive it away.

He had to trust the rest of the band to reach Cliona.

He turned away from the square and stared at the dragon. His heart raced, and he wiped his hands on his pants.

Meshell sidled closer, and he could almost feel the excitement radiating off of her. This was what she lived for. With death itself bearing down on them, she found happiness. "You staying?" she asked.

"Yes."

Her smile grew even wider. "Together, then?"

"Together."

48

Damion pulled at Cliona's arm. Behind them, a storm of teho raged as Father and his friends met the best of Damion's warriors. And off in the distance, the dragon came. She could feel it, closer than it had ever been since that night at Aysgarth.

Its anger radiated off the sands of the wastes, and Cliona swore the air heated as it approached.

She sensed its pain, the barb driven deep within that responded to Damion's crude commands. She wanted to run to it, to take its pain away and allow it to be free.

Damion would kill her if she tried.

Damion pulled at her again, but she resisted. They were fighting for her! To follow Damion meekly into the temple betrayed their efforts.

Which, she suspected, was why he'd brought Zachary. An easy victim to force her to act.

Zachary would welcome the punishment, but that didn't change Cliona's feelings. She was furious at Zachary still, but she couldn't blame him. She'd folded to Damion's threats just as quickly. The mere mention of causing someone innocent to suffer had won her cooperation.

She cursed herself, but she wouldn't be able to watch as Zachary was tortured. So she slowed him down, but didn't dare resist too strongly.

Cliona caught sight of Irric and Solveig charging into the temple square. Both reminded her of dancers. From a distance, it looked so gentle, but even Damion's best warriors fell before their teho blades.

They came for her, but not fast enough. The dragon would arrive in moments, and the main door to the temple was only a few feet away.

Damion pulled one more time, then formed a teho sword in his hand.

Before he could threaten her, someone transported off to their left. Cliona assumed it was one of Damion's soldiers, but when she looked, all she saw was a shadow rushing at Damion.

The exchange lasted but a moment, teho filling the space between two masters.

Damion's sword, already in hand, saved him. Cliona filled herself with teho, ready to aid her ally. She saw the blades flicker together and break apart.

The duel was over before she knew what had happened.

The shadow retreated and disappeared, leaving behind a trail of blood.

It was Ari.

The shadow reappeared above them, shading Cliona from the glaring sun. Two darts, thrown one after the other, came for Damion.

He knocked the first one aside with his sword as he dodged the second.

The second punched through the ground, leaving a crater where it hit.

This was what it was like when kolma fought, gods from another age, joined in battle one last time.

Ari disappeared as blood splattered on the ground between Damion and Cliona.

The delay allowed Solveig to reach Damion. Irric held off Damion's personal guard.

The ground shuddered as Damion's teho blade met Solveig's thin manifestation. The woman who Cliona thought of as a scholar danced forward, her blade constantly seeking Damion's life. Damion withstood the assault with ease.

Solveig advanced, and Cliona dared to hope. The dull crack of teho striking teho echoed in the square, and she felt every impact in her bones. Any one of those cuts would be enough to slice her in two. They'd probably be enough to slice a building in two.

Damion never gave a step. Though Cliona couldn't say how, he slowly pushed Solveig back while keeping an eye on her. Before it could become a full rout, though, Ari reappeared, grabbed Solveig, and vanished. A moment later, he transported Irric from the square.

The dragon was too close.

A dark cloud came over Cliona's thoughts. Even the band fled from Damion.

Which meant that if she wanted to live, her only hope was herself.

Damion would kill her once her usefulness ended. He liked his world neat and tidy, and those who opposed him were like dust that needed to be swept away. When he yanked her into the temple, she wondered if she would ever stand in the light of day again.

Her gloomy thoughts didn't last long.

The temple was too wondrous. When Damion's soldiers had found it, the doors had been sealed shut. They were opened an hour ago. The interior was more preserved than even Marjanna's home, and the walls were in extraordinary condition. Paintings depicting the taming of the wild greeted her eyes, and any thoughts of the battle beyond the walls soon became a distant memory.

She studied the paintings. In them, she felt the artist's appreciation for the natural world, which jarred harshly with what she believed of the stamfar. In legend, they fought ceaselessly against the land, carving out an existence with their own blood. In the book she'd grown up with, the illustrations of famous battles made the wilds appear terrifying. Animals dripped blood from the corners of their mouths while sharpened teeth formed terrifying grins.

Not here.

These paintings showed not blood, but sweat.

It meant something, but her mind refused to put the pieces together.

Damion pulled her violently out of her thoughts. "Where is she?"

"I don't know." Marjaana's journal had never said. But this was a temple to the stars. Higher levels would be considered more sacred than lower ones. She considered lying, but Damion watched her too closely. "I would guess she's as low as we can go."

Damion led her and Zachary deeper into the temple. They found a set of stairs that led both up and down. Damion put his hand to the wall and light appeared in the ceiling, the same way it had in Marjaana's home. Damion took the stairs two at a time.

He was moving faster than he should have. An exploration of this building, done well, should have taken hours, or days. Who knew what traps the stamfar left to guard their secrets?

It was the band outside, she realized. Confident as he seemed, Damion wanted the artifact and wanted to leave without a decisive fight.

Damion was worried.

For the first time since Ari's attack failed, Cliona felt a glimmer of possibility.

Attacking him was pointless. He'd beaten both Ari and Solveig, and he was on guard against her.

But there had to be something she could do.

They continued their descent, passing three underground levels. The stairs ended at a long hallway. At the end of the hallway they found a thick door that again reminded Cliona of Marjaana's home. Before she could utter a warning, Damion put his hand to the door and filled it with teho. She heard something click within the door, but nothing else happened. He turned to look at Cliona. "Why isn't it opening?"

She looked over the door, seeking some sort of instructions. But there were none. "I don't know." Whatever locked the door required more than just teho, but she couldn't begin to guess what that might be.

Damion swore and manifested his long teho blade.

"Wait!" Cliona shouted, but she was too late.

Damion carved the door into pieces.

On the other side, two enormous human-shaped teho demons stirred to life.

49

"Any ideas?" Hakon asked. The dragon was less than a minute away.

"Kill it. Don't die," Meshell answered.

"Oh, good. I was worried you didn't have a plan."

Meshell grinned. "Should we take the fight away from the rest of the battlefield?"

Hakon liked the idea. Though it would cut them off from easy aid from their allies, it hopefully prevented the dragon from interfering with the band rescuing Cliona.

He ran across the roof and leaped. He glanced down at the street several levels below, savoring the feeling of flight. He landed on another roof, Meshell a step behind him. They ran across this roof and repeated the act. When he landed, Hakon slid to a stop.

The dragon was close now, near the outskirts of the city. They only had moments.

The dragon roared again. The building trembled beneath his feet as though it might collapse.

Then the battle began.

Hakon dove to the side as a pair of massive jaws tried to

bite him in half. The rush of air from the passing creature sent him tumbling uncontrollably. Talons raked the rooftop where he'd just stood. When he found his feet, he saw that half of the roof was now missing.

The dragon launched itself straight into the air, slowly spinning as it did.

Meshell stood on the other side of the roof, eyes wide, looking up at the sky.

They'd fought dragons together before. They'd driven many far past the western boundaries of the empire. He didn't remember any like this, though. This one was ancient, perhaps old even in the time of the stamfar. Hakon's legs felt weak as he watched it ascend.

He wasn't sure he could beat Damion, who was a pup in comparison.

The dragon reached the apex of its climb, hovering in the air for a long moment like a bird floating on an updraft. Then it folded its wings in and dove straight for them, falling faster and faster.

There was no defense against such a strike.

Hakon, already at the edge of the roof, turned and jumped a moment before the dragon hit the building. The ancient structure split like a log under the axe, the crack of shattered stone sharp in Hakon's ears.

Without momentum, his jump wasn't strong enough to carry him to the next roof. Debris pounded into his back as he stabbed his sword into the side of the adjacent building. Edged with teho, it slid smoothly through the wall until Hakon twisted the blade, arresting his fall.

He dangled in the air for a bit, his mind slow.

The sound of rubble shifting brought his attention back to the dragon. He punched the wall and made a handhold in the stone. Once secure, he pulled his sword out of the wall and sheathed it, then punched the wall again. One fist-sized crater at a time, he scrambled to the roof.

The creature gave him no time to rest. By the time Hakon stood on the roof, the dragon was shaking the last of the rubble from its wings. It reached out with its mighty claws and swiped at him.

Hakon leaped back, and the claws took the part of the roof he'd just been standing on. He reversed direction, hoping he was faster than the dragon.

Blood on fire, Hakon drew his sword and leaped off the roof at the creature, bringing his sword down on top of its head.

It was a killing blow. His cut would have sliced through a mountain of stone without slowing, but against the teho-armored scales, it barely scratched the dragon.

He only succeeding in enraging the beast.

Hakon landed on his feet in front of the dragon.

It swung another powerful blow, and this time Hakon met it with his sword.

The choice was a poor one. It didn't have anything to do with teho, but the laws of nature. The dragon was enormous, and many times Hakon's weight. The strength of its blow alone knocked Hakon off his feet and into the side of a building.

He blinked the dust out of his eyes in time to see Meshell enter the fray. She threw teho darts at the dragon's eyes, but the dragon moved its head, allowing the attacks to scratch its scales instead. Its tail snapped out and struck Meshell like an enormous whip.

The blow blasted her through a building north of Hakon. The only evidence of Meshell was the human-sized hole in the wall. He still felt her teho, so it hadn't killed her, but it would take a bit for her to recover from that attack.

He stumbled to his feet, unsteady from the hits he'd taken. He held his sword in front of him, but after everything, he wasn't sure it posed even the slightest threat.

Hakon thought of Cliona and her insistence that she had touched this dragon.

He couldn't imagine.

The dragon swiped at him again, but Hakon saw the shift in weight and ran. The claws tore into the building behind him as he ran, just a step ahead of the attack.

Hakon felt the wind as the claws missed behind him.

The building collapsed, throwing up a thick cloud of dust that choked Hakon and blocked his sight.

The dragon's tail caught him across the chest, and for a moment, he knew nothing.

He skidded hard across the street, the pain returning him to awareness. He groaned and pushed himself to his feet, the world tilting wildly underneath him as he did.

The dragon seemed to have lost interest in him, and as the dust cleared, Hakon understood why.

Meshell fought the dragon, somehow standing in front of it without making a quick journey to the gates of death.

For several seconds, Hakon just watched.

Meshell's fighting style was beautiful to watch. Her speed and anticipation of the dragon's moves kept her a step ahead of the creature.

She wasn't losing, but unfortunately, she wasn't winning, either. None of her attacks had any effect on the dragon.

Her attack gave him a moment to think.

Any normal cut, even one from Hakon's sword, was pointless.

But if he could slide his sword under a scale somewhere vital, they might still have a chance.

Meshell started to lose her fight. The dragon was hemming her into a corner, restricting her mobility.

Hakon let his eyes wander for a precious second, looking for some advantage the terrain might give him.

When the idea first occurred to him he dismissed it. It was madness, even by the bizarre standards of the band.

But Meshell only had a few seconds before the dragon landed another powerful blow. He wouldn't let anything happen to her.

Hakon leaped as high as he could and clambered up the side of a building, punching whatever hand holds he needed.

He focused on keeping the teho within him flowing smoothly. He leaped from one roof to the next, and then to the one after that.

Then he was behind the dragon.

Before he could tell himself how poor of an idea it was, Hakon leaped one last time.

He landed on the back of the creature's neck.

It snapped its head straight into the air, and Hakon held on. It roared, deafening Hakon and leaving a ringing sound in his ears.

Then it launched itself into the sky.

Any thought of trying to kill the dragon fled. Panic set in as the creature rose higher and higher, leaving the battlefield of Husavik far below.

Hakon took a deep breath, pushing the panic away.

It faded, and in its place he discovered something new.

He could feel the dragon's teho raging beneath him. Something dark and cold kept it in a constant state of rage, always interrupting the flow of teho through its body.

Had Cliona opened herself up to that?

If so, she had more courage than him.

The dragon spun and then descended, roaring again at the unwelcome rider on its back.

Hakon remembered why he was here. He looked for a likely target between the scales.

He found one.

But he was so focused as he drew back his arm for the stab that he missed the building.

The dragon twisted so that its back gouged into the structure, and Hakon was wiped off the dragon's back in less than a heartbeat.

Hakon fell to the ground and coughed up blood.

The teho that ran through his body granted him an incredible amount of protection. But it didn't make him invincible.

He got to his feet, and though his breath came in ragged gasps, he thought he could still fight.

Then Meshell was at his side, eyes wide. "How are you still alive?"

Hakon coughed up more blood, but he was already starting to feel better. His body was healing faster than usual. "I have no idea."

They both looked up as a shadow passed overhead.

Their next round with the dragon was about to begin.

50

The two teho demons attacked as though they were mirror images of one another. Damion summoned that same enormous sword and cut. But the first teho demon caught the sword with its hand, stopping it in place.

Damion barely had time to swear before the second demon lashed out with a whip of teho, wrapping around the kolma's leg and pulling hard. Damion lost his balance and was pulled into the darkness of the room beyond.

As Damion fought against one demon, the other turned its attention to her and Zachary. A whip appeared in each hand, and it spun them in a lazy pattern as it advanced. Cliona hadn't encountered many demons in her past, but when she had, they had been almost mindless creatures.

These didn't seem that way. She swore she saw an intelligence in their fiery eyes.

A whip lashed out at her and Zachary stepped in to intercept it, teho blade in hand. His sword cut at the whip in a well-timed move.

Zachary had either forgotten or didn't care he was

fighting against a creature with more teho. The whip was far more dangerous than his blade. His sword snapped.

Fortunately, his defense absorbed the worst of the blow. By the time the whip hit him, it was little stronger than a hard slap.

The second whip cracked through the air at Zachary. Cliona jumped forward and raised her arm, intercepting the tip. It wrapped around her arm and the teho demon pulled her forward.

As she slid along the smooth floor, she saw that Damion had freed himself from the first demon's whip, and the two were engaged in what appeared to be an even battle.

The second demon pulled her relentlessly forward. She dug her hands into the floor, leaving deep gouges in the stone, but couldn't slow herself. Zachary charged with a new teho blade, hacking at the whip uselessly.

Then the ground rumbled, the whole building shaking. Cliona sensed her teho grow stronger.

The dragon was close.

The teho demon looked up, forgetting about Cliona for a moment. Cliona seized the opportunity to untangle herself.

She felt stronger than ever, her body humming with borrowed power. She looked up, understood, then tackled Zachary to the ground, willing as much teho into her body as it could handle.

A moment later the world exploded. The air was smashed out of her lungs by the force of the dragon's impact. Stone broke against her back, arms, and legs. She and Zachary went tumbling, the whole world twisting around her like a nightmare.

Her back struck something that didn't break. She stopped suddenly, even as more rubble crashed around her. She kept her eyes closed as the dust settled, and when she opened them, she wasn't sure what direction was up. Everything was dark and she had trouble breathing.

She didn't waste time checking on Zachary. If she struggled to breathe with teho flowing through her body, he was in trouble. She pushed against the rubble.

Nothing happened.

Cliona had a vision of her dying here, trapped under a pile of debris. Forgotten for hundreds of years or longer.

She pushed again, but even with her strength, she couldn't make the stone move.

She relaxed, focusing on taking a few deep breaths.

Nearby, the dragon roared. As it once had, the sound was music to her ears. Her teho flowed in time to the dragon's heartbeat.

She pushed one more time, and this time the rubble moved. Just a little, but enough for her to breathe freely.

Cliona pushed some more, and finally, something gave. The stone slid away, revealing a light.

She kicked and scrambled, reaching the top of the pile and pulling herself free. Then she reached down and pulled Zachary out with one arm.

Only then did she take a look around the room.

The dragon sat where the teho demons had once been. Though it seemed foolish to assign human emotions to such an ancient creature, it looked contented. The teho demons were nowhere to be found.

Behind the dragon, Damion moved. Cliona squinted and saw something in the shadows near the back of the room. After a second, she identified it.

A sarcophagus.

This was their last chance to stop Damion.

The band had failed to stop him.

She knew she couldn't beat him. But perhaps she didn't have to.

The dragon was right there.

Damion reached the sarcophagus and ran his hands over it. Though he stood on the other side of the room, she saw the gleam in his eyes. For a few moments, his attention was completely focused on the object of his desire.

She closed her eyes.

Falling into the dragon was easier than ever.

Its teho felt like hers, and she felt the barb within it, altering the flow of teho. Using the dragon's strength as her own, she pulled at it.

It started to move.

Cliona pulled harder and it began to slide out a bit faster.

Then something hit her.

Her head cracked against the back wall of the room. For a few seconds, she couldn't summon a single thought.

Damion came into view, a ball of teho floating above him.

"Naughty, naughty," he said. "Did you really think I would let you take my dragon?"

Her eyes darted to the dragon.

All she needed was a few more moments.

Damion formed his sword and extended it until the point touched her neck. "Try it and die."

Far above them, the battle for the temple increased in intensity. The band hadn't lost yet.

Damion seemed to feel the same.

"Kill them," Damion said.

A sharp pain stabbed in Cliona's side as Damion twisted the spike in the dragon's teho.

The dragon roared again, and this time, there was no

music in its voice. It squirmed, as though fighting for control, but then launched itself into the sky. The blast of teho that accompanied its departure shook the building.

Cliona couldn't reach the dragon anymore.

It was just the three of them. Zachary was struggling into a sitting position. He wouldn't be useful anytime soon, but at least he wasn't dead.

"Will I have any more trouble from you?" Damion asked. "I tire of his company."

Cliona glared but shook her head.

Damion smirked, then let his sword fade. He gestured for her to follow, and she did. When she reached the sarcophagus, everything else faded. A message had been inscribed across the top, and Cliona read what she could of it.

"What does it say?" Damion asked.

"I'm not sure," she said. At the flash of Damion's anger, she held up her hands. "I'm not lying. I see Ava's name, but I don't recognize the words after. It's not 'grave,' though."

Damion frowned. "And the rest?"

"A short description of her crimes. I recognize the words for murder and rebellion, but not much else."

Damion shrugged and created another teho blade. "Stand back."

"Shouldn't we—" Her protest died on her lips at his look. She took a step back.

Damion sliced across the top of the sarcophagus. The sword cut through cleanly, and he pushed the top of the sarcophagus off. The stone grated against stone, but it fell open.

And Cliona met her first god.

51

The dragon didn't attack Hakon, but the temple.

It crashed through the upper levels of the structure and into the space underneath. The sacred building that had stood for hundreds of years fell in an instant. Hakon ran toward the square, Meshell a step behind.

They met the rest of the band there. From the hole where the temple had once been, Hakon heard the sounds of battle.

He felt the dragon, still enraged, striking at something.

And Cliona was down there.

He ran toward the hole, only to be stopped by the appearance of a familiar enemy.

Gunvald, Valdis, and the blonde woman from the road appeared between him and the hole. Gunvald formed a half dozen needles above his head. "It's good to see you again." He laughed at his own joke and launched the needles at Hakon's face.

Hakon didn't know what the limits of his regenerative

powers were, but they were substantial. With the band at his back, he had little to fear from the trio. He knew this.

But the body remembered pain.

And Gunvald had caused plenty of it.

Hakon flinched away, covering his face with his arm. Teho needles hit his arm and stuck.

Before he could master his fear, teho bloomed in all the streets surrounding the temple. More of Damion's soldiers had arrived, even more than there had been when the band first attacked.

The first wave of soldiers had been a feint to draw the band out. Now, Damion's aides brought down the hammer. Teho darts and spears fell from the sky like a storm of dark raindrops.

Valdis took advantage of Hakon's confusion, launching an attack with her short blades. She scored several clean hits before dancing back and rejoining Gunvald and the woman.

"Be seeing you soon," Gunvald said.

They vanished before square was destroyed.

"Hakon!" Solveig yelled.

He ran to her. The other four had gathered close and Irric kept a shield above them. The teho assault hit, darts and arrows digging deep into the ground. Irric grunted as he fought to keep his shield up against the force of so many small impacts.

Tehoin, all dressed in Damion's dark uniforms, flooded the square from all sides. They formed teho weapons as they charged. Hakon guessed there were nearly a hundred.

In any other circumstance, it would be a tremendous force. Against one of the standing armies of the six states, a hundred tehoin would have carved a path through any defensive line.

They'd chosen their enemies poorly, though.

Hakon and Meshell led the counterattack. Damion's tehoin lashed out at them, but they lacked the strength to cut either of the warriors.

Hakon's sword rose and fell. The first tehoin against him tried to defend, but weapons shattered against Hakon's strikes. Between Meshell and Hakon, a dozen fell within seconds. Those close enough to see tried to escape while those behind pushed forward, eager to join the battle.

Meshell knew how he would shift and react, much as he knew where she would strike. They danced as one, a pair of swords that rarely left the other undefended. He fought well with the others, but nothing matched his skill when paired with Meshell. It was almost as if they were guided by something larger than either of them.

While they attracted most of the attention, Irric and Solveig came behind, the other two points of the triangle wedging itself into the enemy. They fought for more space and prevented any flanking attacks against the pair up front.

Ari, as usual, had disappeared, and Hakon felt sorry for any of the tehoin Ari believed were in command. They would be dead before they even knew they were under attack.

Damion's soldiers pressed against them, but the band pushed back harder. Hakon's heart beat loudly in his ears, and he laughed as swung. He felt like a young man again, the band in the midst of their first battles.

After a long time away, the prodigal son had returned home.

And just like in the rebellion, they were winning.

The thrill was short-lived.

A powerful blast of teho appeared behind him. He didn't

turn because he knew what he would see. The dragon took to the sky, casting a long shadow over them all.

Damion's remaining tehoin ran, seeking cover in the buildings across from the square.

With no enemies left to face, Hakon turned his face to the sky, where the dragon circled like an angry god.

Ari appeared in the middle of the triangle. "It'll be coming for us soon."

Teho gathered in the buildings where Damion's soldiers had retreated. A burst went up into the sky, similar to the one that had summoned the soldiers below Aysgarth.

"He's still got more tehoin?" Irric asked.

Ari had his eyes closed. "Feels that way. Reinforcements are coming from his camp."

All eyes turned to Solveig.

"That dragon is the oldest I've ever encountered," Meshell said. "If all five of us fight against it, we *might* have a chance."

"But if we do, we'll have dozens of Damion's tehoin trying to kill us from behind," Irric pointed out.

Solveig didn't need long to reach her decision. "We retreat for now and use the buildings as cover."

Up above, the dragon began its descent toward the square.

Solveig spoke faster. "We take care of Damion's tehoin, then we focus on the dragon."

The others nodded, but Hakon's mind was elsewhere. He was looking across the square at the hole where the temple had once been.

His daughter was down there. He couldn't sense her teho, but he wouldn't at this distance. He just knew.

The rest of the band started to run from the square.

Hakon watched them, torn between them and the hole.

The band wasn't beaten, they just needed to fight wisely. Solveig's decision was the right one. He belonged with them. If the last few weeks had taught him anything, it was that Hakon the father was a lie. A well-intentioned one, certainly, but a lie nonetheless. He was one of the band.

But Cliona was down there.

He couldn't walk one more step away from her, even if it was the wise decision.

The others stopped when they realized he wasn't with them. He smiled at them and waved. "Go on," he said. "There's one thing I need to do first. And thank you."

He turned and let them go.

Damion's dragon landed directly in front of him, ready for their final battle.

52

―――――

Cliona couldn't help but stare. Light filled a chamber inside the sarcophagus. It was powered by teho, much like many of the lights of the stamfar. But it was the chamber itself that held her attention.

A young woman lay at peace inside. From appearance alone, Cliona would have guessed they were about the same age. Except this woman had been buried for hundreds of years.

The woman was completely naked, revealing a slim, muscular figure. Whatever methods the stamfar had used to bury her, they had halted any sign of deterioration. Cliona had expected to find a desiccated corpse, not a beautiful woman in the prime of her life. She looked as though she might wake up and start talking, as though centuries of history were nothing but a short nap for her.

The chamber was as fascinating as the woman. The top half of it was made of a clear material similar to glass, but was no glass Cliona had ever seen. There were no imperfections or irregularities. And though she couldn't guess how, when she touched the material, she sensed the Teho woven into its construction. Even if she wanted to break it, Cliona didn't think she could.

The bottom half was another material Cliona didn't recognize. It wasn't transparent, but was equally sturdy. The chamber had been designed to withstand eons without wear. She felt the faintest of vibrations as her fingers ran over the chamber. It made her wonder if the chamber was alive, even if the person preserved within was not.

Damion broke her away from the study of the coffin. "Where is it?" he asked, as if she knew the answer. He could see everything the same as her.

In her rush to examine the chamber and the woman within, Cliona had forgotten about the artifact.

She examined the coffin again, looking for anything that might be the source of the legend Damion had pursued. But Ava was completely naked. She didn't hold anything, nor did she wear any jewelry. Even her hair was devoid of orna-mentation.

Whatever Damion sought, Cliona didn't see it. There was no artifact.

Damion laughed, and he sounded like a man close to cracking. He'd risked everything for the artifact.

She thought of the words Damion had shown her back in Aysgarth, the entry from Torsten's journal.

Now, the secret of her strength lies buried with her.

It took her a few seconds, but something shifted in her mind. She understood.

Torsten, and by extension, his pupil, Damion, believed that the secret had been a physical object.

She looked down at Ava.

There was no artifact.

Ava's mind held the secret.

Damion paid Cliona no mind. His laughter grew until it

filled the broken room. It was almost loud enough to mask the sounds of the battle raging above.

She almost blurted out her realization.

They had found the secret! And with it, the possibility of changing the world. She wanted to shout her realization to anyone who would listen.

She pressed her lips firmly together. Her hand rested on the chamber, no longer out of curiosity, but out of a desire to protect it.

Her resolve hardened. It didn't matter what Damion threatened. She would learn Ava's secret, and she would share it with the world.

Damion's laughter stopped. Without warning, he formed a teho blade and cut down on the chamber with a casual flick of his wrist.

Cliona dove out of the way, and teho met teho.

Damion's blade shattered against the chamber.

Damion cursed and formed a new teho blade. He looked at Cliona, and she wondered if he was about to attack her. Had he decided that her use to him was at an end?

He glanced up, to where Father and his band were fighting. Waves of teho rose and clashed with one another, reassuring Cliona that the battle wasn't over.

When Damion grinned, it froze her blood solid.

Zachary chose a terrible time to stumble toward them from the pile of rubble.

Damion turned, took a few steps, and drove his blade deep into Zachary's stomach. Then he let the blade fade.

Zachary's eyes went wide. He took a halting step forward and dropped to his knees, looking down at his stomach as though he couldn't believe what had happened.

Damion smiled again at Cliona. "Wait here. I need to

find your father, and then we can finish this once and for all."

Damion vanished.

She ran to Zachary, who was still on his knees. Blood poured from the wound, and Cliona cursed Damion. The stab had been perfectly placed. It was fatal, but painfully slow. Though he could have granted Zachary a clean death, he instead made him suffer. He made Cliona suffer.

Zachary was no fool. He knew the outcome as well as her. But when their eyes met, she was surprised by how calm he was. "I'm sorry. I should have done more to keep you out of this."

"Don't talk," she commanded. "Save your energy."

He smiled. "There's no point, and we both know it." He grimaced as his weight shifted. "If you survive this, would you look after my sister? She'd make a far better scholar than me, and the further she is from father's schemes, the better."

"You can look after her yourself."

"You're a terrible liar."

Cliona bent down and kissed him.

When they parted, his smile was even wider. "Thank you."

She sat next to him. Up above, the battle had grown in intensity, but here it seemed so far away. She felt like there was something she should say or do, but nothing came to mind.

So she sat beside him and looked up through the hole, wondering how the battle fared above. When she looked at him again, his eyes were closed. His breath came in uneven, shuddering efforts.

As she watched him, a sudden determination seized her.

She could sit here by his side as he died, or she could try

something. She looked up again. There was no safety up above. But Zachary was going to die anyway, so even if she failed, nothing was lost.

Cliona felt teho flowing in her limbs, stronger than even yesterday. With the dragon this close, she felt nearly invincible. She picked Zachary up in her arms, his size more of a problem than his weight. Her arms were barely long enough to cradle his wide body.

Then she looked up and planned her route. She crouched down and leaped upward, ascending through the hole the dragon had made, one broken level at a time.

It was time for her to join the band in their battle.

53

———

The dragon didn't attack Hakon. It writhed in place, as though trying to get comfortable. Its eyes flashed, but it suffered in silence.

Behind him, someone coughed.

Hakon spun around, afraid Damion's soldiers had transported to attack him.

But the rest of the band stood there, weapons drawn. When he noticed them, they stepped up to join him in a line. "I thought you were going to run," he said.

"Not without you," Meshell said.

Before he could answer, the dragon's behavior changed. Its whole body shuddered.

Then it charged.

The band scattered, not wanting to be targeted by the dragon. Ari, Solveig, and Irric threw teho at it while Meshell and Hakon closed in from opposite sides. Hakon looked for a gap in the scales to slide his sword into, but the dragon twirled too fast for him to find one. He jumped back, then leaped over the tail as it snapped at him.

The dragon's wings flapped as it lifted into the air, forcing everyone back.

Behind them, Damion's tehoin sensed their moment. They launched attacks at the band. Meshell and Hakon ignored them, but the others had to defend both against the tehoin and the dragon.

It was a losing battle.

Then the dragon shifted its attention and flew into one of the buildings Damion's tehoin were using for shelter. The collapsing structure crushed both the dragon and anyone inside.

"What?" Meshell asked.

"I have no idea," Hakon answered. Dragons always disliked tehoin, but wasn't this one under Damion's control? The dragon was acting erratically, as though pulled in two directions by different masters.

The rubble of the building shifted as the dragon pushed itself free of the collapse. It extended its wings in a cloud of dust and shook itself off. It half-writhed, half-flew toward the band, landing only a few dozen feet away.

It shuddered again, more violently than before. To Hakon, it looked as if the dragon was being attacked by a dozen invisible demons it was trying to shake off.

The dragon coiled on itself, and Hakon took a step back. "We need to get away."

Before they could run, the dragon became a tornado of motion.

There was no reason to its moments, no greater purpose. It lashed out at any building or person nearby. Hakon suffered a glancing blow from one of the claws, sending him spinning to the ground. Meshell helped him to his feet as they retreated. Buildings collapsed as the dragon's tail sliced through them.

A few of Damion's soldiers attacked the dragon, which only enraged it further.

Its movements were impossible to predict.

The band retreated further, maintaining a loose circle. Fortunately, the dragon didn't seem to have any particular interest in them. Its fight was with whatever demons tormented it.

"I never thought I'd see a berserker dragon," Irric said.

Hakon nodded, worried what would happen if it did turn its attention to them. Against this, they had no chance, even together.

"Maybe we should think about retreating from the square," Meshell said.

They all turned around when they felt teho behind them.

Damion appeared, a wide grin on his face. "Going somewhere?" he asked. A large blade formed in his hand, at least twice as long as a normal blade.

Hakon didn't even have time to take his stance. The dragon launched itself at them, its first direct movement in several minutes. He wasn't sure if the dragon was aiming for them or Damion, but it didn't matter. Those who could formed shields.

The dragon hit, sending the band tumbling in all directions.

Hakon tried to run, but got caught up in one of the dragon's claws and thrown across the square. He bounced and skidded, coming to a rest near the center of the square.

His body hurt. Teho protected him from breaking, but its use took a toll. Nor was it an impenetrable shield. Cuts, scrapes, and bruises ran from shin to shoulder. Exhaustion tempted him with the promise of one last sleep.

He rolled over and looked at the sky. He didn't know

how to defeat the dragon, nor did he know how to defeat Damion. Perhaps one final sleep wasn't the worst idea.

In the distance, he felt the band fighting against the dragon. They accomplished little, but still they tried.

They always fought, no matter the odds.

He'd been like that, once.

"Get up." The voice was harsh. Hakon craned his neck to see Damion standing not far from him.

"I'll kill you lying down if you want, but it will be more satisfying for me if you're on your feet fighting." He spat into the dirt by Hakon's face. "At least this trip will have been worth something."

Hakon took a long breath. Teho still raged within him, pulled from its normal pathways in his body by the dragon. It gave him more strength, but little control. He stood and took a few practice cuts with his sword. He was in no condition to fight Damion. "Where's my daughter?"

"Dead," Damion said.

Hakon took his stance.

The lie revealed Damion's concern about this duel. He was trying to anger Hakon. And it gave Hakon confidence.

Hakon's giant sword met Damion's long one, neither giving into the other. The blades broke apart and met again. Hakon pressed forward. Damion would be used to people trying to stay out of the range of his long sword. A closer fight favored Hakon.

At least, Hakon hoped as much.

Damion gave up ground, but Hakon didn't let him escape.

Damion snarled and vanished, reappearing a moment later well behind Hakon. He formed several spheres of teho and launched them, one after the other. Hakon deflected one and dodged another, but it wasn't enough. The third caught him, knocking him backward.

Once his balance was lost, Damion seized the upper hand. The spheres came at Hakon from every direction, battering him. For a moment, the grip on his sword loosened when one hit him in the arm. He gripped it tighter, but the assault was relentless.

Across the square, the band wasn't having any better luck with the dragon. The four of them working together were doing all they could just to survive.

No help would come from that direction.

Another series of impacts forced him to his knees. One sphere rocked him across the cheek, and another landed on his chin like an uppercut delivered by a giant. Hakon struggled to hold onto thoughts and his consciousness.

The hits ceased, and Damion formed his sword once again. "Come," he said, "and let's finish what you started the night you came to murder my master."

54

———

Cliona's surge of strength didn't last long. She jumped to the second level, then found the stairs and took those. Zachary weighed on her arms by the time she reached the ground level.

The temple, and the beautiful paintings it once contained, was gone.

In search of an artifact that didn't exist.

She would make Damion pay.

Cliona found a corner of rubble where she could lay Zachary. No place in Husavik was safe, but this was as good as one could expect. She put his hand against his chest and felt him breathe. He had some time, but not much.

She looked over the shattered wall. Bodies wearing dark clothes lay everywhere.

The dragon writhed madly, a tornado of claws, teeth, and tail. Her attempt to free it had only caused more suffering. It fought four of the band, and they barely seemed able to survive.

On the other side of the square, she caught movement.

Damion and Father dueled.

Or, more accurately, Father endured a beating at Damion's hands. Spheres of teho pummeled him and he wobbled unsteadily on his feet.

She almost rushed to him, but then stopped.

Her presence wouldn't change anything. If anything, it gave Damion another weapon to use against Father.

The dragon was their only hope.

She ducked behind the wall and closed her eyes.

Joining the dragon was harder than it had been the times previous. Its anger formed a wall she fought to breach. She squeezed her eyes tightly, focusing on the feeling of their teho flowing together.

Her own teho responded, growing more uncontrollable with every heartbeat. The pain in her side sharpened, and she gasped for breath. How long had the creature endured this pain?

She didn't pull at the blockage the way she had before. The longer the effort took, the more likely it was Damion would stop her before she succeeded. She examined its contours, and after a few moments, she thought she understood how it worked.

Cliona twisted and pulled. At first, the darkness within the dragon's teho didn't move.

Then it began to slide.

Damion's response came immediately. A cold wall of teho tried to snap shut between Cliona and the dragon. But he'd done it to her several times, and she was ready. Needles stabbed into her mind, but she didn't let go.

It slid faster.

And then it was out.

Cliona let it go, and it was as if it had never existed. The teho running through her body calmed, a small reflection of the change happening within the dragon. She opened her eyes and peered over the wall.

Damion was staring at the dragon, horrified.

The dragon launched itself into the air. Cliona inclined her head as the dragon soared higher into the sky. The sight brought a smile to her face. If nothing else, it would fly free, hopefully never in bondage to a human again.

Damion fell to his knees, mirroring Father's position. Unlike Father, he returned to his feet quickly. He looked toward the temple and saw Cliona before she could duck.

He vanished.

Hakon blinked. His thoughts were slow, as though he needed to dig through thick mud to bring them to the surface. The dragon had flown into the air, but it hadn't returned.

Damion vanished, too.

The teho within him calmed, returning to the normal paths he was used to. His thoughts came quicker and he felt the bruises across his body begin to fade. Across the square he saw the band. They all still lived. Then Ari disappeared.

Motion to his left drew his eye.

Ari and Damion fought, their exchange of teho too fast for the eye to follow.

He saw the back of Cliona's head, barely visible over a bit of wall, one of the corners of what had once been the temple.

Ari was protecting his daughter.

The other members of the band ran toward the temple.

The world snapped back into place, and Hakon was on his feet.

He took two steps and stumbled, his balance not quite

returned. He crawled forward on hands and knees, scrambling toward Cliona.

Cliona pressed her back against the wall, trying to get as far away from Ari and Damion as she could. She could follow their exchange, but also knew that any of the attacks that passed between them would kill her.

Ari fought valiantly, but Damion was stronger. For a few precious seconds, the duel seemed like it could go to either warrior. But with each exchange Ari fell further behind.

She expected him to transport away, but he never did.

He kept fighting, even as the duel turned against him.

A few seconds later, a dart took Ari in the shoulder. Then another in the opposite hip, and finally one through a leg. Ari dropped.

Before Damion could land the killing blow, he was attacked by a blur of teho blades.

Cliona couldn't follow Meshell's movements, and neither could Damion. He gave up ground, scrambling backward so he could put a shield between him and her. She pounded against it helplessly.

Darts appeared in the air above Damion, but instead of pointing at Meshell, they pointed at Cliona. They sped toward her, and then Meshell was there, blocking them with her own body.

It came down to a matter of strength, and Damion's was greater. Meshell collapsed to the ground, a half dozen darts sticking out of her chest. Her teho prevented them from penetrating too far, but she was still out of the fight.

Behind her, she heard Solveig cry.

· · ·

HAKON FOUND his way to his feet. Ari and Meshell were down, and Solveig and Irric were rushing in like fools. By attacking separately, they played to Damion's strength.

But Solveig had seen Ari fall, and feared the worst.

She would see no reason.

All Hakon could do was run faster. With every step he gained ground, but he would not be fast enough.

They would have to hold out for a few precious seconds without him.

Solveig fell a moment after she reached Damion. She overreached, too eager to cut Damion down. Blood poured from a deep cut on her right leg.

Irric maintained his composure, but Damion refused to engage him in a sword fight. He retreated, attacking with teho darts from every direction. Irric had no choice but to throw up a shield that completely protected him.

Which was exactly what Damion wanted. Then the battle became a mere comparison of strength.

Damion forced Irric to his knees under a relentless barrage of teho. The last of Irric's strength faded just as Hakon reached the battlefield. Hakon swiped away the teho dart meant to kill Irric as his friend collapsed, unable even to support his bodyweight.

Damion smiled as Hakon approached, then vanished, transporting himself behind Hakon.

Hakon turned, but Damion already had the spheres formed and under control.

Hakon tried to defend himself, but he had no answer to Damion's tactics. Blow by blow, Damion drove him back. A sphere struck him on the forehead and put him on his back, staring up at the sky once again. He struggled to a sitting position and saw that Damion had released the spheres in favor of his teho sword.

The boy was willing to fight properly, but only when victory was certain.

Hakon spat blood.

Damion looked around at the band, broken at his feet. "You're pathetic. You've been given all the time in the world, and what do you waste it on?" He focused on Hakon. "Starting a family? *We're gods!* You could have anything you wanted!"

Hakon pushed himself to his feet, swaying as he did. He lifted his sword, which felt heavy in his hands. The tip wobbled back and forth.

They passed one another, and Damion easily avoided Hakon's clumsy swing. Damion's own sword cut deep into Hakon's chest, slicing right down to the bone. Had Hakon been anyone else, it would have cut him in two. Hakon collapsed again, and he didn't think he would be getting up anytime soon.

"Pathetic," Damion repeated. He walked toward Hakon and raised his sword. "Your time has passed."

"Not yet it hasn't!"

Hakon saw a flash of long, blonde hair as Cliona attacked Damion.

Cliona swung her fist, and Damion barely dodged.

She pursued, punching at him whenever she came close enough. She was faster than him, but her lack of experience showed. It didn't matter how quick she was if he could predict her moves.

But she refused to let Damion win. Father and the band fought for her. The least she could do was fight for herself.

She backed Damion up to a wall, but when she swung at him, he vanished. Her fist shattered the wall.

Damion reappeared behind her, and she launched herself at him again.

She wanted to punch the smile off his face, but he kept dancing away, his grin growing wider and wider. He didn't even try to fight back.

Cliona stopped. All she was doing was entertaining him.

But what else could she do?

A shadow passed overhead. Cliona didn't dare close her eyes, but she reached out to the dragon, wondering if they might help each other one last time.

The connection came easily, and it only took Cliona a few seconds to make herself understood.

The expression on Damion's face changed as he realized what was happening. His smile vanished, replaced by a sneer.

He disappeared, then reappeared right in front of her, teho blade in hand. He drove it into her chest.

For a moment, the teho in her body fought the blade.

But Damion's strength was too great, and he pushed harder. Somewhere, far away, she thought she heard someone call her name.

The blade broke through her teho, stabbing through her breast and out her back. A bright agony exploded in her chest and her limbs went limp. Damion held her up on his blade. Then he swore, let his blade disappear, and formed a shield.

The dragon hit Damion a moment later, one of its claws kicking him across the square and into a building beyond.

Cliona fell to the ground as though she didn't have a bone in her body.

The dragon stopped and landed between her and Damion, then turned to her, its snout sniffing at her as it neared.

She blinked and Father was there. He had tears running down his face. It was the first time she'd seen him cry since Mother died. She'd been so angry then, and she was sorry for that now. But there was no reason for him to cry. She and the dragon had defeated Damion.

His tears landed on her forehead, and he wiped them off, his hands surprisingly gentle for such a large man.

Her body felt cold, and she tried to snuggle closer to him.

A memory, long forgotten, came to the surface. Her as a young girl, lying awake in bed, terrified that the creatures of the wild would break through the wards around their home and eat her. Mother couldn't comfort her. No matter what words and explanations Mother gave, Cliona knew the wards were going to fail. Then Father had come in and held her in his arms. He said nothing. He just held her close. She felt the muscles in his arms and heard the steady beating of his heart, and as sleep took her, she knew she didn't have to worry.

His arms were still strong, and his heart still beat steadily.

She didn't have to worry.

She reached up her hand, and the dragon brought its nose down to touch it.

It was the most glorious feeling. The small stream of her teho joined with the river of its, becoming something greater. For the first time, teho flowed smoothly between the two of them, and nothing could interrupt it.

She looked up at Father and smiled.

She was in his arms.

And that was a good place to be.

55

———

akon felt the moment Cliona stopped breathing. Her hand dropped limply from the dragon's snout. With her in his arms, he felt the teho stop flowing through her body.

His body convulsed in a silent sob.

Solveig pulled herself through the dust to reach them. She left a trail of blood behind her. She stretched out her hand and grabbed Cliona's other arm. Then she closed her eyes. "I'm sorry, Hakon."

He barely heard her.

Memories swallowed him whole. As a baby, she wailed while he held her in his arms, pacing the dining room in a futile attempt at getting her to fall asleep. As a child she grinned at him as she hung upside down from her knees on a tree near their house, her hair glowing in the last light of the day. Her laughter echoed across time, high-pitched and full of joy. He saw her as a young woman, asleep by the window with a book open across her chest.

He brushed the hair back from Cliona's face.

There would be no more memories.

He took each one and tried to burn it into permanence. He'd lived so long. He remembered so many names without faces, and so many friends without sound. Memory was fallible, but he wouldn't allow himself to forget.

Never Cliona.

She looked peaceful for the first time since they'd met again. There was even a hint of a smile on her face. He ran his hands through her hair, his tears falling freely. "I love you, girl."

Hakon looked up. The dragon remained, and if he didn't know better, he'd say it looked sorrowful.

For the first time, he stared into the eyes of a dragon. They were deep and intelligent, and as he looked, he swore he saw a flash of something familiar.

He wiped the tears from his eyes and stared again. Had he imagined it?

Off in the distance, the building Damion had been kicked into began to rumble.

Hakon spared the event a quick glance, then returned his attention to the dragon. Gently, he laid Cliona's body down and stood up. He stumbled toward the dragon and extended his hand, the same way he'd seen Cliona do.

The dragon tilted its head and leaned forward, so that Hakon could run his hand along the side of its head. He felt the teho within the dragon, and his eyes went wide.

He turned to Solveig. "Heal her."

Solveig shook her head. "It's too late. There's nothing I can do."

"Heal her wounds," he demanded.

The front wall of the rumbling building exploded outward, and Damion stepped through. He walked with a limp, but the teho emanating from him was stronger than ever. The band, broken as they were, wouldn't have a chance.

"Just do it." He left Solveig no time for argument.

Hakon stepped closer to the dragon, well aware that it could devour him with one quick bite. He dropped to one knee and bowed his head. "Will you help us?"

When he looked up, the dragon was bowing its own head, offering a place on its back. He stood, grabbed his sword, and climbed on.

"Hakon—" Solveig said.

Hakon looked back at Damion. The man stood about a dozen feet away from the building, but approached no closer. The teho raging within the boy was fearful. Hakon tore his gaze away. "Keep them safe," he said, "and thank you."

He had no desire for a long goodbye. The dragon seemed to understand his wishes. It spread its wings and flew.

Hakon had lived a long time, and his life had been one rich in experiences. Despite whatever tragedy he'd endured, he never took for granted the gifts he'd been given by fate. But he'd never experienced flight. The force of the dragon's ascent pushed him down hard against the creature's scales, and he became dizzy as Husavik shrank rapidly beneath him.

Then they were gliding, the dragon making a lazy circle high above the city. From up here, he could see the curve of the planet, and everything below seemed so small.

Was this how dragons usually felt? The concerns of the world felt so far away, so petty.

No wonder they didn't like humans much.

He closed his eyes, feeling the teho within the dragon.

Cliona had spoken of a sense of communion with the

ancient creature, of teho flowing back and forth between them.

Hakon swallowed his fear and let go of his tight grip on his own teho.

It was like opening up a set of floodgates. Teho filled him, more expansive than anything he'd ever imagined possible. He'd been a fool to think he could ever fight this dragon. Its teho was as vast as the universe itself.

And he wasn't alone.

He smiled.

"Together," he said.

The dragon circled again, and Hakon felt it gathering its power. Connected as they were, the teho was Hakon's as well.

The dragon folded its wings and dove back toward the city. Hakon clenched his legs tightly against the dragon's neck and held on with one hand, leaning close. The wind pulled his hair straight back, and the clean air wiped the tears from his eyes as he squinted.

Faster and faster they fell. Teho filled every cell in Hakon's body, and he felt lighter than air.

With his other hand, he reached back and drew his sword.

He'd never felt stronger.

Husavik grew quickly. The buildings became larger, and Hakon saw the hole where the temple had once been. Something small glowed in the bottom of the hole.

Whatever it was, he doubted it was worth this.

Nothing was worth this.

Damion formed a shield and launched several teho darts at the dragon.

It slid to the side, avoiding the darts with ease.

Damion focused on defense, forming a shield even a stamfar would be proud of.

The boy was right about one thing. He'd developed the strength to become a god in this world. Torsten would have been proud of his pupil.

Hakon leaned his weight forward and relaxed his thighs' grip on the dragon. He brought his feet up and together, so that they were planted on the dragon's back.

They were only a few hundred feet above Husavik now, and still the dragon gained speed. Hakon saw the band, gathered together under several layers of shields.

He wished them well, and thanked them once more in his heart.

Hakon let his body absorb even more teho from the dragon. Cracks opened up along his skin that leaked both blood and light. He roared, and the dragon roared with him.

A hundred feet from the square, he launched himself off the dragon.

The dragon spread its wings, slowing to a rapid stop.

Hakon made the very last part of the journey on his own.

He raised the sword high above his head, then brought it down with all the force and will he could muster.

Sword met shield. Teho clashed with teho, and Damion's shield held.

But only for a moment.

Hakon's sword slowed, but cut through the shield. The explosion of teho blew dust in all directions for hundreds of feet, but Hakon finished his cut.

He smiled as he crashed into the ground.

They expected Isira, but none of them so soon.

Hakon lay on the ground, staring up at the wispy clouds that floated through the sky. He felt the tremendous teho that always accompanied the stamfar and slowly rolled to his feet.

Solveig could find nothing physically wrong with him, but his body constantly ached. It hurt even worse when he tried to use teho. For now, though, that seemed a small price to pay for still being alive. Had he attempted the same feat with only his own teho, he would certainly be on the other side of death's gate.

So he shuffled over to where Isira stood, looking over their camp with an inscrutable expression. "Hakon," she greeted him. "You look the worse for wear."

"It's been a rough few days."

"Show me," she commanded.

She had never been much for small talk. He turned toward the hole in the ground. Several of the others were sitting up, but Irric and Meshell still slept. Only Solveig stood and joined them. She, too, walked with a limp. She'd put most of her strength into healing the others. Her own body fixed itself slowly.

Isira looked into the hole, then glanced at Hakon and Solveig. "I'm not waiting for you two to make it down the stairs." She reached out, grabbed them, and transported them down to the bottom. Hakon was silently grateful. He hadn't been looking forward to the stairs, either.

Isira walked to the chamber. Solveig and Hakon shuffled after her.

The stamfar studied it for a moment, then looked up. "What can you tell me?"

Solveig shrugged. "It's Ava."

Isira raised an eyebrow. "I can read the inscription, too, you know. It seems she was quite the criminal. So why didn't they just kill her?"

"No idea," Solveig said. "It was Torsten's obsession."

Isira's eyes narrowed as she studied the chamber again. "What is your intent?"

"We don't really have one," Hakon answered. "We only wanted to rescue Cliona and stop Damion from further bloodshed. And we weren't sure what you would want."

"I know nothing about this woman," Isira said. "So bury her and leave her as the other stamfar intended."

"Both Torsten and Damion believed in her legend enough to risk everything for her," Solveig pointed out. "She might help us fight against the wilds."

"And she might try to subdue the six states," Isira replied. "You could barely fight Damion. What chance would you have if she disagrees with your principles?"

Neither Solveig nor Hakon had a good answer for that.

Isira snorted. "When will you learn? You meddle and meddle, always striving. Let humanity find its own way and let the stamfar die in the memories of the young. They don't need gods anymore." She paused. "Leave her be. The risks that come with waking her are too great."

Her tone gave no room for argument.

Solveig, to Hakon's surprise, pushed harder. "May I take her to Vispeda?"

Isira shot her a suspicious glare. "Why?"

"I'd feel safer if she were in the vault under the academy. At least then I'd know she was undisturbed."

"No place on the continent is more remote than Husavik."

"And any of Damion's soldiers could transport here in a moment. I can't keep a constant eye here."

Isira considered for a moment. "Fine, but don't even try to study the chamber. I don't want her woken. Speaking of Damion's soldiers, what happens to them?"

"They've been fleeing for the past few days," Hakon answered. "I assume they're running back to Aysgarth."

"What will you do about them?"

This time, it was Hakon's turn to shrug. "For now, nothing. Damion was the threat to the stability of the six states, not Aysgarth."

"Maybe there's hope for you after all." Isira held out her hand, and Solveig and Hakon took it. A moment later, they were up at the temple grounds above. She turned to go.

"May I ask a favor?" Hakon asked.

Isira glared at him. "The fact that you still draw breath is the greatest favor I'm willing to grant you."

"It's my daughter."

"What about her?"

"I'd like you to store her body in one of the pods you imprisoned us in."

"Hakon—" Solveig cautioned.

"No," Isira said. "I'm sorry your daughter died, but—"

"Examine her," Hakon said.

Isira gave an exasperated sigh.

"It'll only take a moment," Hakon insisted. "I wouldn't ask without reason."

The stamfar stared at him for a long moment. "Show me."

Hakon nodded and led the way to one of the tents. He opened the flap. As usual, Zachary was there, sitting next to Cliona's body as if he were a guard dog. If Hakon was fortunate Isira let him live, the boy was doubly fortunate Hakon let him live. The only reason they hadn't let him bleed to death was because Solveig had seen Cliona carry him from the basement of the temple. His daughter had tried to save him.

Since then, the boy had barely left Cliona's side.

Isira ignored Zachary and went to Cliona. She rested her hand on Cliona's forehead and closed her eyes.

Less than a minute later, she opened them wide. She turned to stare at Hakon, who nodded.

Her decision came quickly. "I will."

"Thank you."

Then Isira was gone, and with her, Cliona's body.

Zachary started. "What did you do?" He tried to get out of his chair, but he didn't have the same healing powers as the band. Of them all, he was still the weakest.

Hakon pushed him back down. "She can keep Cliona's body safe. Better than we can."

Zachary sputtered, but Hakon wasn't in the mood for questions or arguments. He held up his hand. "It's for the best, and you have no say in the matter."

The boy slumped in the chair, and Hakon took pity on him. "Keep your faith."

He left the tent and shuffled out into the light of day. The warmth of the sun felt good on his face. Meshell had woken from her slumber, and when she saw him emerge from the tent alone, she came to him. "She took her?"

"Yes."

Meshell leaned against his arm. "Good."

Her fingers intertwined in his, and together they looked up to the sky.

THE ADVENTURES CONTINUE!

Top o' the morning!

I hope that wherever you are in the world, and whenever it is you're reading this, that you're doing well.

First, as an author, let me thank you for reading *Band of Broken Gods*. Whether this is the first book of mine you've read or my twenty-first, I hope that you enjoyed it. There have never been more ways to be entertained, and it truly means the world to me that you choose to spend your time in these pages.

If you enjoyed the story, rest assured the adventures of Hakon and the band are far from over. They mysteries of their world remain, but the truth isn't far away.

Look for the next installment of *The Saga of the Broken Gods*, coming fall 2021!

And if you're looking to spread the word, there's few better ways to support the story by leaving a review where you purchased the book!

Thanks again!

Ryan

April 19, 2021

DIVE DEEPER INTO THE STORY

Sometimes, it's hard to know how to end a story. There are books where the final scene is pretty obvious. *Band of Broken Gods* was not one of them. I liked the way the final chapter ended, but I also knew this book needed an epilogue.

My problem was that I had several to choose from. They all did a decent job of wrapping the story up, but some introduced elements of the next story better than others. In the end, I decided to go with the scene between Hakon and Isira because it kept the story a little tighter and a little neater.

But it meant sacrificing another scene I'd written from Zachary's perspective.

It's a scene I really like, taking place a while after the events of *Band of Broken Gods*. I've expanded it into a short story (and taken out some of what would be repetitive now that you've read the epilogue in the actual book), but I still really enjoy it, and I hope you do, too. If you'd like to read it, you can visit:

www.waterstonemedia.net/lone-wolf/

And if you pick it up, I hope that you won't mind staying in touch. I typically email readers once or twice a month, and one of my greatest pleasures over the past five years has been getting to know the people reading my stories.

If I'm being honest, email is my favorite way of communicating with readers. Whether it's hearing from soldiers stationed overseas or grandmothers tending to their gardens, email has allowed me to make new friends all over the world.

Email subscribers also get all the goodies. From free books in all formats, to sample chapters and surprise short stories, if I'm giving something away, it's through email.

I hope you'll join us.

Ryan

ALSO BY RYAN KIRK

Saga of the Broken Gods

Band of Broken Gods

Last Sword in the West

Last Sword in the West

Eyes of the Hidden World

Oblivion's Gate

The Gate Beyond Oblivion

The Gates of Memory

The Gate to Redemption

Relentless

Relentless Souls

Heart of Defiance

Their Spirit Unbroken

The Nightblade Series

Nightblade

World's Edge

The Wind and the Void

Blades of the Fallen

Nightblade's Vengeance

Nightblade's Honor

Nightblade's End

Standalone Novels

Blades of Shadow

The Primal Series

Primal Dawn

Primal Darkness

Primal Destiny

ABOUT THE AUTHOR

Ryan Kirk is the bestselling author of the *Nightblade* series of books. When he isn't writing, you can probably find him playing disc golf or hiking through the woods.

www.waterstonemedia.net
contact@waterstonemedia.net

 facebook.com/waterstonemedia

 twitter.com/waterstonebooks

 instagram.com/waterstonebooks